# Moonbow over Charleston

### TERRY WARD TUCKER

RADIANCE PRESS



ISBN 978-0-578-51347-8



Book design and layout by Booknook.biz

Cover Design by SM Savoy Designs

# Dedication

*for Tony, baby whisperer*

# Moonbow

What words of light
In ebony night
Of dark blue silver stars
A delicate dance
Doth speak of romance
A moonbow speaks of ours.

E.E. Jacks

# 1.

## Larissa

Larissa Harold tiptoed up the front walk of the low-rent project apartment she shared with her mother. Pressing an ear to the door, she heard Bob Barker shout from the TV, "Susie Smith, come on down." The audience screamed as if the gray-haired show host were handing out hundred-dollar bills.

Larissa gritted her teeth, then bumped her forehead, on purpose, against the metal door facing. A rerun of *The Price Is Right* meant Jake, Mom's current live-in, had control of the remote. Anyone would think if a single mother's welfare check paid the cable bill every month, she'd be the one picking what to watch. Lifetime Movie Network maybe, or the Hallmark Channel, not some ancient game show Jake or Pete or Jimbo liked. Or once last year, a guy who actually called himself Shark Face. Anyone would think.

Stepping into the apartment, Larissa slipped off her backpack and let it drop to the filthy welcome mat. It landed with a thud. She rubbed her shoulders where the straps had dug in. "You're late," Jake said without taking his eyes off Door Number Three. "Where you been?"

The girl ignored her mother's boyfriend. "Hi, Mom," she said. "Anything to eat?"

Jake got louder. "I said *where you been?*"

Larissa went into her room and slammed the door. She turned the lock in the doorknob for effect, not because it made her feel safer.

Closing her eyes, she whispered, "Five, four, three, two..." Her mother did not disappoint her.

"Larissa?" she said through the hollow door. "Can I come in?"

"I'm hungry, Mom. Is anything left?"

Female footsteps clicked to the kitchenette, dishes rattled, footsteps clicked back to Larissa's door. "Unlock it, baby. I've got Chef Boyardee."

Larissa let her mother in and took the plate of ravioli. She sat on the side of the bed to devour it. Mom handed her a canned Mellow Yellow and watched the ravioli disappear. "Don't get him started tonight," she said. "He's been a snake all day. Beer don't agree with some people."

Larissa scraped the plate clean and chugged the soda. Mom slumped down beside her and fiddled with the drawstring on her child's worn-out hoodie. "Girl," she said, "why do you wear this ratty thing every day, hot as it is in Charleston?"

The teen shrugged one shoulder. Mom gave up on small talk and went back to the important thing. "I'm asking you, L, as nice as I know how, don't make him mad tonight. The super said we're gonna get kicked out on account of the noise."

Larissa set the Mellow Yellow can on the empty plate and handed it to her mother. "That was good, Mom. Thanks for saving it for me." She hugged the woman who looked like an older, heavier version of herself.

"You're welcome, honey. There's another can of ravioli if you want me to heat it up later. You're always so hungry."

"I talked to Mrs. Hammond again at school today. You know, about going to college to be a nurse."

Mom squinted anger. "I hate those school people. All the time telling you stuff we can't do."

"I've got the grades. Might be a scholarship or something."

"Why you want to try to do that, L? Why?"

"Already told you...to get a job, a real apartment. But for you and me, not..."

"And I'm telling you. Stop messing with Jake. My back's still killing me from last time."

"I need to take a shower, Mom. I feel...a little dirty."

# 2.

# Miss Posey and Bedon

Nighttime. Charleston. July. Air so muggy you could break a sweat standing still. Miss Posey Montague, ninety-year-old insomniac who weighed one pound less than her age, jerked the leash on her pig-shaped Boykin spaniel, Hamp, and called him a lowdown mule. Hamp, short for General Wade Hampton, pulled the sparrow of a woman off balance by ignoring his leash and lurching along the sidewalk of Murray Boulevard like a juiced-up battery toy. It was hard to tell if short fat Hamp was panting every breath from being choked to death by Miss Posey or from the sticky South Carolina heat. On this particular sauna of a night, either could have wrung the lifeblood out of a bull gator in his prime.

Dr. Bedon Lautrec Calhoun, Sr. settled deeper into his rocking chair pillow, the same corduroy cushion that had shaped itself to the peach of his backside ten years earlier. From the safety of his piazza, Bedon took a long slug of his iced tea to gird himself up for an encounter with Miss Posey, known neighborhood crank. Right on time, tiptop of ten p.m., she and Hamp blundered by his wrought iron front gate, lyre-designed by Philip Simmons, famous artist among those in the know. "Evening, Posey," Bedon said when he had no choice but to speak. "You and that mutt are better entertainment than the blather on my television set."

Hamp pretended not to recognize his neighbor's voice. He worked himself into such a barking frenzy that his mistress had to swat him with the leash loop. Whack. Silence. Then a pained yelp accompanied by improved behavior on the part of the trainee. General Patton couldn't have done better by him.

But tonight Hamp wasn't the only malefactor in need of straightening out. "Don't you get familiar with me, Bedon Calhoun," said the old maid. "I'll not hesitate to beat you like I beat this dog. I'm still your elder by two decades."

She tugged so hard on Hamp's leash his front feet rose a foot off the sidewalk. The sturdy little Boykin looked like a trick pony pawing the air.

"I see how terrified he is," the threatened Dr. Calhoun said to his nemesis, who couldn't hear him due to the decibel level of her own protracted tirade.

"I'm not the only one around here thinks you're cracked, sir. Everybody's talking about it, how you roost up there on your piazza every night like some concrete gargoyle. I tell'em, I say, 'When Hildie died, he just gave up on livin' himself.' Why else would a perfectly good physician shut down his medical practice and go home to vegetate like a potted plant on his own front porch? What's it been, five years now? Pathetic is what it is. And me having to get naked in front of that wet-behind-the-ears, fresh-out-of-medical-school upstart in Mount Pleasant. Had to let him look at my hemorrhoids this morning. 'I'll have to take a little peek,' he says to me like I'm senile. I don't know which is worse, him or you looking up my rear end."

"Go back home and count your money, Posey. And take that poor abused animal with you. I'm fine right here by my lonesome."

"Can't you think of anything better to do than commune with a dead wife? Where's your imagination gone?"

Bedon lifted his tea glass and proposed a toast to his crotchety neighbor. "To a heartwarming tender lady I'm always delighted to see. G'night now, Posey."

He leaned over and balanced his now-cold smoking pipe across the ashtray stand next to his chair. He'd made that stand in his garage workshop six years earlier, a time when he'd felt more like himself, not some stranger with a hole in his heart.

Muttering as she departed, "tender lady" dragged Hamp in the direction of her Murray Boulevard mansion seven doors down from Bedon's lesser mansion. The good doctor massaged his forehead as noise of the epic struggle between spaniel and owner grew faint. He rested his head on the back of the padded rocker and tried to nap, though he knew he wouldn't be able to. He'd found out the day he buried Hildie that solitude never tires of ruining the slumber of its victims.

Rising from the rocker and stretching his legs, he descended the piazza steps and shuffled toward his front gate, taking the tea tumbler with him. An odor of rotten eggs drifted up his nostrils. The essence of pluff mud, famous Southern perfume better known as marsh yuck, had come free with the deal when he'd purchased his house four decades ago. He blew out through his nose like a racehorse as he crossed the street to lean on the iron railing that kept tourists from falling into the harbor. Sometimes he could still appreciate his expensive view, especially after dark when the moon shone bright and new. Sometimes, but not tonight. Tonight he wondered what it would feel like to climb over the railing and jump. Could salt water filling his lungs hurt any worse than this slow death by loneliness? Bedon thought not.

He drank off the last inch of his tea and rested both elbows on the railing. Mesmerized by moonlight, he stood still a few moments, then, uncomforted by the extravagant lunar radiance, he threw the empty tumbler as far out as he could over the black water. It made a puny splash in a wavelet. "And that, you old codger," he said to himself, "is about what your life is worth."

# 3.

## Carriage House Intruder

latter and clang. Bedon alerted to sounds of the neighborhood rogue raccoon burglarizing his trash can again. He had to forsake all poor-me thoughts and his harbor view and return home to defend his garbage.

On a mission now, he seized the golf club lying next to his rocking chair, kept there as a weapon in anticipation of this very moment, and made tracks for the backyard to confront old mask face.

Sly as a shadow, the raccoon scampered behind the carriage house at the far back of the lawn, disappearing among the tangle of honeysuckle vines the carriage house owner had been meaning to clear out since early spring. Wary of rattlers, Bedon slowed his hot pursuit despite being aware no self-respecting diamondback would take up residence within the city. Still...

Darkness hampered his vision. Was the carriage house door standing open? Did the lock not catch when he pulled it shut that morning after mowing the lawn and putting the mower away?

Under his breath, he said to the invisible intruder, "Outsmarted yourself this time, Zorro. A new but not improved hiding place."

Clinks and clanks. Scrabbling sounds. And was that a growl? Bedon, his golf club poised high in the air, issued a command. "Come out, bandit. Federales got you cornered."

No more noise. No more movement. The urban hunter reached inside the carriage house door, taking care not to place a sandaled foot in some dark danger zone – rats certainly do reside in a few luxury hiding places downtown – and switched on the light.

No raccoon shot past. No rattlesnake slid between his feet. Only rusty rakes and hoes welcomed him, plus a giant collection of oversized art canvases, unwanted vestiges of his late wife, Hildie's, favorite pastime. A few stacks of those moldy canvases appeared to have grown taller over the years, reaching chest height and higher now. Bedon elected not to venture into this hard evidence of chaos theory that had been percolating in his carriage house the five long years since Hildie's demise. Not at nighttime when nocturnal wild animals roamed free. "Come out, Bat Man," he said as a last threat. "You're on animal control's most wanted list."

Another moment of silence convinced the hunter the rascal had foiled him again. He turned off the light and closed the door, checking this time to make sure it had locked tight. "Justice is patient," he said to the balmy evening air, "as patient as an old man with nothing to do."

But the night's excitement was not over. The moment Bedon heard the works of the lock tumble into place, a cry fainter than a newborn's penetrated his good ear. He fumbled for the key under the geranium pot by the door. His hands trembled as he worked with the lock that was six months overdue for a squirt of WD-40.

As he shook the doorknob, he realized with a start that someone was shaking it harder from the other side. The door flew open. Bedon jumped back. Something, or someone, plunged through and landed in a sprawl on the flagstones at his feet. He raised the golf club, but the human form, after moaning and writhing about for a second, went deathly still.

Bedon backed into the carriage house and hit the light switch again. Still gripping the golf club, he dropped to his knees on the wet grass. When his eyes adjusted, he could make out that the person prone on his flagstones was not an axe murderer, but a girl, adolescent judging from her size, all bloody and unconscious.

As he knelt beside her, the physician Bedon still was at his core leapt to the surface of his consciousness. His brain kicked into medical mode, a function it hadn't accessed in months. He checked her pulse, her breathing, tested all four limbs for breaks. Satisfied it was safe to move her, he utilized the adrenaline still pumping through his system to carry her into the main house.

After settling the small stranger on the couch in his back den, he picked up the phone to call 911. But after pressing nine, he hesitated for some primordial reason that never revealed itself to his rational mind, no matter how many times after the fact he tried to force it to the surface.

Dr. Bedon Lautrec Calhoun, Sr. – widower, father, grandfather, stand-up citizen, retired doctor, church member and lay preacher, honorable gentleman who never stepped to the left or right – hung up the phone for good that night. He closed the blinds of his den, blinds that hadn't been closed in ten years, fetched his black medical bag from the cabinet section of his built-in, knotty pine bookshelf, and began to treat the wounds of a young girl who would change his life forever. He knew nothing about her, not that she was extraordinarily intelligent, or had dreams of transcending poverty through becoming a nurse, or had been given the name, Larissa, by a mother who would have been overjoyed to find out that in Greek it meant "Cheerful One."

As Bedon worked on his unknown patient's cuts, the only time she acknowledged his presence was to complain a bit without opening her eyes about the shots of lidocaine he administered in her chin and cheek. She did not protest as he closed the curved gashes in her flesh with the tiniest stitches he had ever sewn. And with every suture, he felt a certain something gaining strength inside his own heart, something like the beginning of a slow heal.

# 4.

## *Stitches*

Thomas Turner, the nickname Hildie had given her husband's prized grandfather clock, struck twelve midnight. For weeks, Bedon had been awake to witness this regular event. But tonight, of all nights, even with the peculiar circumstance of a small quiet visitor sleeping on his den sofa, he lay breathing easy in his leather chair, his big bare feet propped high upon matching ottoman, and snoozed right through it. Walter Edgar's beloved book, *South Carolina: A History,* lay open in the snoozer's lap to page two hundred and forty-four, Chapter Ten, "Threats: Foreign and Domestic." Which made sense as a choice of reading material considering the reader himself had so recently let a stranger into his home.

The stranger had been snoring on Bedon's sofa well over an hour. She awakened on Thomas Turner's twelfth chime, sat straight up, and flung off the blanket with which her rescuer had covered her.

"Who are you?" she said to her groggy host. "Is that a clock somewhere?"

"Oh, hello." Bedon said, waking up slowly, rubbing his eyes. He lowered his feet from ottoman to carpet and pulled himself forward to the edge of his chair. "What did you say? Something about a clock?"

"Like a gong. Are you telling me you didn't hear that?"

He looked at his watch. "Oh, it was Mr. Turner splitting the night in two. That's what midnight does, you know. How do you feel? Looks like you've got your color back."

She remained seated, but glanced around the den, fearful, trying to determine the quickest way out. Bedon explained more about Mr. Turner in the coolest tone he could muster. "It's a grandfather clock. Strikes every hour, on the half-hour and quarter-hour, too. My wife used to tell everybody it struck twenty-four the day I carried her over the threshold as a bride. She didn't know Henry Clay Work was my favorite songwriter. I love every tune he ever penned, except for that heartbreaker, 'Marching through Georgia.'"

Larissa licked her dry lips and swallowed with great effort. "I don't know what you're talking about. Where's the door?"

"Behind you. No one's trying to hide it. Follow the yellow brick road to the kitchen. The back door is on the far side." He stood up, still gripping the book he'd been pretending to read. "Want something to drink before you go? A Coke, maybe? I keep them here for my grandson and his girlfriend when they come by, and I can certainly put old Dr. Edgar aside…" He held up the heavy volume, so she could see he meant Dr. Edgar was a book, not a real person. "… long enough to pour one for you over ice."

"I don't like Coke. I like Mello Yellow." She joined him in standing, a bad mistake given what she'd been through over the last few hours. Pain contorted her face. As she felt for its source, her fingertips encountered the sutures in her chin. Her knees buckled. She sat back down so hard that Bedon was glad the sofa was there to catch her.

Observing her with a medical eye, he said, "Dr. Edgar doesn't usually have such a stunning effect on people. He'd be thrilled to hear you were almost overcome at the mere mention of his name." He placed the book topmost on a stack of others on his lamp table. "Those are stitches in your chin and cheek. You'll have to keep them clean."

"Are you some kind of doctor, like that Dr. Edgar guy there?" She pointed to the thick blue book.

Bedon had to laugh at that. "Oh, my, no. Walter's a real doctor, an academic. He wrote that big tome all by himself. Me, I'm a lowly physician. Used to be, anyway. Still licensed, but don't go to the office like I used to."

Pale again, she gathered enough strength to ease herself up and make her way through the archway to the hall. From there it was a straight shot to the brightly lit kitchen. Bedon followed her at a respectable distance. She stopped and looked back at him after opening the door to the outside. He was standing next to the fridge, as far away from her as he could get and still be in the same room. "Thanks," she said. "I don't know how I got hurt or how I got in this house. I don't even know who you are."

"For starters, I'm the owner of the carriage house, where you were hiding."

"I did figure that much out. I'm not dumb." She wiped her nose on her hoodie sleeve, a childlike move rendering null and void the fierceness in her voice. Bedon waited with restraint to see what she'd do next. He did not have to wait long. "Well," she mumbled, "see ya...I guess." Then she vanished into the night with the same abruptness with which she had appeared. No warning. No explanation.

# 5.

## Sooner or Later, Stitches and Personality Must Come Out

A week and a day passed. Then at midnight once more according to Thomas Turner, she showed up again, this time on the moss-covered back steps to Bedon's den. It was a door he never used, in fact, kept a cedar chest in front of it on the inside, which made answering her timid knock a test of determination. Yet sliding the heavy chest to the side and hassling with the frozen door lock proved worth the trouble. The good doctor beamed at her, delighted to see the improved condition of his odd little patient.

"Hey there," he said. "Been wondering about you. A week? More than a week? How'd you get along with your stitches?"

She touched the red line on her chin that was crisscrossed with tight black sutures. "My mom said whoever put them in for free has to take them out for free. She tried to make me tell, but I wouldn't."

"Why not?"

"I don't know. Can you work on them now?"

"Sure, come in."

She looked around the den, checking off details in her memory. Bedon shoved the cedar chest back in front of the door. He walked over and fetched his medical bag from its home in the bookshelf cabinet, where he'd hidden it from the curious eyes of his daily lunch visitor – grandson, Bedon Lautrec Calhoun, Jr. (nicknamed Buddy, to lesson confusion). And why did the respectable doctor hide his own bag? That was one more question to add to the lengthening list for which the respectable doctor had no answers.

He motioned her to follow him. "Light's better in the kitchen," he said. "This way. But you already know which way, don't you."

She lagged behind in the hall to scan a grouping of photos starring Buddy at different ages. Birthday parties, graduations, vacations of all sorts – snowboarding sugared mountain slopes, kayaking turquoise waters.

Bedon glanced over his shoulder to see what was holding her up. "Great pics, all right," he said when he saw what had captured her attention. "My grandson, Buddy, calls it scene staging. A second before the happy shot, the star's getting his backside warmed up with the business end of somebody's hair brush."

She averted her eyes from the wall. "Sorry. There're so many. I couldn't help but..."

"Look all you want. No charge."

She hurried to catch up with him. He showed her which chair to sit in at the kitchen table. "So," she said, "did you tell him about doctoring me?"

"Who?"

"You know who. Your grandson."

"No, I didn't."

"Why not?"

He thought a minute, but was unable to come up with an answer, not an unusual happenstance these days. "Beats me," he said. "But that's not important. What's important is why your mother lets you stay out so late."

She accompanied her response to this insult toward her mother – at least, she interpreted it as an insult whether Bedon meant it to be or not – with a couple of perfectly executed head-rolls, defiant moves foreign to her host. Said she with practiced toughness, "I don't know the answers to stuff you ask me, mister, like you don't know the answers to stuff I ask you. Which means we both know the answers to everything, but aren't telling each other anything."

The physician, whose intention was nothing more than helping a poor and needy one, peered into her insolent green eyes. "I didn't get all that," he said and thought he was being convincing.

She swiveled a last expert "roll" out of habit. "You did so get it. You just think it's cool to play like you didn't. I told you before, I'm not dumb." Her performance was genius, should have been on TV.

"Uh-huh," he said, impressed. "Well then, you also know I can't clip stitches out of a moving target."

She glared back at him. "The thing I've been wondering," she said, sounding as if she might be accusing him of something, "is why you didn't call 911 that first night. My mom does it all the time."

Bedon imitated her one-shouldered shrug. She threatened him with her eyes. "Making fun of me isn't any cuter than playing dumb. I knew you wouldn't tell me, 'cause I knew you wouldn't know yourself."

She reached out and thumped him hard in the chest. He hunched over and grimaced, fooling no one present. "This conversation is wearing me out," he said. "I can't follow it, and I can't treat a wiggle worm. Do you want me to take these stitches out or not?"

"What do you think, mister? They itch."

# 6.

## Bedon Helps Larissa; Larissa Hurts Bedon

Larissa held her head still and looked up Bedon's nose while he clipped her stitches out. Bored, she began counting a group of dark brown moles the size of pin pricks on his forehead. Five, six, seven, eight...nine. With nothing else interesting to look at, she decided to interrogate the suspect.

"How old is he, your grandson?"

"Twenty-eight."

"Does he live here with you?"

"Used to. His mother and father got killed in a car wreck, my daughter and son-in-law. But Bud's all grown up now. Goes to law school over town, has his own apartment."

"And you're paying for it. Sort of like paying for him not to live here."

"Bingo."

She paused before getting to what she really wanted to know. "Are you some kind of rich perv?"

"What?"

"You know, a pervert."

Bedon's face went burgundy. He blinked, then blinked again.

She raised her eyebrows. "You don't have to go all mental about it. I was just asking."

The doctor's hands and forearms began trembling so violently, he drew a drop of blood on yanking out the last stitch. "We're done here," he said. "You can go."

She looked into his watery eyes – cracked-marble irises, light blue with darker blue outer rings – and lowered the pitch of her voice. "I know you're not a perv. Kids watch too much TV. True crime. I know I do."

"Tell your mother to put peroxide on those places tonight."

"I'll do it myself if we have any. I'm going to start taking classes soon to be a nurse."

Bedon dug in his bag and produced a dark bottle. "Here's a freebie for Florence Nightingale. Three percent peroxide." He set the bottle on the table, shuffled over to the sink, turned the cold water on full force, and began washing his hands and face.

The sight of his bent back made her regret what she'd said even worse. Getting up from the table, she picked up the peroxide bottle and imitated Bedon's shuffle on her way to the back door. Hesitating, she turned and studied her good angel as he toweled off his face. Then she apologized again in a voice almost inaudible. "I didn't mean it. It was a stupid thing to say. Sometimes I'm not as smart as I look." She paused, working her mouth and eyes. "Thanks for sewing me up the other night. I probably would've bled to death."

Bedon, his cheeks now flushed and damp, turned around and faced her. Leaning backward against the sink for support, he said, "You would not have bled to death. Facial lacerations always make people think that. Lots of scary red. Now go home. I don't even want to know how you got the stinking cuts."

Tears pooled in her eyes. "I didn't mean it, and you know I didn't. Everybody gets mad at me."

The good angel's eyes blazed. He clenched his jaw as he crossed the kitchen to where she was standing. Reaching behind her, he pushed the door open and stepped to the side, somehow managing to execute both moves without touching as much as a thread of her jacket. "Go...we're done here." His words had such force they assaulted his own ears as well as hers.

She flinched. "Okay, okay. But you don't have to be so hateful about it." Halting a second, she changed the subject. "I guess you've decided not to call DSS on me about the la-cer-ations." Another pause, a deadly silence, then, in a voice as regular as one might use to make a comment on the weather, she dropped a bomb shell on her host. "Lacerations aren't all that's wrong with me." And in one smooth motion she unzipped her hoodie and stuck out her small, yet obviously pregnant belly. It looked as though she'd stuffed a cantaloupe under her hot pink tee.

Bedon stared at her abdomen a full ten seconds without moving a muscle. He had to shake himself to break the trance. "You need to go home to your mother. This thing here? My treating your face? It's over and done with."

"My name is Larissa, but you don't care." She stepped sideways through the open door, pausing long enough to force him to look at her face. "Who's Florence Nightingale, anyway?" she said. "Your wrinkledy old girlfriend? I'll bet you don't talk mean to her like that, do you, Dr. Quack."

# 7.

## Enter Buddy

Next day at twelve when the sun was high and hot, Bedon stood sweating in the shade of his backyard grand oaks. From a distance of twenty yards, the old man contemplated the door of his carriage house. He held a key in his right hand, trying to decide whether or not to use it. Perspiration trickled down his back under the white, mesh-vented shirt his grandson, Bud, had given him for his birthday. Then a toggle switch flipped in his brain, and the aging gentleman began a slow journey across his yard via the flagstone walkway he'd laid in himself. He locked the door of the carriage house and dropped the key into his pants pocket.

Buddy strode up as his grandfather was twisting the doorknob to the building to make sure it was secure. "Hey there, Pop," he said. "Locking your trash in?"

"Locking my trash *out*."

Buddy nodded. "Yep, yep, yep. Ronnie raccoon again. Don't tell that trigger-happy Sol Jacobs next door. The guy needs some serious target practice, and if you ask me, a new can of Right Guard. Whew-wee."

Bedon chuckled as he mopped the sweat off his face with a dingy handkerchief that compromised the trendiness of his shirt. "Nobody ever accused old Sol of smelling like jasmine. Let's go in and get your lunch. I'm not hungry myself."

The two men headed toward the main house. "Where's Caroline?" the older Calhoun said to the younger as they walked along in step. "I thought she was coming with you today?"

"Stood me up. Stood us both up. Heartless little hussy would rather go shopping for engagement rings with her mother than eat lunch with us two cave men. I think she and her 'muh-tha' should marry each 'uh-tha' and leave us out of it altogether."

"I'm not the one marrying her."

Buddy stopped long enough to kick a pebble back to its home in the driveway. He said as he resumed walking, "You know what, Pop. Neither am I, and somebody ought to break the news to the girl. You've always said you'd do anything for your only grandson."

"Not that. I'd rather face a barracuda."

# 8.

# Buddy Calhoun, Valedictorian?

"We're a reasonable family, aren't we, Bud? To my knowledge none of us has ever spent more than a night or two in jail. And I'm okay as fellows go, right?"

Bedon asked these unusual questions of his grandson while they were eating their midday meal. But his grandson wasn't paying attention. He was too busy chomping his way through a kitchen-table spread of fried chicken and heirloom tomato sandwiches loaded with Duke's mayo and McCormic's black pepper, favorite brands of none other than Elvis, the king. (This midday meal was courtesy of a widow from the church who'd gotten ideas into her head about courting and marrying the most eligible widower in the congregation, Dr. Bedon Calhoun.)

Buddy gnawed the meat off a greasy chicken leg with the relish of a Neanderthal, Caroline being correct in her observation of his habits, and washed it down with sloppy gulps of iced sun tea...don't hold the Dixie Crystal.

"Haven't ever thought about whether people think we're nuts," he said. "I ranked ninety-four out of ninety-five academically in my senior class at Porter Gaud. That ought to count for something. Pass the salt, will you? The only thing'd make this plate prettier would be some of Grandma Hildie's 'whupped' potatoes. I miss her." He smacked his lips and licked each one of his fingers with individual care.

Bedon handed his progeny a napkin and considered the lifelong plight of Caroline, if by some miracle she landed him permanently. Forcing himself not to comment on Buddy's table manners, the loving grandpa posed another question, though he expected no straighter answer than before. "And who ranked ninety-five?"

Bud drained his tea glass and breathed out the famous aaah sound that passes for manners in Southern male company. "Bo Gaillard, my best friend in all the world, ranked dead last. I was thrilled for him when he achieved that high honor."

A supersonic belch erupted from Bud's esophagus, followed by another a tad less deafening. "The only reason Bo didn't place ninety-six was that Bubber Holston transferred to public school first semester our senior year. He went over to Wando High where every guy on the football team weighed over three hundred pounds like he did. Left Bo and me competing for last on class rank. And I guarantee you, I would not have let Gaillard beat me out if it hadn't been for that hot-lipped little French teacher I got a crush on. Studied my irregular verbs to impress her every day and pulled too many A's on oral conversation. 'Je t'aime toujours. Je t'adore toujours. Plus que Frogmore stew.'"

Buddy's grandfather snickered. "I thought you were valedictorian and Bo was salutatorian."

"Nuh-uh, we had that fake graduation program printed up saying we were just for your sake. The truth would have been too painful. You didn't have to face reality about little ole me 'til I washed out of The Citadel the first fifteen minutes of my knob year. Good thing College of Charleston takes rejects."

"I have to tell you, Buddy, it irritated me no end you didn't go to medical school."

"Why you want to say that to me, Pop, when you know good and well I wanted to be a rock star?" Buddy picked up two oily drumsticks he'd stripped clean of meat and tapped out a rhythm on the kitchen table. Bedon tried to hand him another napkin, which Peter Criss (original drummer for KISS who'd somehow taken over Buddy's body and was now in full performance) rejected outright. Peter accompanied his creative drumming with original lyrics. "I made," – tap, tap, tap – "six thousand, seven hundred and eighty-six bucks," – tap, tap, tap – "playing in my fabulous band the first four years after I graduated from college, most of which I spent wisely on riotous living and the rest of which I squandered." Tap, tap, tappity, tap, with a flashy, eight-second jungle-drum roll for a rousing rock star finish, a real crowd pleaser.

"Your old grandpa is still thanking his Maker you didn't achieve stardom, although I don't know why you decided to become an attorney instead of a doctor...after you crashed back to planet earth, that is. Guess you aren't going to change your mind at this late date, a year into law school."

"And doing all my studying right here in my own home town, so I can come over to your house and eat free lunch every day. And go to summer school like now. I found out last month that lawyers have to write up all their cases in a foreign language called legalese. My advisor told me I needed some extra tutoring in it. Made me enroll in his 'optional' class for eight captivating weeks. I don't know why. I think I write good. Who'd-a-thunk Charleston would ever open up herself an attorney mill?"

Buddy tilted his straight-legged chair back and belched again. Bedon tilted his own chair back and belched in self defense, though as a lesser expert. The rear legs of the two ladderbacks made four more dents in the ancient red linoleum. When Hildie was alive, she didn't permit husband, child, grandchild, or anyone else to scuff her weekly application of pine scented Spic and Span.

"Your grandmother wouldn't take kindly to us gouging pits into her floor," Bedon said.

Bud expressed his disagreement by letting the ladderback he was occupying fall forward with a clunk. "Look, Pop. Grandma Hildie's been dead and gone way longer than my rock band, may they both rest in peace. She ain't worried about her linoleum no more, and you shouldn't be, neither."

Bedon rested his elbows on the table and rubbed his forehead with the heels of his palms. Buddy got up and began depositing dishes and silverware into the sink with excessive noise to make the task sound difficult. When he finished, he took a short break to observe his grandfather's behavior. "What is it they call those headaches, Pop? T.I.A.'s? One more reason I want to get a nurse in here to help you. Or at the least, Aunt Pauline and Uncle Lawrence."

"No, not them. And a T.I.A. is a mini-stroke, not a simple headache."

"If you say so, but keep your aspirin bottle handy, just in case. You never know."

"Aspirin is for heart attacks, not strokes. Why did I ever think you'd make a good doctor?" The elderly man sat up straight and pulled himself together. "And you didn't answer my question."

"What question?"

"About whether we're considered a decent family."

"Oh, that. Let's see. If you don't count Aunt Pauline... How many times has she been in the loony bin? If you don't count her, I suppose we're good as any. She's an in-law, not blood kin. Who gives a rip anyhow?"

"I don't know. It occurred to me people might think I'm getting cracked in my old age, living in this barn of a house all by myself for so long. Do you think I'm...cracked?"

Buddy soaked a paper towel in hot water and wrung it out in the sink. "Let me tell you something, gray man," he said, while wiping crumbs off the tabletop straight onto the floor. "A person who thought a man like you was cracked would be cracked himself." He wadded up the towel and free-threw it into the trash can with a swish. "Did you see that? I nailed it. Eat up with talent is what I am. Look-a-here, Pop. Have you been watching 'Dr. Phil' again?"

# 9.
## Larissa Returns, Battered Worse

Metal on metal. Glass on glass. A series of feral yelps. The kind of nocturnal fuss sure to offend persnickety dwellers South of Broad Street. Random lights blinked on, illuminating the windows of homes on both sides of Bedon's. He jumped out of his piazza rocking chair, aware that night noise of this variety could mean only one thing, and it wasn't the masked bandit.

Fuzzy minded from dozing, no flashlight in hand, the elderly homeowner stumbled down the side piazza steps on his way to the backyard. In his haste in the purple darkness, he came close to tripping over her. Quiet now, she lay immobile on the dew-damp back lawn.

Sol Jacobs' shaky voice split the darkness next door. "Need any help, Bedon? You know I keep my derringer loaded."

Bedon guessed, hoped, prayed his frail neighbor of forty years hadn't ventured beyond his own back stoop. He called to him as loudly as he could, for his frail neighbor was more deaf than he. "Raccoon again, Sol. Go on back to bed before your rheumatism kicks up. I'll call animal control in the morning. And put that Howitzer back in your gun safe."

The response he received was the irritated sound of Sol's back door banging shut. After which Bedon noticed for the first time his own palms had begun to sweat. He wiped them on his pant legs, muttering something under his breath about Sol being "a blind loose cannon, literally."

On straightening up, he stared at the long row of eight-foot oleanders separating his and the Jacobs' backyards. It was clear no one, not even a person with good eyesight, could see through those pink-blossomed monsters. Yet, he could not bring himself to begin trying to help the troubled girl at his feet, not until Sol's windows and the rest of his neighbors' windows had faded to black again.

When the last lamp winked out, Bedon squatted down beside her. She remained on her stomach, silent, tranquil, her face buried deep in monkey grass that had long since outgrown its welcome as a border around Hildie's swan hydrangeas. He eased her over onto her back to assess the damage, impossible even with the help of reflected glow from a high gibbous moon.

She stirred. He spoke. "Whoever is doing this to you has got to be locked up. This time I'm calling DSS."

Bolting upright, she bumped his nose with her forehead. "No, no. They know us. They'll try to put me in another foster home." She got to her feet with difficulty. "I'm going. I'll find somebody else to help me."

Shifting mental gears, Bedon became Dr. Calhoun of the good old days, the one who had enough physical strength to prevent a combative patient from getting the upper hand. "You're going all right, back to the kitchen for more medical attention. Otherwise, I'm calling the police."

As strong as he thought he had become, she broke away from him easily and hurry-hobbled around the side of the house toward the miniature front lawn. Her destination appeared to be the sidewalk, which would provide a quick escape route. Bedon followed in a clumsy gait, at which point Miss Posey, accompanied as usual by Hamp, spied the homeowner, but not the fugitive. On hearing Hamp snuffling up the sidewalk, the "fugitive" managed to drop to her knees and out of sight behind the wisteria trellis flanking the side piazza.

Miss Posey pulled Hamp up short. "What the devil are you doing, Bedon?" she called out to her favorite, if cracked, neighbor. "You scared the living daylights out of me."

"I, uh...was chasing that raccoon again. He got back in the carriage house, you see..."

"You were not. Hamp would have jerked me clear to Ropemaker's Alley if he'd smelled a raccoon. Poor dog hardly ever gets to chase."

"Maybe it was a cat then. I don't know. It's gone now, whatever it was."

"Why don't you go to bed like a normal human being? People already…well, you know what people already think, you up all hours like a vampire."

"And what do they think about you, Posey? Up all hours like a vampire yourself."

"I don't care. My time has come and gone." She returned her attention to Hamp, who was making a valiant attempt to chew his leash in two. "Stop that, Wade Hampton, you ungrateful mongrel. Make haste. You're going home to bed like a normal dog and some normal people."

It wasn't until "Lady and the Tramp" had bumbled away that Bedon realized his legs had turned to jelly.

# 10.
# Accepting Help, Rejecting Pity

Qarissa made sure Miss Posey and Hamp were out of hearing and sniffing distance before she tried again to elude her pursuer. Bedon, despite his weak knees, managed not only to catch up with her, but to overpower her, akin to overpowering a sick puppy.

They tussled as he guided her up the piazza steps, through the front door, across the foyer and down the dark hall to his den. "If you didn't want my help, why did you come back here?" he said, huffing on some words, puffing on others. He made her sit down in his armchair, then fired the question again. "I said why did you come back here?"

She answered this time by staring mute at two blank TV screens, one on top of the other, that were occupying the far corner of the room. It was an eye-catching arrangement of monitors, all Bud's idea. That is, using the old furniture-style console TV as a base for the new, fifty-six-inch plasma screen, joyfully referred to by Buddy as "the bomb," that he'd convinced his pop no red-blooded American male could live without, the purchase of which, according to Bud's best friend, Bo Gaillard, was the most superior idea Buddy had ever hatched in his entire history of superior ideas.

Bedon almost made a remark about the futility of his angry little visitor watching two TVs, neither of which was turned on, then remembered he'd caught himself doing the very same thing last week after lightning had run in on his breaker box and shut down all things electrical in the house for four hours. Welcome to downtown Charleston. He decided against trying to explain to his patient the atypical logic behind the odd setup of his home entertainment system, and to focus instead upon her problems, not his own.

After a moment of intense medical evaluation, he said, "This appears to be an ordinary female pout. I'm used to them. Hildie was a master. Nod your head yes if I need to get my black bag. But to tell you the truth, I'm more concerned about your baby at this point."

She didn't look away from the two TVs as she spoke. "Must be okay. I never get any sleep for all the kicking." She rubbed her eyes with both fists like a child. Bedon hated seeing how dirty and tear-streaked her face was. She spoke again, flatly. "My arm's bleeding, though." Sliding forward in the leather chair, she began unzipping her hoodie.

"Wait," Bedon said. "I'll get my bag. And we need to move to the kitchen, fluorescent lights in there, if you can tear yourself away from that intriguing drama on Channel Zero. Though I have to agree with you. I'd rather watch a couple of blank screens than most of the shows they have on now-a-days."

# 11.

## A Serious Girl Makes a Serious Threat

Qarissa ignored Bedon's lame attempt at humor. She got up and headed toward the kitchen. By the time her rescuer had found his bag and joined her, she was sitting in the same chair as before, jacket pushed back off her shoulders, dirt and blood on her t-shirt, dirt and some other unrecognizable gunk on her face, shivering as if the temp in the room were freezing instead of stuffy hot. Dr. Calhoun did not sit down when he saw how bad she looked in the light. He went straight back to the den to get one of Hildie's handmade throws to put around his patient's thin shoulders.

"All right," he said with false cheerfulness. "Let's have a look. And you're sure I don't need to check the baby?"

"I told you, it's okay." She held her hand forward, palm up, so the kind man, on whom she had no choice but to depend for an hour or so, could examine her inner arm. The kind man, unprepared for what he was about to see, winced on being confronted with four, blood encrusted band-aids covering a wound in the tender white area just below her left elbow. "What? Why didn't you say something when I was strong arming you before?" So much for false cheerfulness. He peeled off the band-aids and examined the deep gash. "This is worse than your face."

"Other doctor said I got a high threshold for pain."

"What other doctor?"

"At the emergency room. I have to go there sometimes."

Bedon turned away for a second, rubbed his temples, then turned back. "I shouldn't have said anything about it being bad. Unprofessional. Guess I'm losing my edge in my old age. But something's got to be done here."

"Duh. Faster you sew me up, faster I leave."

"No, I mean something about your...situation." Pause. "Who's hurting you at home?"

"Same person who always hurts girls like me. Mom's latest boyfriend. I sassed him good last night."

"Hell's bells. What would he do if you hit him?" He turned her arm back and forth to look at the wound from different angles. "How old are you?"

"Eighteen. And I did hit him."

"You're not eighteen, and I'm not a fool."

"Seventeen then, and neither am I."

He pulled his eyebrows down into a deep V and glared at her. She gave him her signature, one-shouldered shrug. "Sixteen-and-a-half," she said, returning his glare, "and I'm not going back to any foster home. I'll run away first. I'll kill myself."

Electrified by her last three words, Bedon now found himself on the wrong end of the stare-down. He gave in and busied himself with cleaning her cut. "Don't look," he said. "I have to give you shots in this to deaden the pain."

She refused to turn away, did not flinch or shed a tear when he pushed the needle deep into her torn flesh. He monitored her behavior without comment. After the last injection, she spoke to him in an emotionless tone, belying the fact he'd just jabbed her four cruel times. Her low voice had no more feeling than if she were ordering take-out from Domino's. "I want to know why you locked the door last night. Is it a secret?"

His eyes assured her he didn't know what she meant. "The storage building," she said. "I've hidden there tons of times, and it's never been locked before."

He stopped working and looked at her face. Oh, those ruddy cheeks, those defiant eyes. "Bugs and spiders," he said.

"I'm not afraid of bugs and spiders, and neither are you. It was me you wanted to keep out."

"No, other critters, the four-legged kind. Dogs, raccoons." He resumed tying off the last stitch and began the bandaging process. From the beginning of the whole procedure, Larissa had watched every detail of his work as closely as any good nursing student.

When he finished, she tossed her head and said in a bored voice, "Doesn't matter if you keep it locked forever. I won't need a place to crash for a while. Jake took off last night."

"Mom's boyfriend?"

"Uh-huh. Left after this." She glanced down at her arm. "But if he comes back, I don't know."

"I have to report you to somebody. Did you say your name was Larissa?"

"No, I said it was Rainbow in the Mist. My third grade teacher read us a story one time about a Native American princess with that name, so I went home and tied an old shoelace around my head and stuck a nasty pigeon feather in back and went around the apartment the rest of the night making my mom and whoever her boyfriend was at the time call me Rainbow in the Mist. And you don't really have to report my situation to anybody. You just want to get me off your own back."

Bedon kneaded his forehead, trying to avert the headache he felt coming on, then he said to his new patient, "Now that was a roundabout folk tale, Miss Rainbow in the Mist. But I do have to make a call. He might kill you next time. What about your mother? Why doesn't she do anything?"

"Don't talk about my mother. She's good, perfect. No one could ask for a better mother. Not unfit like those DSS case workers say. I hate women like that, with their plastic briefcases and dumb-dumb shoes. They creep me out so bad."

Bedon reached into his bag and pulled out a bottle of pills. He walked over and filled a glass with water from the kitchen faucet.

"I don't need those," she said. "Shots haven't worn off yet. And you know stuff like that wouldn't be good for the baby."

"They're for me, not you." He shook out two pills and downed them with one gulp of water. "My head feels like someone's beating a drum inside it."

"Probably that nutty clock. I'm not coming back here to bother you anymore. And you can't call anyone and tell on me, 'cause you don't know my last name or where I live or anything else. And they'd ask why you didn't call before."

He re-opened the bottle, shook out two more pills, and swallowed them dry. She gave him a disapproving look. "I'm going," she said. "Thanks for this." She held up her bandaged arm. "And don't worry about the stitches. I can cut them out myself since they aren't on my face. I've done it before, being a nurse almost and all." She slipped her hoodie back on and zipped it to hide her baby bump.

Bedon stared down at Hildie's red linoleum, all pocked and punctured, so dull in places it looked black instead of red. He sighed, walked over to the pantry/broom closet by the back door, and disappeared inside. Larissa followed him and peeked in to see what he was doing. She saw as he took two keys with white plastic fobs off a nail beside the light switch, the same nail pinning a Lowcountry wildlife calendar to the wall. He looked hard at the keys in his hand, then hung one back on the nail and held the other out to Larissa. "Be careful about bugs in that old building," he said, "or worse than bugs."

She refused the key. He waited a long time before hanging it back up with its twin. "Well, you know where it is if you ever need it. I used to keep it under the geranium pot outside the carriage house until someone broke in..."

They left the closet and moved to the back door. She flipped her hood up and said, "I know you're not a perv. Sorry I asked you that last time, after you helped me and everything."

"Forgiven and forgotten. You're sure you don't want me to call the authorities to stop this madness right now? I was thinking last night your mother may not know about the baby."

She pointed a forefinger at her temple. "I meant it when I said I'd kill myself if you sic DSS on me. Watch this." Pulling an imaginary trigger, she yelled out one horrifying word, *"POW!"* Then she dropped her head forward on her chest, feigning unconsciousness.

Bedon, shocked beyond anything he'd ever experienced, could not say a word. When recovered enough to speak, he did so with concentrated intensity. "Don't ever do that again. When you think or talk about violent things, you might wake up one day and find yourself acting them out. What's the matter with you? Are you crazy?"

"Nope, it's just how it is. You don't call DSS, and I don't scare you anymore with talk like that. Deal?"

"Boy oh boy, you're one tough cookie." He looked down at the floor a second before confronting her hostile eyes again. "Okay then," he said. "I won't call. But you...you have to straighten up before it's too late. What you just said? Just did? It's dangerous stuff."

She snorted, a reply the meaning of which he could not decipher. He jingled the change in his pocket to try to calm himself, an absentminded habit in the same category as someone else's one-shouldered shrug. Then, again with no warning, she faded from sight among the black shadows South of Broad Street. Neighborhood of nice. Natural habitat of the Bedon Calhouns of the world, not of a schoolgirl acquainted with poverty and violence. Her natural habitat was...well, which resident who slept every night in an elegant bedroom in an elegant mansion would ever know about Larissa's natural habitat? And which of them would even care?

# 12.

## Desperation Spawns a New Way to Help

Bedon didn't sleep five minutes the rest of the night. For hours, anxious *what-if* ideas chased each other around in his skull like a pack of devils. The next morning when he went outside to unlock the carriage house, and to leave it unlocked for the girl who was far more disturbed than he'd first guessed, his hands shook so much he had trouble dealing with the key. Even dropped it once and had to conduct a hands-and-knees search through the slimy grass shoots between his flagstones, a difficult task that added a strobe light effect to his already high red alert thoughts of self recrimination. I shouldn't have fallen for that act of hers, he fretted. Should've gone ahead and made the call. Just digging this hole deeper.

After too much time spent trying, he got the key to slip into the lock and the uncooperative door to pop open. When he stepped inside, the condition of the building's interior gave him a pang, not because he was sentimental about it being Hildie's former art studio, for though he hadn't begrudged her the pleasure of having it, he never took seriously her aspirations as an artist. But, oh, how he hated the sight of perpetually junky spaces. Hildie had thought Lowcountry tourists needed more paintings of Rainbow Row on East Bay Street and the sweetgrass basket ladies on Meeting and Market, and, her personal favorite, the Palmetto-tree-framed view of Charleston Harbor from her own front porch. Thus, she'd spent six months and thousands of dollars turning an insignificant carriage house into quarters Michelangelo would have envied, to include the installation of a combo AC/heat window unit to keep Charleston's extreme summer temperatures from melting her expensive Winsor & Newton oil paints.

Trouble was the renovation itself sapped its project manager's creative energy. After she had finished wasting a good portion of Bedon's retirement savings on her ill-conceived project, she lost interest in its original purpose. Never again did she paint a picture of Charleston's high battery or the marketplace or anything else historic. And that was how Bedon became proud owner of the neighborhood's most expensive storage outbuilding. As far as he could see, the only thing of value in the collection of rubbish inside was his beloved John Deere mower with its yellow and green mulch bag attachment, which would fit just as easily in the garage. Everything else could go.

"You're going to have to find new digs," he said to a tiny gray bat hanging upside down from Hildie's dolphin-shaped ceiling light fixture. "A new ministry is about to take root here."

# 13.

# Buddy Worried Sick, Bedon Worried Sicker

"Where are you, Pop?" Bud said as he burst into his grandpa's kitchen for lunch. "Would you believe I got a B+ on my independent research study after failing it last semester?"

Bud's mood plummeted from jubilant to miserable when his grandfather came into the room looking downcast and disoriented. "Pop...man, you look terrible. Is your head hurting that bad? We have to get you to Doc Belton."

Bedon sat down at the table and put his head in his hands. "It'll pass, always does. Say grace and eat. I'll catch up."

Buddy looked at the table laden with ham and tomato sandwiches and perspiring glasses of sweet tea. "You don't have to do all this for me, Pop, not when you feel bad. I should be doing it for you."

He sat down opposite his grandfather and waited. After a few moments, the pale senior citizen took a sip of his tea and put a napkin in his lap. Composed now, he said to his concerned lunch pal, "See there, I told you it would pass."

"Why don't we go on to the doctor," Bud said. "You know it's hard to tell the difference between a T.I.A. and a major stroke."

"I'd know, don't you think? It's my head."

"Okay, but don't take any aspirin today. In fact, don't take aspirin ever again. Throw all the bottles away."

"Sure as I did, I'd have a heart attack and some first responder would ask me where my Bayer was. Seems like you and I have this same conversation once or twice a week."

"What do you think is causing them?" Bud said. "You've had two with me here. Have there been others you haven't told me about?"

"Stress, maybe. It's what they say causes everything."

"If that's the case, I won't make it through tort class next semester without falling out of my seat dead as a hammer."

Buddy's beloved granddad smiled and nibbled at his sandwich. "If I feel another one coming on, I'll check in with Doc Belton. But you know there's nothing he can do. Mini-strokes are sneaky."

"Promise? You'll call him?"

Bedon, his eyes now as serene as a Lowcountry sunset, regarded his grandson's knitted brow. "Don't worry, Buddy boy. I know I'm all you've got, except for that knock-kneed girlfriend, Caroline, bless her heart. How is she today? Still dreaming about a wedding at Wide Awake Plantation and a canned Carnival honeymoon cruise?"

"Buddy boy" did a fake gag with his forefinger.

# 14.

# A Glance Down Memory Lane

Later that same afternoon, Bedon backed his '68 Chevy pickup close to the carriage house door, killed the engine, and hopped out. It was a young man's "hop," for which he paid in hip pain and a limp the next two hours. His usual custom was to take a nap after eating lunch with Buddy, but today he wanted to haul off the trash he'd spent the morning in the carriage house secretly bagging up. Eight leaf bags full. No wonder Buddy had started talking doctor visits when he saw how tired his grandpa looked at lunch time.

After lobbing the last bag onto the truck bed, the weary laborer went back inside the building to do one more walk-through before leaving for the dumpster. He checked the tiny bathroom to make sure the water was still connected. The sink and potty both worked fine. So did the showerhead, though it was a good ten minutes before he was able to make sure. It took that long to drag out all the half-painted canvases Hildie had stashed in the stall behind her Perry Ellis designer shower curtain. Bedon felt grateful his late wife had no way of knowing black mildew had created horror house designs on her pricey curtain and its plastic liner.

The last two trips to the truck to deposit the dusty canvases were exhilarating, completing, once and for all, the trash removal component of Dr. Calhoun's new project. Hildie had nothing on him now in the way of pseudo creativity. Bedon just hoped his own project would be less misdirected. One last check inside the empty carriage house reminded its owner that deep cleaning would require another day's work, maybe two. He would have to scour everything before he could begin the fun part: painting the walls, ceiling, and trim, and, if he got ambitious enough, staining the wooden floor.

The empty parking lot of Bedon's red brick medical building proved without a doubt that the office was not open for business. And, according to the terminal condition of the sago palms in their faux stone planters on either side of the driveway, hadn't been for some time.

Bedon drove his loaded truck around back where he knew he'd find the same old green trash box standing as faithful as an apostle on its concrete platform. Miller's Pharmacy, the business next door, also used the giant dumpster, which meant the closing of Dr. Calhoun's medical practice did not alert the city to transport the rusty relic to a better address.

Dr. Calhoun put his work gloves back on and began throwing the trash, bag by bag, canvas by canvas, over the side of the box. The truck bed was empty in less than twenty minutes, a tenth of the time it had taken to fill it, what with all the bagging, breaking for lunch with Buddy, and having to load the pickup with no help.

When done, the exhausted retiree took off his gloves and leaned against the hood of the truck. He stared at the back of his office building, then decided to use the last bit of energy he had left to walk around front and peek inside. There were seven steps up to the narrow front porch. Bedon found himself having to use the handrail to brace himself as he climbed the stairs, a new necessity since his last visit. But the bright white vinyl letters affixed to the glass front door remained the same, "Dr. Bedon Lautrec Calhoun, Monday – Friday, 9 a.m. – 5 p.m." The letters suggested the conscientious doctor himself might still be somewhere back in the maze of examining rooms, listening to symptoms and writing out prescriptions on a paper pad, computerized prescriptions being too impersonal for the day of gentlemen MDs.

Bedon shaded his eyes and peered through the glass door. He scoped the waiting room with its high-dollar leather chairs, knockoff Oriental rugs, and Bailey & Griffen wallpaper. "Always hated those phony rugs," he said aloud, then turned to skip back down the first three steps and limp down the last four.

# 15.
# How to Decorate a Safe House

Bedon sat in his piazza rocking chair brooding about the pretty little daybed and ten-by-twelve pink frieze rug he had bought at Value City the day before. The set of twin mattresses for the bed, along with the pastel pink rug a twenty-something clerk had spent a quarter hour convincing him would be needed to pull the room together – "really make it pop," she'd said – had been collecting moisture under a tarp in the back of his truck since purchase, reason being their buyer couldn't figure out how to get them into the carriage house without attracting the attention of neighbors. Thomas Turner struck midnight with more emphasis than usual, declaring a simple solution. Move everything in at night, genius. That way you can take your time and avoid nosiness.

Bedon broke a sweat hefting the rolled-up rug onto his right shoulder. It wasn't heavy, just cumbersome, the reason he'd put it off to last. He had already moved all the boxes in, most of which were full of parts and pieces for the daybed. The cheerful assurance printed on each box - Easily Assembled at Home - left the doctor suspicious. This "easy" job would have to be tackled later. Right now, it was all he could do to stagger inside with the rug.

As he propped it against the bathroom door, the novice moving-man/decorator took great pains not to leave scrub marks on the fresh pink wall paint. So far, he had been laboring by the backyard security light, but more detailed work would require higher wattage.

He turned on the ceiling dolphin, and, realizing with an uh-oh that the door to the outside was still standing open, snapped it off again. What good would the window shades he had installed that morning do if he couldn't remember to keep the door closed at night when the ceiling light was on?

He kicked the door shut before hitting the wall switch again, after which the moving-man/decorator changed hats and became expert assembler. He looked around and considered what needed to be done first. The rug would have to be unrolled and put in place, then the daybed dealt with. He had to lean against a wall as the reality of assembling the daybed beast sank in, with its innumerable parts and big trundle drawer designed to house the lower single mattress. For a few moments, Bedon couldn't deal with the prospect. He felt too tired or too old, though he couldn't tell which. It was easier to think about arranging the other things he'd brought in, the ones that didn't have to be put together.

Six or eight jumbo Wal-mart bags, all overflowing with pink pillows and white frilly bed linens, lay strewn about on the bare floor, along with numerous other acquisitions he had surmised a teenage girl might like – two pink blankets edged in satin, four framed puppy posters, two framed kitten posters, a white marsh mallow robe with matching slippers, and an extra large bag of good smelling stuff for the bathroom he'd had to do some guessing about as he shopped the aisles of Bed Bath & Beyond.

It took two hours to put the bed together and make it up, the complicated nature of which caused him to come down with one of his all-systems-stop headaches. Dizzy and in pain, he sat down on the new bed that, when the trundle was in, resembled a too-tall sofa. After the throbbing pain in his temples subsided, he was able to scan the room once more to assess his progress. Not bad. Not bad at all.

Bedon, relieved there was only one more big item left on his to-do list, looked forward to a second trip to the furniture store, where he had to pick up the small chest of drawers that went with the bed. There hadn't been room in the truck to haul everything home at once. He stood up again and eyeballed the empty wall opposite the ultra-feminine bed. Narrow though the space due to the placement of the bathroom door and a super skinny closet, the chest would definitely fit. Both pieces of furniture, chest and bed, were made for a child really, not a teen, so the chest of drawers would be light enough for him to haul in from the truck with no help. He'd already made a mental plan to take the drawers out and carry them in one by one, then to roll the chest itself in on the old hand truck he kept stored in his garage workshop. And now, though he hated to admit it, he could see the overzealous store clerk had been right in trying to convince him to buy a matching mirror to hang over the chest. Good thing a second trip to the store was already in the offing.

He tried unsuccessfully to blink the last vestiges of his head pain way, then took a pill bottle out of his pocket and went to the bathroom to get some water. The spotty mirror above the sink caught his eye. He leaned forward to examine his reflection up close. "Looking a little worse for the wear, old man," he said. "And the kicker is, she probably won't even be back."

# 16.
# Rainbow in the Mist Returns

But a week later, on Thursday morning to be exact, Bedon found out he had been wrong. At half past ten, he unlocked the carriage house to put a reed diffuser fragrance bottle inside – lavender mint, his first purchase ever online – and discovered a note on the bed.

> Hello,
> Did you fix this room up for one of your granddaughters or somebody else special like that? If you did, I won't come back around and get it dirty.
> Check yes__ or no__.
> Sincerely,
> Rainbow in the Mist
>
> By the way, I clipped the stitches out of my arm last night. It didn't hurt. And the baby is still kicking. I knew you would ask me that.
> R

Bedon smiled – Rainbow in the Mist, indeed – and considered what she had meant by "check yes or no." Was it yes, you can come back? Or yes, you cannot come back? He gave up trying to figure it out and used his pocket ballpoint to scribble a response across the bottom of the paper.

I don't have any granddaughters. I fixed the room up for you.

He started to add Do you like it? Which struck him as juvenile, so he stopped while he was ahead. The good report about the baby and no mention of more knock-abouts at home were the only facts he needed to know.

# 17.

# To Take the Key or Not to Take the Key

The note Larissa left was a good thing. It made Bedon feel better about her welfare. But then she didn't come back for days and more days, or at least there was no evidence that she had. So many days he lost count. Thus, on the hottest night of the summer – ninety-five-plus on the piazza where there was supposed to be a breeze off the harbor, but was not – the moving-man/decorator/ assembler decided to work through his regular evening worry session while sweating it out in his porch rocking chair instead of prowling about inside the house like a nervous feline. Was she in danger? Was the baby all right? And why did he care so much?

Here he was again, sleepless at midnight, growing roots in the same old rocker on the same old piazza, smoking the same old pipe. The ritual had become a springboard to pondering obsessively about what sort of psychosis a man would have to be suffering from to spend wads of cash renovating a carriage house for two different females – first Hildie, the art dilettante, and now this little pregnant stray – neither of whom showed an ounce of appreciation.

But then, in the middle of a pull on his pipe, an apparition drifted toward him from the far side of the piazza. He coughed smoke into the air as he scrambled for his weapon, the trusty Momentus five iron that had never gouged a divot out of a fairway.

Larissa, the apparition, spoke when she saw how badly she had startled her good angel. "It's just me. Don't freak out," she said and hurried closer so he could see her more clearly.

"What? Who...?" he said.

She eased herself down on the top step of the piazza to watch the one-man show he was putting on. Grabbing up his dropped pipe, he stamped out the live coal that had fallen out of it onto the wooden floor. Then he turned the air blue with a few choice words Larissa had never heard before, words not fit for print.

She pulled her knees up to her chest and stretched the zipped hoodie over them all the way to her ankles. "Why do adults tell kids not to cuss and smoke when they're doing both themselves?"

"You and Buddy should get together and write a treatise on the pitfalls of listening to adults. He acts like I'm committing a crime every time I say horse sh..., I mean horse feathers, and every time I light up my pipe."

One last spark that had escaped his size eleven Rockports flared in the darkness next to his left foot. He stomped it out with the vengeance of Smokey the Bear. "It's a dying art form."

"What? Cussing?"

"No...the pipe."

"Seems creepy," she said.

"Creepy? The way you and Bud carry on you'd think I was chasing the dragon."

"The what?"

"Never mind."

She shifted her weight from one hip to the other and said, "Still creeps me out."

"Okay, I see this is going to be another one of those circular conversations that goes nowhere and leaves me by the side of the road."

"I'm not talking about the pipe now, Marlboro Man. I'm talking about the storage building."

"Ah, the storage building. The carriage house. The new safe house. What in the world is creepy about pink and white ruffles on everything but the toilet seat? I can tell you one thing, I will never understand women. Creepy? Horse you-know-what."

"People on TV and at school say girls my age shouldn't talk to strangers. Not take gifts and stuff. Somebody might be weird like online sometimes." She stretched out her legs and squirmed about on the hard step.

Bedon, still jumpy from the pipe mishap, pulled another rocking chair close to his own before sitting down to repack his Mark Tinsky. He pointed to the empty chair. "Sit there. You don't have to pretend you're not pregnant in front of me. I'm still a doctor. And for the record, young people do need to be careful. Are you afraid of me?"

"No, but that's the problem. I saw on TV guys do things to get you to trust them, then they start thinking they own you and act real mean when you try to get away. It's on all the time, stuff like that. True crime."

"True crime. I don't know what to say except you're right. I just thought since you've had so many injuries at home, you could use a place to hide out now and then. That's the sum total of what the carriage house is about. It's a safe house, if you need it."

"Saying 'sum total' is dumb. It's like saying sum-sum or total-total. Why don't you go ahead and say it three or four more times, or five or six?"

"I already told you, I can't handle round-and-round tonight. There's such a thing as being a smart alec. I know. I spend time with Bud."

She ignored his remark about Buddy that on Bedon's part had been no more than a pitiful shot at self defense. Cocking her head in make-believe surprise, she said with make-believe sweetness, "Do you feel sorry for me?"

"Matter of fact, I do. My brain is telling me to call somebody right now to get you some help. But my gut is telling me you meant it when you said no more foster homes, not to mention that other awful thing you said. It's what you call finding your can between a rock and a hard place."

"Your can?"

"Your rear end."

"Well then why didn't you say rear end instead of something stupid like *can?*"

"I guess I was trying to talk young like you and Bud. Didn't work, did it."

She thought a moment, but not about Bedon trying to talk cool, about something else that had been on her mind. "So how many keys are there to the carriage house?"

He gave her a quizzical look. "Two. But you know that. You saw them on the nail in the kitchen closet. I'll give you both, so you won't have to be afraid of some old geezer barging in on you."

"Geezer?"

"Yeah. That would be me, a worn-out old geezer." He got up and went into the house. When he returned, he stepped toward her, being careful not to get too close, and handed her the keys. "I hope those will makes you feel safe. But you really do need to start locking the door when you leave. If you don't, some other prowler might take over your territory."

"You could be lying...about how many keys there are. Maybe you've got more than two."

"What do you think?"

She narrowed her eyes at him and said in a soft voice, "That they're two."

Bedon remained silent while she picked at the tiny graphic of a wrecker emblazoned in gold ink on one of the white plastic fobs. *Modern Mules – For All Your Towing Needs.*

"What's your name?" she said to her good angel without looking up.

"Bedon Lautrec Calhoun, Sr. You can call me Bedon or Dr. Calhoun, whichever."

"What does your grandson call you?"

"Pop."

"Sounds like a drink out of a soda machine. What is he, an idiot?"

"No, smart. Smarter than I ever thought about being."

"You mean smart alec. That's what you said before."

"This time I mean smart as in head smart."

"You have to say that. He's your grandson. I'm going to call you Bedon. My name is Larissa, like I told you the other night, but you can call me Rainbow in the Mist if you want to, or just Rainbow."

"Anything's fine with me...Rainbow in the Mist."

"I'm not going to tell you my last name."

"Doesn't matter. The important thing is for you to have an escape route if things get dangerous where you live. Carriage house. Safe house. Bottom line."

"I know," she said and reached over to give back one of the keys. "Bottom line, sum total, bottom line, sum total..."

He took the key from her on reflex. "Don't start that again, young lady."

She slipped the remaining key ring onto her little finger and held it up with a jingle. Moonlight winked off its polished metal. "I ain't afraid of kooky old men like you," she said, "or bugs or spiders, or even snakes."

"Glad to be lumped in with such good company."

She stood to leave and touched the scar on her chin, the doing of which had become a habit. "What happened to the old bike that used to be out in the building? It's a long walk from the project when you're preggie and somebody's been beating up on you."

"Beyond repair. Got rid of it during my cleaning spree. I'll round up a better one for you tomorrow. New, maybe."

"Thanks, if it doesn't cost too much...and I was wondering, if you could get me some of those stuffed animals to put on the bed like girls on TV have in their rooms. I stole a panda bear once from Dollar General. The clerk called the police, and I got threatened with juvie court. Didn't even get to keep the dumb bear. My birthday's not too far away. Whatever you buy me can be for that. I won't ask for anything else. My mom gets a check every month."

But Bedon wasn't listening to her prattle any longer. He was thinking of what might come up if he googled the words "stuffed animals."

Larissa realized his mind had wandered. "I guess I'm too old for junk like toys," she said. "Ought to be asking for groceries for my mother."

"Ask away, Miss Smart Alec."

She giggled. "Better than being an old geezer like you."

# 18.

## Bedon Wears Out His Credit Card Again

For the first time since Hildie's passing, Bedon's memory served him accurately. He knew he'd seen a pile of stuffed animals and the books that went with them on a table at the Preservation Society's Book and Gift Shop at the south end of King Street. He bought one of each: Emmett, the schnauzer; Legare, the lizard; and Hermie, the hermit crab. As an afterthought, he left the animals at the cash register and went back to get the books that had inspired them, babyish though they were.

Next came a visit to Charleston Bicycle Company, the elaborate shop on the Savannah Highway where Bedon found himself purchasing something far more grown-up and expensive than a bag of stuffed animals and picture books. He put a white Fendi Abici Amante Donna two-wheeler bicycle on his Visa card. And to go with it, the clerk had no trouble talking him into a helmet, saddle bags, and a wheel lock. The good doctor allowed himself to be led like a dumb ox up and down the aisles of the store by this young man, for the good reason he remembered with respect the wisdom of a former young clerk's suggestion that a particular mirror over a particular chest would be a most excellent investment. In short, Dr. Calhoun did not want to have to make a second trip to the bike store.

Once he'd gotten back to the old home place South of Broad, the new shopping addict derived as much fun from putting out his purchases in the carriage house as he used to derive from putting out Santa Claus for his daughter (Buddy's mom) when she was little, and for Bud after the life-altering car wreck.

A Build-A-Bear almost as big as a real cub was the last animal he placed on the daybed. He'd allowed a third adolescent clerk at the Citadel Mall Build-a-Bear Workshop Store – she reminded him of Larissa – to dress the brown bear in a rock star outfit in hopes it would please little Rainbow in the Mist. He went so far as to raise his right hand and take the formal oath to care for Fuzzy Wuzzy, this to the delight of a set of pre-school twin girls who were having their birthday bears dressed up like princesses, all paid for by their plump Grandmother Nettie. Out of vain largesse, Nettie was merrily maxing out her own VISA like there was no tomorrow on behalf of her granddaughters.

Bedon wasn't positive, but he suspected Grandma was trying to flirt with him. She followed him around the store like a birddog, asking who he was buying the darling rock-and-roll bear for, where he lived, if he lived alone, if by chance he'd like to go on a senior citizen bus trip to Branson, Missouri in November to see seven country-western stage shows and eat buffet dinners every night for a solid week. Bedon couldn't get out of that store fast enough. In his hurry to get to the mall center walkway, he tripped over a box of stuffed baby bears and almost fell into a plastic duck pond filled with real water. The last he saw of Nettie, she was clattering along behind him through the food court on her black patent kitten heels, hollering out her phone number.

# 10.
## Happy Birthday and Merry Christmas

"Mom thinks I stole it."

Larissa, Bedon's still occasional, though welcomed nighttime visitor, again occupied the steps of her benefactor's front piazza. This time she had no eyes for the pipe-puffing master of the porch. She stared, entranced, at the gleaming new Fendi designer bicycle leaning in elegant repose on its kickstand in the middle of a certain old geezer's herringbone brick walkway. The bike's chrome handlebars glinted in the halogen glow of Murray Boulevard's row of security lights. Its jet-black tires emitted the smell of new rubber, jet-black saddle bags the smell of real leather.

"It's for your birthday and Christmas and next year's birthday," Bedon said. "Set me back a bundle. I'm worried about someone stealing it from you, not to mention the danger factor of you riding it in your condition."

She got up and rubbed her lower back, then padded down the steps to admire the bike at closer range. "Beats walking, Santa. I'll register it at the police station tomorrow with its serial number and my name. I know all about how to do that, 'cause I stole a boy's bike once when I was twelve. He left it in the school rack one afternoon and forgot to chain it up. I took it while he was in the Dixie

Convenience Store on the corner, buying ciggies every day of the week. He lied about where he was to his father, told him he was at soccer practice. I heard him when he said it."

She paused to flick a non-existent speck of dust off the slender seat of the bike. "His I'm-the-most-fabulous-stock-broker-in-the-world fa-h-h-h-ther had the po-po looking for his baby boy's cheap-wad bicycle by six that afternoon. They came straight to our apartment complex. Lots of stolen bikes end up there. I know that now, but I didn't know it then. They found the bike right beside our front door, matched up the serial number and the boy's name with their records, and that, dear Santa Claus, was that."

She stuffed her hands into her jeans pockets and slowly, proudly, circled her new, paid-for-on-a-charge-card bicycle that this time had been given to her fair and square. "I never understood why those police officers let that boy's dad holler at me so much, like I was a murderer or something. Embarrassed his kid big time. Next day at school he came up to me and said he had an old bike at home I could have if I wanted it. I said thanks, but I'd rather go ahead and steal a new one. He laughed, and I laughed, and we were friends after that, sort of."

Bedon blew out a lovely blue smoke ring to give himself time to formulate his next question. "If his dad thought he and his son were so much better than everybody else, why didn't he have him in a private school?"

"Oh, the middle school we were going to was special, one of those magnet schools for kids who score high on some test. I don't know how I got in, except my fifth-grade teacher felt sorry for me and made some phone calls. Any-hoo, she didn't expect me to go over there and start stealing other kids' stuff, which is exactly what I did every little chance I got. Bikes weren't all I walked off with. Rich kids are careless about leaving jackets and things lying around, anything not attached to their bodies. Their mamas and daddies can always buy more."

"Have you stolen anything from me?"

"Nope."

"Why not?"

"'Cause you aren't a snot. You treat me like a real person. Want me to tell you something funny?"

"Sure."

"Those magnet school teachers thought they were uppity-ups, 'cause they taught in a school for smart kids. I think they'd gotten the idea it made them smarter themselves somehow. I never gave 'em the time of day, but some of the rich kids looking for help with grades to please their parents, so they could get more jackets and bikes and stuff, would schmooze those teachers to their faces and then talk smack about 'em behind their backs. And the ignoramus teachers never suspected a thing."

"And you're in what grade now?"

"Eleventh. By the way, Jake came back last night. Mom was so happy she made tacos for supper. I ate five with double guacamole and sour cream."

# 20.
## Jake

After Bedon had watched Larissa ride away on her magical bike, he went back inside to check his medical bag. News of Jake's return had thrown his worry impulse into overdrive. He felt the need to get prepared in case his only patient came back later needing attention.

After piddling around in the den and kitchen for half an hour, he started upstairs to bed carrying a tall iced tea. On the second landing, he stopped and rested as Thomas Turner struck eleven. On the final chime, Bedon slumped his shoulders like a veteran insomniac and turned around to make his way back down to the main floor. The piazza rocker would think he'd lost his mind if he left it unoccupied the hour before midnight. Perhaps the rocker would be right.

It began raining hard as the tired man schlepped across the covered piazza toward his chair. The nasty weather blip would for certain keep Miss Posey and Hamp from taking their nightly stroll. Bedon let his body slide into the comfy rocker. Resting his head on its back cushion, he dozed off to the music of Lowcountry frogs croaking their raspy welcome to the downpour, which did not let up until Bedon had slipped into deeper slumber. It was then someone rattled the catch on his front gate and startled him awake. He grabbed his golf club and groaned at the stiffness of his calf muscles as he struggled out of the chair. "Who's there? Is that you, Posey?"

A male voice answered in a slur, "Posey? How many girlfriends you got, old man? I came over here to find out what kind of advantage you're taking of Larissa."

Bedon stared down the walkway and saw a dark, hulky shadow staggering toward him. The alarmed doctor backed to his front door and slipped into the safety of his foyer. He was about to shut the door against present danger when a second, louder commotion erupted on the side lawn. He poked his head back outside and watched a smaller shadow fly from the side of the house with the furious intent of attacking the hulk on the walkway.

Screeched the smaller shadow (Larissa) at the larger shadow (Jake), "Get away from here, you animal." She began beating him about the head and shoulders with what looked like a rubber flip-flop. "You had no right to follow me here," she said. Thwack. "I'll break your neck." Thwack. "I'll crack your skull." Thwack, thwack, thwack, thwack, thwack.

Not exactly the kind of language and behavior one would expect from a darling girl who enjoyed referring to herself as Rainbow in the Mist. *"I'll smash your ugly face!"*

Larissa's blows to Jake's head with her flip-flop and her repeated verbal attacks exploded like exclamation points in the darkness. Bedon recognized her voice. Dashing out the front door, he raced down the piazza steps like an older man who might have been an athlete in his younger days. Someone, and he was the only reasonable someone in the vicinity, had to stop this insanity. No pregnant girl should be engaging in dangerous behavior of this sort, not even toughies like Larissa.

Jake, the hulk, off balance from being beaten, as well as from alcohol if the reek of bourbon in the air were any indication, covered his head with his hands and turned about in a slow circle. On realizing he was too drunk to defend himself, Rainbow in the Mist threw down her rubberized bludgeoning instrument (the worn-out, blown-out flip-flop, size five narrow) and went after him with her bare fists and feet. Jake lowered his head and hunched over. She grabbed hold of his shoulders and climbed onto his back, wrapping her legs around his waist.

Bedon seized the hood of her jacket and pulled hard. "Get off him," he said. "You're going to hurt the..."

She let go and wriggled out of her hoodie, which left Bedon standing there holding the empty outer garment with no one left inside it. He dropped the hoodie to the ground and grabbed the small assailant's wrist, enraging her so much she turned around, balled her free hand up into a bony little fist and delivered a well-placed punch to Bedon's right eye socket. Blinded for a second, he groped about until he got hold of both her wrists and would not let go despite her spitfire efforts to break away.

*"Stop...now...stop,"* he yelled, which, inexplicably, inspired her to fight harder.

Jake, though still operating in an advanced state of alcohol muddle, figured out Bedon had somehow restrained his attacker. He gathered himself up like an ogre, walked over to the struggling twosome and pushed them both to the ground. Like a couple of clenched high school wrestlers unable to withstand gravity, Bedon and Larissa landed face to face in a pile of pine straw the homeowner had been planning to use for mulch around his late wife's Lady Banks rose bushes.

The old man got to his feet and made a show of raising his fists at Jake. "You can't do that," he said in an embarrassing tenor brought on by stress. Though from the look of things, Jake most certainly could "do that," even when falling-down drunk.

Which was why Bedon found himself forthwith on the ground again, flat on his back deep in his own well-tended plot of Bermuda grass. This time he made no attempt to get up, just lay there blinking at a couple of moons adrift in Charleston's night sky. Turned out he didn't need to bother getting up anyway, for Larissa had already regained control of the maelstrom. This time she made sure Jake did no more damage by sneaking up behind him and knocking him out with the blunt side of the shovel that Bedon had left propped against his late Hildie's tallest crepe myrtle.

When sure she'd been successful in vanquishing the hulk, Rainbow in the Mist hurried back to her aging protector's side. "Are you all right?" she said, breathless.

The doctor, still on his back in the grass, put a hand to his injured eye and covered it. Larissa leaned closer. "Did he hit you? In the eye?"

"No, you did."

"Me?"

"Yes, and it smarts bad."

"I'm sorry. He must have followed me. I was going into the carriage house when I heard him around here in front. Are you hurt anywhere else? Can you get up?"

Bedon allowed her to help him to a sitting position. He closed both eyes and waited for the T.I.A. headache that never came. "Been a long time since I got knocked down. Twice, I think it was. Guess I showed him."

Larissa pulled her defender to his feet and walked him to the bottom piazza step where he could hold onto the iron railing. Hulk moaned and turned over in the grass. But before the drunkard could right himself, Larissa marched to his side and gave him a hard kick in the ribs just to make him feel better.

He grunted. "You little freak. I'll fix you, wait and see."

Bedon, deluding himself with the thought he still might have a thimble full of fight left in his own trembling muscles, threatened Jake in a loud clear voice, albeit from the porch steps where he was still hanging on, because he couldn't stand up by himself. "Get out of my yard, you skunk, or I'll call the police. There're laws against child endangerment."

The "skunk" exhaled a cloud of essence-of-Kentucky-bourbon as he hauled himself up off the grass. "Don't you worry, man. I'm leaving. She ain't worth goin' to jail over. Child endangerment, eh? You're the one ought to be thinking about that."

Bedon and Larissa watched as the would-be criminal stumbled out the front gate and down the sidewalk. She giggled. Bedon snapped his head around and stared at her with his one functioning eye. The other had swollen shut. "It's not funny," he said. "What am I supposed to do when he comes back?"

"Oh, it's funny all right, Dr. Pirate. He's going in the opposite direction of our apartment like the Einstein he isn't. Couldn't find his way back here if he had a map. Wasted, remember?"

Bedon cupped a hand over his blind eye to avoid being called Dr. Pirate again. He said, less annoyed, "I don't care about that mad man anymore. I'm concerned about your baby. Can you tell if it's all right?"

"One time...just once, I wish you wouldn't ask if my baby is all right. My baby is fine. Now let's go inside, so I can work on your eye. I'm a nurse almost, in case you forgot. That's how I know you're supposed to put raw meat on it."

<h1 style="text-align:center">21.</h1>

<h1 style="text-align:center">Pop's Got a Shiner</h1>

Buddy breezed into the kitchen whistling and singing the jingle from the used car commercial he'd just heard on his Super Bee radio – *"Impress pretty women with a pre-owned ride. Interest free loans for a year be-sides."*

He came to a halt at the table and stared at it in disbelief. No sandwich, no fried chicken, no hunk of cake, not even a glass of tea. The hungry, thirsty law student changed from whistling a happy tune to wrinkling a worried brow. "Pop?" he yelled as he made his way to the den. "Where are you, man? Lunch ain't gonna fix itself."

"In here, resting. Took a little tumble last night."

Buddy turned pale when he saw Bedon lying back in his chair with a cold pack on his right eye. "You did that in a fall? How in the world...let me see." He lifted the ice pack from Bedon's eye and gasped.

"It's better now," his grandfather said, peeking through a slit in the purple flesh of his eye socket. The mass of tissue was so pulpy, it looked like a fake black eye purchased from Hokus Pokus Costumes. "I've been keeping ice on it all morning. It was swollen shut 'til a little while ago."

"Get up, Pop. We're going to the doctor, right now."

"No, no, I've turned the corner on it. I can see okay. That's all any Board certified doc not padding his receivables should be looking for. I'll just have to walk around for a week or two looking like I was in a bar fight."

"What did you hit going down? I don't see how you could've done this in a fall."

"To tell you the truth, I don't know. Doesn't matter, though. All's well that ends well."

"I'm supposed to be seeing after you, Pop. This thing's gotta be addressed. Have you looked at yourself in the mirror?"

"I'm a doctor. I'd know if something more needed to be done. Always best to let the body heal itself."

"We have to get somebody in here to help you. I can't sleep through my ambulance-chasing classes in peace if I'm worrying myself to death about whether you've fallen and can't get up. Maybe we ought to get you one of those gizmos to wear around your neck like those old ladies with false teeth advertize on TV. Or am I gonna have to give up wine, women, and song and move back in my old room upstairs?"

Bedon waggled his head like an irate bull elephant. "No way," he said. "It hasn't been a year since I got you out of here. Talk about the boomerang generation. But if you're bound and determined to shorten my life through the poison of proximity, get yourself in the kitchen and make me a corned beef brisket sandwich, double mustard, the fancy brownish kind that tastes terrible. And bring me a glass of tea with a bendy straw – there's a box of them in the cabinet over the stove - and my Zippo lighter and Tinksy pipe and pack of tobacco, and a fresh ice pack and a dry towel. This one here's soaked through...if you're still feeling so moved to 'see after me.' And don't forget my robe and slippers. They're in the walk-in closet upstairs. You know where my bedroom is, third floor."

"Yes, sir. Three flights up, three flights down. Up...down. Up... down. No elevator. We gotta get somebody in here to help you, Pop."

# 22.

# Mountain Vacation Misery

Strange how T.I.A.s worked on Bedon. You'd have thought a scuffle like the one he had with Jake and Larissa on the front lawn would have made them worse, but the opposite was what happened. For six weeks, no headache of any sort appeared. Bedon knew it was six, because it was the same number of weeks Larissa had been shunning the carriage house.

Glad for the respite, but not glad for the constant secret fretting he found himself engaging in over her advancing pregnancy sans prenatal care, and less glad for the constant arguing he kept letting himself get sucked into with Bud on the pros and cons of bringing outside help into the house, Bedon retreated once again into the wasteland of loneliness.

No wonder the time for his annual mountain vacation with his only living brother, Lawrence, and his only living sister-in-law, Pauline, slipped up on him. And, no, a deteriorating memory caused by the T.I.A.s did not bring on this mental lapse. Bedon forgot about the vacation for the simple fact he did not want to go; moreover, had stopped wanting to go ten years back, right after Lawrence and Pauline had picked up and moved to Central Florida to be what they called snowbirds. And, Bedon knew the only reason his "poor relatives" insisted on the annual mountain trip was he always foot the bill.

Buddy didn't want to go to the mountains, either, and he displayed much more strength of character concerning the matter than did his grandfather. Grandson came to the conclusion the only way to solve the problem was to stay at home, or, if he had to show face for a little while, not to stay the whole week. He revealed the basics of his new plan to his parasite relatives from the Sunshine State while talking to them on the phone. Bedon stood by and beamed with pride at his grandson's courage, while, on the other end of the line, Pauline thought up so many questions designed to shame her great nephew into resuming his regular holiday with "the fam," that Buddy couldn't think up enough lies to answer them all, which, curiously, didn't seem to offend Pauline in the least. Lawrence, either.

As time for the trip drew nearer, Buddy grew desperate to sharpen his plan to rifle-shot precision. He had no choice. Its successful execution was the only thing standing between him and clinical insanity. If he failed, he knew he'd have to follow his grandfather in jumping off the same cliff the old man always said he felt like jumping off whenever things in his own life backed up like a clogged toilet.

After intense analysis, Buddy decided to initiate the first phase of his operation simply and boldly: Pick up Pop early on the pre-determined September Saturday morning and drive him to the dreaded vacation destination, High Hamilton Inn right outside Cashiers, North Carolina, crime scene of the week-long marathon of torture-by-talk inflicted on Bedon and Buddy every fall by Great Aunt Pauline, dear wife of Great Uncle Lawrence.

Now then, and let us be clear about this, empty headed Lawrence could be endured on most days, no problem. But Pauline was a different hyena. Buddy responded to her noise pollution by threatening homicide or suicide, sometimes in quick succession, every time he had to spend more than one evening in her presence. A lot of years this had been going on. A lot of years and a lot of suffering, not that Pauline cared. She'd been making it her business since Buddy was a little boy to drive him nuts over the course of the third week in September year after year after year.

Which was how it came to be on the first morning of the current "holiday," that Buddy, Bedon's official chauffeur for the drive up, was glancing every once in a while over at his grandfather, who sat silent and sullen in the shotgun seat of his grandson's 1971 Dodge Charger Super Bee. "It's okay with me if you sulk all the way there," Bud said to his miserable passenger. "I myself have been thinking of getting professional help on dealing with difficult relatives, present company excluded. Maybe the thing to do is start a support group or something."

"I don't want to talk about it," his grandfather said. "It's worse than going to a cocktail party downtown or some awful charity event. I feel like jumping off a cliff."

There it was again, the infamous cliff. Bud knew mention of it meant his pop had about reached its edge and was gazing off into the wild blue yonder with an unhealthy longing. The old man closed his eyes and put on a less than convincing act of dropping off to sleep, the daytime prerogative of the elderly. Bud knew he was playing possum.

"That's right," he said, "leave me to suffer the anticipation alone." He pressed the accelerator pedal until the speedometer needle hovered at ten miles over the speed limit. This amounted to a pitiful show of powerlessness, but it was all Bud had to hold onto at the moment. With grim resolve, he returned to his not-so-secret "plan," his only hope of enduring with a semblance of adult maturity one dinner with Aunt Pauline, all the while trying as hard as any psychotic underachiever could, to inject reason into unreasonable proceedings.

To be fair, there was always one upside to this money-bleed of a trip each year. Uncle Lawrence was great company, mostly by sheer accident, yet he still managed to sneak a measure of levity into whatever abyss his boss-lady-of-a-wife – Perilous Pauline – shoved him into. Bedon and Bud both liked talking to Lawrence, although they hadn't succeeded in having a real conversation with him in a decade. His wife's Gatlin gun spray of words prevented any common exchange between common people within a geographic range the size of Alaska.

Bud's bad mood soured more when he thought about his impending dinner with the terrorist, Pauline, and the terrorized, Lawrence. Auntie P would launch a full-out frontal attack as soon as they sat down at the table, the first volley of cannon balls always being lobbed in the form of a series of anecdotes about her and Lawrence's annual side junket to Reptile, Rhino, and Rodent Heaven on their drive up from Florida. According to Pauline, seasoned tourist that she was, last fall when they'd visited the popular Kissimmee attraction, its owners had added a colony of poop-throwing rhesus monkeys to its family of terrifying animals in order to lure more Yankee visitors with their bulging wallets into their sinister collection of animal lairs. Buddy didn't want to know what new exotica the park owners had thought of to add this year. A few beds of South American fire ants perhaps (truthfully, South Carolina fire ants, since the recent infestation). Or a thousand-gallon aquarium tank full of man-eating, red-bellied piranhas with a sign next to it reading: "Enjoy the Fantastic Feeding Experience of Our Favorite Finned Friends - Every Hour on the Hour."

"Lawrence is right," Buddy said to his possuming grandfather on the other side of the car. "A paying customer sure as heck can expect excellent value for his dollar at Kissimmee's brand of Heaven."

## 23.
# Fine Dining with
# Great Aunt Pauline and
# Great Uncle Lawrence

Anybody who booked a week at High Hamilton Inn and didn't take advantage of the all-inclusive "American Plan" would be missing out on the fabulous nightly buffet and be forced to eat from the menu, which would cost twice as much, three times if you ordered appetizers and desserts all around. The Calhoun party of four buzzed through the salad and hot bars like chain saws through a pine thicket. Along with a couple dozen other American planners, the Calhouns concentrated on filling their chilled salad plates with variegated greens, cut-up tomatoes, and boiled egg halves. Then, with no break between courses, they piled up bigger plates with baked or fried chicken, mashed potatoes and four or five cooked-to-mush green vegetables. French hard rolls that came pre-baked off the Sunbeam truck nestled in red plastic serving baskets on each dining room table. If you wanted butter, you had to get foil-wrapped squares of it out of the salad bar ice bed and take them with you to your table with not a pretense of assistance from the wait staff.

Buddy helped his great aunt into a chair after she had completed her lengthy sojourn through both food lines. On sitting down, she gazed sad-eyed at the diners nearby who were perusing their leather-bound menus. "I'd so like to try the t-bone steak for a change," she said in the special whine she reserved for hard times and pity parties. "My bridge table ladies say it's flavorful enough that Otto - y'all know Otto, the maitre d' here - well, Otto recommends leaving the A-1 Steak Sauce off altogether. But I guess I'll never know." She emitted a deep sigh accompanied by a disappointing examination of the fatty chicken quarter cooling in a puddle of congealing grease on her plastic dinner plate.

Bud comforted her. "Now, now, Aunt P, you know you aren't supposed to be eating red meat. The only reason Pop didn't set up a tab for you and Uncle Lawrence to order a-la-carte off the menu all week is he's concerned about your health."

Pauline sighed again. "I suppose it would be more expensive," she said, "and considering how our dear generous Bedon invites us up here every year as his guests and insists on paying for everything himself like he always does, well, I can't complain. Our dear Lawrence might be rude enough to fuss a bit. We all know about that ornery streak he tries to keep covered up. But never me. I'm not the one without good taste."

Then she realized as she looked at the food piled in layers on her plate that she certainly was "the one without good taste." And her valiant, though failed effort to saw off a bite of her baked chicken quarter verified it, for the poor fowl was suffering from rigor mortis. Pauline soon gave up on the chicken leg and sought solace in spooning a few tough green peas into her mouth, the kind that would go pop every time she chewed.

The poor woman had to swallow extra hard and guzzle down half a tumbler of sweet tea before being able to continue her witty repartee. "Do you have any news for us, Buddy?" she said. "We're your closest relatives, just dying to share every little detail of your life. You've been seeing that same darling girl an awfully long time."

Socially smooth Pauline – "socially smooth" being the rare personal trait Auntie P thought she possessed in abundance; she

believed this with same rock steady faith with which she believed
in Social Security – displayed a row of flawless false teeth in a smile
equally as false.

Her great nephew, Bud, understood that his great aunt's sideways
question about his girlfriend would go something like this loosely
translated: "Still dragging your feet on getting married, Buddy?"

"Talking about Caroline?" he said. "Oh, we broke up again. I'm
dating a girl in the ink industry now."

"Ink? What?"

"A tat artist. You know, tattoos. Tramp stamps. She's got a little
studio up in North Charleston where she specializes in secession
battle flags, red and white being her favorite colors and all. Misty says
high up on the shoulder blade is the best place to put'em. That's her
professional name...Misty. Her real name is Bambi, but she doesn't
want to go by anything formal like that in her professional business
dealings. This girl is so talented, she can knit, smoke a cigarette, and
talk on the phone at the same time she's driving down I-26, and she
can show you how to use your back muscles to make a secession flag
tattoo look like it's waving in a Lowcountry breeze."

While Great Aunt Pauline was trying to marshal enough brain
cells to process whatever tidbits of nonsense were dropping like Rocky
River pebbles out of Buddy's mouth, Great Uncle Lawrence stumbled
from the buffet line over to the table and sort of fell backwards into
his chair. Lawrence had a balance issue brought on by inner ear
troubles men of the dignified age of eighty-two-or-three often suffer.
His Chinet premium dinner plate clattered onto the table before him,
dislodging a lone Brussels sprout that rolled unnoticed across several
ketchup stains on the grayish/whitish tablecloth.

Lawrence nodded approval at Bud's description of his new love
affair with the Queen of Ink. Buddy would have elicited no happier a
reaction from his great uncle than if he'd reported his new girlfriend
was preparing to sacrifice home and tattoo parlor to become a
missionary on the foreign fields. Bedon, however, did not react so
positively. He knew, as well as he knew his own name, there was no

hope of going down any logical road of discussion over dinner, yet he could not bear to see the journey made worse by his smart alec of a grandson.

"Enough," he said to Buddy. "I'm not in the mood for baloney tonight." Then to his sister-in-law, "You were asking what was new in Charleston, Pauline, before the monkey at the table turned into a wise acre. But you of all people know how Charleston is. Same old, same old."

The puzzled expression on Pauline's face caused by Bud's ill-advised commentary on the ink industry melted away in the sunshine of Bedon's interest in conversing with her one on one. The leading lady became her scintillating self again, dazzling her three male relatives with a grin, the thin upper and lower lips of which were still smeared artfully with Revlon moisturizing lipstick (hue, Cherries in the Snow) since its wearer had not eaten quite all of it off yet.

"I'm sure you're right," she said to the object of her affection (Bedon, not Lawrence). "Everything in small Southern bergs is so predictable. If it weren't for the Palmetto Bug Stomp Dance that the leading cultural folks put on every so often, people in Charleston could fall asleep for ten years, then wake up one morning and start carrying on business as usual like no time at all had passed. I couldn't stand it personally. Too slow for an urbane woman like me. I've adopted the past modern world view."

"Past modern?" Bedon said. "Urbane? I don't think..."

Pauline's galloping ignorance got Buddy so tickled he choked on a chunk of fried drumstick meat, his most favorite delicacy. Recovering, he gave his grandfather some good advice. "Don't try to straighten that one out, Pop. Past modern, post modern, what's the diff?"

"Yeah, what's the diff?" said Uncle Lawrence, exposing his own dentures in a grin that was, unlike Pauline's, utterly sincere.

Bedon's face glowed nuclear with disapproval of Bud's behavior, yet he was unable to stop his out-of-control grandson from collapsing into a laughing fit so raucous it attracted the attention of every guest in the dining room. Bud's face approached the color of red hibiscus as his guffaws escalated from ordinary punct-u-a-tions to that rare type of hysteria characterized by a disquieting vacillation between cackling and crying.

"Hush up," Pauline said. "Everyone in here is looking at us. What's wrong with you?"

"I don't know. Ha ha. Go on, Aunt Pauline. Ha ha ha. Your chit-chat thrills me so." Then the crazed nephew meted out further embarrassment for his table companions by blowing his nose horn-like, after which he gagged up the same piece of floating chicken that had now somehow managed to get itself lodged behind his left tonsil. Under Otto's glacial stare (you remember Otto, the maitre d'), Bud almost regained control of himself, and would have if he hadn't made the mistake of looking at the face of Uncle Lawrence and then at the face of his grandfather. All three men burst out laughing at the same time, but not even Bud's "innocent" humor was enough to keep Bedon from banishing him from the table to endure the loss of any possible involvement with the dessert cart.

Whereupon the offender headed for the real bar, not the food bar, through the grandiose archway on the far side of the dining room. He confessed his sins to the bartender, who offered him a sympathetic ear, but no absolution. Insanity on the part of his patrons was not a new phenomenon to the middle-aged man mixing drinks. Buddy continued chuckling into his iced ginger ale (no alcohol for a guy facing a four-hour, night drive back to Charleston), while the bartender polished shot glasses to a high sheen. As he worked, he offered up to his new customer the insight of a shaman. "Dude," he said to Bud, "I don't know what sent you off the edge in the dining room tonight, but whatever it was, you need to stay away from it."

"I lost my mind, man, and it's still lost. Snicker giggle."

"Yes, sir," said the bartender, "that rubber chicken on the buffet line is a real scream."

Buddy wiped his nose on a paper napkin embossed in gold with the High Hamilton Inn logo, an inaccurate pen-and-ink drawing of a rhododendron blossom. "It's my aunt, my great aunt," he said.

"Every time she opens her mouth, she gives me a different glimpse into a different wing of that "House of Usher" brain of hers. I don't know why it shocks me so. I always know it's coming. It's happened a million times. But then, when it does, I can't stop myself from going bonko and laughing like a mental patient, which is stupid, 'cause it ain't no laughing matter. The woman's only goal in life is filching money and other junk from my granddad. I'm serious. Her only goal."

# 24.
# Home Is Where the Heart Is

And so it was Buddy left High Hamilton Inn with the same relief one might leave a war zone. Bedon, the bereft, stayed on, and the longer he stayed, the more depressed he became. Pauline never lost an opportunity day or night to twist him through her personal kaleidoscope of emotional sturm and drang, but that didn't affect him nearly as much as his heart-concern for a certain poverty-stricken young girl back home.

He lay awake nights in his lodge room wondering with no way of finding out, for to ask Buddy to check into the situation was not an option, whether Larissa had come up against any circumstance that would force her to take refuge in her newly refurbished safe house. The only thing the good doctor knew for sure was he'd left his charge a note on the carriage house daybed listing the dates he would be gone, this after he hadn't seen her for six weeks and was beginning to think he'd never see her again.

Bedon's preoccupation with what was going on back home accounted for Pauline's constant trouble getting him to listen to her monologues at meal time, tea time, or any other time. "You're so distracted, dear," she'd say. "Are you sure your doctor is treating you properly for those stroke episodes?" Meaning, "I hope to high Heaven your doc is *not* treating you properly, because the sooner you kick off, the sooner Lawrence and I might come into some of your rusty old moo-la."

What joy, what joy, when Buddy phoned Bedon on Thursday morning to ask his accommodating pop if it would be inconvenient if he drove up and brought him back home two days early, since Bo, Buddy's best though broke friend, had invited him to go on an all-day offshore fishing excursion that both fishermen, according to Bud, would have to *"put on plastic, but it was well worth it to go into debt for the chance to hook a blue marlin."* That was Buddy's subtle way of asking his grandpa to pay for the jaunt, knowing full well he'd say yes.

Bedon, the bereft, turned into Bedon, the ecstatic. Never mind his checking account had about succumbed to diarrhea from all the money he'd found himself spending on Buddy and the other two mooch relatives in his life, Pauline and Lawrence, plus all the coin he'd run through trying to help Larissa. Not that he cared, not while basking in the glow of news he was going home early, *hallelujah!* He packed his belongings in ten minutes and parked himself in a rocking chair on the front porch of the inn's common building where he could see every vehicle venturing onto the property.

"But he won't be here for another three hours," the femme fatale Pauline said to her deserter. She had joined him on the porch for a last loving tete-a-tete after finding out about his impending departure. In Pauline's mind, she was not only a femme fatale charmer, but the most irresistible femme fatale charmer since Blanche DuBois in *Streetcar Named Desire*. She leaned to the side in her own rocker to get into the face of the "charmed" (Bedon) on whom she had been crushing all her adult life with the hormones of an ovulating Orca whale. "Oh, Bedon, don't go yet. We...I...need you so."

Pauline projected spittle onto the "charmed's" cheek when she said the word *so*. Bedon, losing his patina layer by layer, pulled out a handkerchief and wiped her spit off his face in a way suggesting it might be poisonous. He then spit a few words of his own back at the more skilled spitter. "Buddy said he's coming to take me home, and I don't want him to have to wait around when he gets here." The anxious grandfather then re-focused with the intensity of a pit bull guarding his Gravy Train upon the scenic entrance of the resort, as if by visualization alone he might be able to manifest his grandson's Super Bee zipping up the black asphalt.

Pauline deepened the crease between her eyebrows. "And what are Lawrence and I supposed to do the rest of the week all by ourselves?" She stood up then and positioned herself squarely in front of her brother-in-law in order to block his view. The annoyed Bedon stretched over to her left side to try to see around her.

"I don't know," he said, "the same thing you do in Florida all by yourselves. I already took care of the bill, if that's what you're worried about."

Auntie P pursed her drawstring lips. "Well…it was the decent thing to do. You invited us."

Bedon leaned around to her other side, but Pauline's wide-load frame was sufficient to obstruct the moving image of a Mac truck barreling down the drive. "Come on, Pauline, if you'll get out of the way, I'll tell you about a sign I saw in the lobby. They're having a craft show in Cashiers tomorrow. You and Lawrence can go over there and buy yourselves some jars of organic mountain honey and one of those homemade bluebird boxes to put up on a pole at that Florida campground site y'all stay on in the wintertime."

Pauline sighed and sat back down beside her hopeless romantic of a close relative, though not related by blood, which made it all right for her to flirt with him shamelessly. Undaunted by his rebuffs, she reached deep into her inner soul and found her best theatrical voice, low and throaty…resonant, ardent. "Bedon, darling, please. Look at me for one second."

Caught off guard by her tone, which sounded as though Darth Vader had taken possession of her vocal chords, he obeyed his sister-in-law's request to *"…look at me for one second."*

She smiled into his blue orbs, wooing him with her own yellow-green cat eyes as intensely as Scarlett O'Hara wooed Ashley and Rhett, sometimes both at the same time. The gifted Pauline managed with huge effort to produce the faintest teary glisten on her corneas as she blink, blink, blinked her bald eyelids at her prey. "Oh, Bedon, darling, just promise me this one thing, that you'll consult a doctor the minute you get back home. I'm afraid our dear Buddy isn't seeing after you like he should."

"Bedon, darling" flared his nostrils as wide as a loggerhead's. Pauline misinterpreted this as pure passion instead of the final end of his wits to which her brother-in-law had come. The frustrated Bedon shot a few more spiky blow darts in his pursuer's direction to the purpose of defending his grandson. "Buddy sees after me exactly the way he's supposed to see after me," he said. "He's my best friend, my only friend."

Passionate Pauline was about to say more, but Uncle Lawrence lumbered up and spoiled what she thought was a tender moment on its way to becoming an intimately delicious tryst with her adoring and adorable secret sweetheart (dear Bedon). Lawrence poked his wife in the shoulder with a skeletal finger. "Come on back inside, honey bun," he said to his faithless wife. "They're starting Bunco in the parlor. We might win an extra piece of rhubarb pie."

# 25.

# Worrying About the Welfare of a Waif

When Buddy dropped Pop off at the Murray Boulevard house late in the afternoon on Thursday, his grandfather's expression communicated unadulterated joy. *So glad to see you, lovely house of mine on the harbor. If I could, I'd kiss you right in the mouth.*

Greedy grandson stuck around long enough to accept a check from generous grandfather of an amount hefty enough to cover his and Bo's whole fishing trip. Buddy was so overcome with gratitude, he gladly toted – without Bo's help, naturally – Bedon's rollerless, fifty-five pound suitcase, circa 1951, upstairs to the master bedroom and dropped it onto the bed for ease of unpacking, a job Bud was sneaky enough not to get involved in. Hustling back downstairs, he joined his pop in the kitchen where they both got into major fidgeting fits, Bedon trying not to give away how badly he wanted Buddy to make himself scarce, and Buddy trying not to give away how badly he wanted to make himself scarce.

Said Bud while jockeying for the back door, "I'm grateful for the check, Pop, but I got a life of my own, you know. You don't care if I borrow some of your fishing gear to use man-yana, do you? Two blue marlin are waitin' for me and Bo out there in the Atlantic

89

Ocean as we speak." He went through the motions of pulling back an imaginary rod and casting for an imaginary fish. "Why don't you come with us...bring your wallet."

"I'll pay extra not to. You can have whatever cash is left in the snowman cookie jar."

"That would be all of four dollars and thirty-five cents. I already cleaned it out. Bye-bye now. I know your heart is breaking over being separated from Pauline. Guess you'll have to drown your sorrows in Ovaltine."

"I'll get by," Bedon said.

"Well, so long again, gray man. I'll call you when we get back."

When the door slammed behind the "grateful" young fisherman, Bedon walked over, snapped the deadbolt in place with emphasis, and said to his departed grandson, "So long, yourself."

And that's how it came about the good doctor was at home on a night when Larissa didn't expect him to be. She had checked and double checked his vacation dates on the note he'd left, though it did her no good since the writer of the note had changed his schedule mid-trip.

After Buddy had left for his apartment, Bedon went outside to inspect the carriage house. Disappointed to find no evidence of a visitor, he decided to skip smoking his pipe on the piazza and go to bed early. Exhaustion had caught up with him. It would have caught up with anyone who'd endured careening down the curvy mountain road from Cashiers at twenty mph over the speed limit with Buddy Calhoun at the wheel.

The weary traveler crawled into bed and turned off his bedside lamp. He attempted to quiet his mind with prayers and *Bible* verses he'd memorized as a child, yet, try as he might, he could see nothing behind his closed eyelids, except yellow highway signs with black icons depicting snake curves ahead.

He tossed. He turned. He wondered if he'd assumed correctly Larissa had not been there while he was away. What would that make? Seven weeks, almost eight? He knew she was fastidious. The spa towels and washcloths in the bathroom remained unused, the comforter on the bed undented. For all he knew, she could have stayed there three or four days, then cleaned the place up. He knew from living with Hildie all those years that females had a domestic gene most men were missing.

He reached over, turned his lamp back on and settled himself to read some in the Walter Edgar history book he'd brought upstairs. To the photo of General Robert E. Lee on his bookmark, he said matter-of-factly, "If you don't put me to sleep, Johnny Reb, nothing will."

# 26.

# Larissa Takes Advantage

Sure enough, half way through Chapter Twelve entitled "Quest for Order," Bedon crossed over into dreamland where he resided blissfully until two a.m., whereupon a familiar noise woke him. Though muffled, there was no mistaking the rhythmic bass beat of a sound system playing somewhere outside his house, from a car on the street, maybe, or a neighbor's TV.

Bedon's good ear picked up the sound, because he'd gotten used to hearing one like it every day at noon when Buddy wheeled into the driveway in his souped-up muscle car. Not music exactly, just an insistent drumbeat that invaded the chest cavity of everyone in earshot and would not stop thumping inside the rib cage until its power source was shut off.

Bedon waited, half thinking he might detect the fumbling noises of Buddy as he searched for the house key under the flower-garden-in-a-terra-cotta-pot just inside the front gate, and as he let himself into the house to crash for the night. But Bud hadn't done that in months, and he surely wouldn't do it tonight what with having to get up before dawn to go out on a charter trawler with Bo, who would oversleep for certain and have to be dragged out of his own house in a comatose state by Buddy to make sure they got to Shem Creek Marina in Mount Pleasant on time for their five a.m. boarding.

Bedon shut his eyes and listened harder. He realized the noise was not coming from the front yard. Its source was somewhere in the vicinity of... His feet hit the floor in a trot. He did not slow down, not even when he realized he'd left his robe and slippers behind. His size elevens on the stairs out-thumped the bass drum now sending shock waves all around the peninsula. And what was the origination point of these powerful vibrations? Bedon's own carriage house, no doubt about it.

The upset homeowner skidded to a stop at the door of his outbuilding and tried the knob with a jerk. It was locked. He kicked at the wooden door with a bare foot and swore at the pain, then he shook the knob so hard it bruised the palm of his hand. Like magic, the pounding from inside ceased, and the strip of light beneath the door went dark. At the same instant, Bedon's reliable and irritating next-door neighbor, Sol, began waving a 270-volt flashlight around from his back stoop. He could have assisted a nighttime landing of a Boeing 787 *Dreamliner* with that thing.

"Bedon?" Sol shouted. "What's going on over there? My Rachel is saying someone's beating on a steel drum. I can't hear a thing myself, but she sent me out to check."

Bedon whispered another quasi curse word before shouting a response at his neighbor. "Go on back inside, Sol. It's just me. I tripped over the wheelbarrow I left out this afternoon."

"All right then," Sol said, "but you know I keep my Spring Double Eagle Colt .45 loaded for bear, and my derringer. Call out if you need me."

"Sheeze," Bedon stage-whispered. "It's the burglars getting blown up I'm worried about." Then in a voice not much louder, "Larissa, open this door right now. I know you heard what Sol said about his guns. He shot his own son two years ago when he showed up over there to turn the security alarm off for the fourth time in a week."

Bedon watched as the knob turned and the door creaked opened. His "helpee" poked her head out. "Did he kill him?" she said. Her eyes caught the light of stars fourteen million miles away and as many years burned out.

"No, he didn't kill him. Shot him in the foot by accident. You do understand it was an accident, right? We had to drag the poor guy over here, so I could fix him up in my kitchen to keep the police from getting involved."

"Uh-huh, same kitchen you fixed me up. You run a regular clinic in there, don't you. Want to hire me as your nurse?"

"Let me in. We have to talk about noise level."

"Do you have a gun, too?"

"Yes, back in the house, but it belongs to Buddy. And I don't keep it loaded. What difference does it make?"

She tried to close the door in his face, but he stopped it with his naked foot. She gave up attempting to force it when he yelped. And that was when he heard laughter from more than one person erupt from behind her in the darkness. He shoved the door back, almost causing his trouble-making little friend to fall down in the process, and then reached past her to flip on the dolphin light.

The cold-busted Larissa flew across the room to join a cluster of young people sitting in a circle on the rug, the expensive frieze carpet that Bedon had bought for her and only her. His eyes spoke the hurt he felt when he figured out what was going on. She'd turned her safe house into a party pad and allowed the stinky rear ends of strangers to occupy her special rug. The disheartened Bedon recoiled upon spotting a gigantic seashell ashtray defiled by Camel cigarette stubs and a small pile of metal tabs from Pabst Blue Ribbon cans.

He stared at the group. The group stared back. "You have to cut out the noise," he said, then frowned at the young people a moment longer before closing the door on the roomful of stale smoke.

# 27.
# Gone, But Not Forgotten

Qarissa followed Bedon out of the carriage house and ran after him as he strode away. "I'm sorry," she said, breathing heavily in her hurry to catch up. "Really, I am. Please don't be mad. I won't do it again. Please…"

Bedon continued walking in silence. She lurched forward and grabbed him by his arm. He stopped and looked down at her with cold eyes, the chill of which stabbed her even in the darkness. In a controlled voice he said, "You'll have to give back your key. I can't have that kind of thing going on here."

"Oh, no, please. I'll make them leave. And I'll clean everything up, and I'll…I'll pay for anything that got ruined."

"Get them out and leave the key under the mat outside the kitchen door. I'm not in the business of running flophouses for savages. Go home and take your gang with you."

She started crying, but he didn't comfort her. All he wanted was to go back inside his house and resume the ordered life he'd known before she had sailed in and shaken it to its foundation, a life in which she had no legitimate part.

The next morning at eight, he opened the carriage house with the key she'd left precisely where he had instructed her. With the exception of a faint odor of cigarette smoke, the place was immaculate, to include the six-by-six bathroom. All the sheets and towels lay in a neat bundle by the shower stall. They'd been used for the first time and probably not by the person for whom they had been purchased.

Bedon collected the bundle of laundry and conducted a last visual sweep of the room. Nothing seemed to be missing except the Build-A-Bear and the expensive bicycle. He shrugged and said aloud, "I don't know why it would matter if she took everything. I bought it all for her."

It was then he spied a note on the bed. Written in pencil on a torn-off corner from a Pabst Blue Ribbon twelve-pack carrier, it resembled a forgotten piece of trash.

I'm sorry. Thank you for everything. I didn't think you would mind if I took Bo Bo Newsome, my teddy bear. So I just took him. Is the bike mine? I wasn't sure, so I took it, too. I need wheels in case Jake gets cranked up at home.
Love ya,
Rainbow in the Mist

Bedon dug in his shirt pocket for a pen to write an answer, re-thought the impulse, re-pocketed the pen along with the note. On leaving the building, he pulled the door shut behind him somewhat harder than necessary, locked it, and rattled the knob, also somewhat harder than necessary. As he walked away, hands deep in pockets, he felt for the silver key several times to make sure it was still there. It was, along with two quarters and a tin of Altoid Cool Honey Breath Mints. Halfway back to the house, he stopped walking and took the key out to study it. For several seconds he stared at the mindless ad about Modern Mules on the white plastic fob. As he traced its crimped edges with his fingertips, the tenderhearted man decided to return to the door and slip the key back into the lock. The butt end of the little key sticking out of the doorknob glinted in early morning sunlight, happy to be back in its rightful place.

# 28.

# Bud Hires Med Helper; Bedon Hates Med Helper

Three more weeks plodded by, then four, then five. Bedon tried to chalk up his effort to help Larissa as a good deed well done, but overwith. Yet too many questions remained hanging in the air like wisps of smoke from his pipe or traces of odor from an ashtray full of Camel stubs. Was she all right? Had she been beaten up at the hands of Jake? Too many upsetting Q's with no reassuring A's.

Buddy continued showing up every day for lunch. T.I.A.s continued showing up when Bedon least expected them. And, because the accompanying headaches had become more debilitating, Bud had contracted with an eldercare service to send a helper in three times a week to do this-and-that for his pop.

"I don't need her," Bedon said one day over a casserole of mac-and-cheese a yearning widow from the church had delivered earlier in the day. He was talking directly to Buddy, though Bo Gaillard was also at the table partaking of the feast. The two younger men were sucking up the cheddar-infused pasta like a pair of Hoover vacuum cleaners. They weren't paying much attention to Bedon's steady stream of acidic pronouncements of hatred against Mrs. Harris, the new med helper.

"Humor me, Pop," Buddy said with his mouth full. "Let her watch soap operas in the den a couple of hours, then send her cellulite booty home."

"I'm getting rid of her altogether," Bedon said.

Bo couldn't resist chiming in from his own stuffed mouth. "Send her over to our house to help Nana. Won't be five minutes she'll be running up Highway 17 toward Awendaw, screaming bloody murder."

"She smells like Bengay ointment," Bedon said.

"Look, Pop, every other time I come over here, your head's hurting so bad you can't see straight. What am I supposed to do?"

"She smells like foot powder. I don't like her."

"Neither do I," said Bo, Buddy's perverse best friend. "She's a bona fide troll. I've seen her. Hey, did you two boys know today is my mom's birthday? I went to Bank of America last week and took out a loan. I'm gonna buy my mama a handwoven sweetgrass basket from Madie down at the open air market. Had to put Red Dog up for collateral. Gonna pay the loan off a hundred dollars a month for the next twenty-five years."

# 29.

# Flight Risk

Bedon gritted his teeth at Mrs. Harris, the helper. She had folded his boxer shorts inside out unlike the way Hildie used to fold them, unlike the way any reasonable person would fold them. He snatched every pair out of his bureau drawer and threw them down at Helga-from-the-health-farm's sensible shoes.

She gritted her own teeth. "I see we aren't in a good mood today," she said, though the high and mighty tilt of her squared-off jaw assured Bedon she could not have cared less what kind of mood he was in.

"No," he said, "we aren't. I'm going out for a drive. Isn't it time you went home?"

"My hours are from one to five. It is now one fifteen, according to your wretched grandfather clock that just went off downstairs. What kind of clock strikes on the quarter hour?"

Bedon gave his unwanted employee a wide berth on his escape from bedroom to hallway. His anger intensified with every step he took down the staircase. So did his jangled thoughts. I can't believe I let her run me out of my own room, where a grown man should have peace and privacy. If Buddy Calhoun were here, I'd wring his thick neck.

The escapee slid into the driver's side of his pickup, checked his shirt pocket for the doctor's appointment reminder card that had come in the mail two days before, and blinked to ease the pain in his head.

"I will not let her beat me down," he said to the steering wheel. "I am a veteran of the Korean War, twice decorated. I will continue to function...continue to function. I'll push past this adversity and continue to...whatever."

As he backed out of the driveway, he knocked over a flowerpot of cool-weather pansies that did not deserve it, and then went on to smash flat-as-a-flitter a pot of rootbound English ivy that did.

# 30.
## Chase Scene

Dr. Calhoun poked along in his truck on his way up Meeting Street like the definitive stereotype of an old man driver. Inching along in slow motion, he crept toward the ramp of the two-and-a-half-mile Arthur Ravenel Bridge leading to Mount Pleasant, that great cable-stayed wonder bridge supposedly the pride of Charleston, but in truth the career capper of a certain political favorite for whom it was namesake. Bedon, still verbalizing his military positive affirmation, *I will continue to function*, in mental preparation for a successful crossing of the big bad bridge, hiccupped when he saw Larissa whiz past on her bike directly in front of his mallard-on-the-wing hood ornament. She sailed through the intersection of Meeting and Calhoun Streets going west on a direct path toward the College of Charleston impact zone.

His doctor's appointment forgotten, Bedon began fretting about nothing but the fact that he was in the wrong lane to turn left. With no deliberation, he exercised all rights afforded him by his silver-gray hair to observe peculiar driving rules, and cut across two lanes of traffic in front of an Escalade SUV and a broken down Mercedes bomb, and let us not forget the EMS vehicle burning rubber from the opposite direction with its right-turn signal light blinking red. Bedon's illegal turn onto Calhoun left a whole fleet of stunned drivers to ponder how old one has to be to get away with driving like that and not get locked up.

Because of traffic and the occasional maniac showing no more respect for rules of the road than the white-haired Bedon had shown, Larissa was able to make far better time on her bicycle than any motorized vehicle traversing Calhoun ever could. Her tracker, Bedon, ran the red light at the King Street intersection, leaving in his wake even more drivers and more pedestrians scratching their heads in disbelief. He drove past the College of Charleston's Addlestone Library in pursuit of the petite bike rider, who looked like, but was not like, any other college student wearing raggedy jeans, an oversized gray hooded sweatshirt, and a bright blue bandana.

On approaching the St. Philip Street crossing, Bedon realized he'd be embarrassed for her to see him anywhere other than his old homeplace on Murray Boulevard, though he couldn't have told you why. He pressed hard on his brake pedal to the consternation of half a dozen drivers in line behind him. His quarry spun on, three car lengths ahead. Bedon followed as she turned left onto St. Phillip Street, and left again onto Logan. He had no clue where she was headed, but kept her Fendi Abici in his sights in a sneaky police surveillance fashion just the same. Though, if he really had been the police, he'd have known right away the red brick apartment complex she was gliding up to was housing for low income families and Larissa's home sweet home.

He allowed his truck to roll by her as she parked the Fendi and secured its front wheel with the chain and padlock Bedon had purchased for her himself. Pulling to the curb a little way down the street, he shut off the truck's engine and made a concentrated effort to slow his racing heart.

Now the questions his subconscious had been pricking his conscious mind to answer began jumping around in his brain like popcorn. Why did you follow her, old man? And why did you go to such lengths to keep her from seeing you?

"To make sure she was all right," he said aloud in the emptiness of the truck cab, "and that her mother's sorry-ass boyfriend hadn't injured her again."

His eyes filled with tears as he checked around to see if anyone he knew had seen him, or anyone he did not know for that matter. Then, leaning forward on the steering wheel, he began sobbing into his shirtsleeve like a child, exhausted and humiliated at not being able to cope.

I should be at the doctor's office by now, he thought. I'll have to go home and face my corrections officer, admit I didn't make it across the bridge. Maybe she and Buddy will try to stop me from driving, take my keys, my license.

Overcome by jumbled thinking, still resting his head on his own hairy forearms, Bedon fell into a peculiar sleep. He looked exactly like the suspicious character he'd been hoping he did not look like, a daytime drunk the local cops ought to pick up and incarcerate. How many times had he called the authorities to have problem people on Murray Boulevard "taken care of?" How many times had he observed and judged them with an ice-cold heart? And now here he was one of them.

# 31.
## Chance Meeting, Not

Bedon would have continued to sleep for hours if someone hadn't disturbed him by tapping on the driver's side window. He lifted his head at the sound, eyes wide and glassy from his recent tears, mouth open, chin wet with drool.

Someone tapped again, this time causing him to look left out of reflex. Larissa smiled at him through the window glass. She made a circular motion with her forefinger, and Bedon turned the ignition key for power to let down the glass.

"What's going on?" she said, still smiling. "I saw you go by when I was locking up my bike. Why didn't you come back and say hi? I waited for you."

He tried to hide the necessity of wiping away his drool. "I...don't know."

Larissa moved closer and stared hard at him. "Are you all right, Bedon? You looked like you were asleep when I walked up."

He inhaled deeply, feeling better in the warmth of her presence. "I'm fine...now. How about you?"

"Okay, I guess. Jake left. He got mad at mom because of me. I'm a...what was it he called me? Oh yeah, a sassy little smart-tail who disrespects adults. Is that not a stupid thing to say for a guy who's living on a single mom's welfare check?"

Bedon chuckled at her spunkiness. "Well, time to go, I suppose," he said.

"Okay. Good to see you. Take care of yourself."

The good doctor's face brightened when he remembered a detail extremely important to him. "Oh, yes. I left the key for you in the door of the carriage house the morning after y'all were making so much noise. But you haven't been back in a long time. Anyway, it's there if you need it. You and the baby."

"I thought I...we...were banished," she said and put a hand on her bigger, yet still hidden belly. "And the baby is fine, if kicking means anything." She hesitated. "Listen, Bedon, you don't have to worry about those other kids. They're not smart enough to find your place again. Inebriated on arrival, if you know what I mean."

"Good," Bedon said, "or bad if you look at it another way. They're just kids. I'm relieved, though." He waved good-bye to her with his fingertips and started the truck engine to leave. She took a step backward and smiled at him again.

He returned her sweet look with a calm expression. He was no longer sweating, no longer fretting. And all the way home he drove like a model citizen, obeying every traffic ordinance, waving car after car in front of him as their drivers attempted to merge into his lane through the clog of tourist traffic, even letting a teenage boy squeeze into the flow of cars from a sliver of an apartment driveway. After the boy's PT Cruiser was safely in front of his truck, Bedon nodded, with the confidence of one who obeys every law on the books, to a police officer maneuvering between vehicles on a standup Segway. The officer saluted Bedon like he might be Citizen of the Year again the way he was once back in the sixties.

Not until the shaky doctor had pulled into his own driveway and was sitting in his truck, stoking himself to go inside to face his eldercare menace, did he realize his head was no longer aching.

# 32.

# Lowcountry Tempest

Bedon waited on the piazza for his electricity to go off. Thunder and lightning storms in Charleston caused residents and businesses to lose power so often that many a downtown restaurateur had coughed up the fifty thousand dollars necessary to buy a generator to keep the tourists well fed on Southern cuisine and well hydrated on Southern Comfort.

Bedon, however, routinely addressed the problem of a power outage with a gas stove, a Coleman cooler, and a few boxes of fifty-cent candles. At the moment, from the comfort of his piazza, he was enjoying a lightning show in the high-flying clouds above the harbor when, blink, all of Murray Boulevard went dark. He looked at his green fluorescent watch face, the one with the huge numerals on it Buddy had given him last Christmas.

Ten o'clock and all was not well. Rain beat harder on the roof as a cool wind off the harbor picked up. When a rocker at the other end of the piazza blew over and crashed into the joggling board, Bedon gave up on the romance of enjoying a storm and rose to prepare for retreat. Time was he would have pulled everything on the piazza close to the wall before going inside to hunker down. But not anymore. "Let it all blow to Georgia and back," he said, stepping inside his foyer and slamming the front door against the elements. "It's enough to rescue my pipe and iced tea, the important things in life." He lifted his glass in a mock toast and took a ceremonious sip of his Louzianne.

It was no trouble finding candles, matches, and a flashlight in the dark. He knew the floor plan of his house so well he could have lived there the rest of his life without a single electric light. Though it did help that flashes of lightning were still illuminating the windows in starts and flares. Thunder continued to roll, but at such a distance it seemed no more threatening than the lightning, until a transformer on a pole in the block behind Bedon's house exploded from a direct hit.

The earsplitting boom caused him to jump, though he was not really alarmed. He'd witnessed the same thing twice last summer. All it meant was the power would be off longer.

"I hope it's this bad at Awendaw," he muttered, while raiding a kitchen drawer for candles, "so that old battle axe won't be able to come over here tomorrow." The WCBD-TV 2 eleven o'clock news header (that hadn't aired yet), played out in advance in his head. *Grand oaks down across all roads leading to neighborhoods in Awendaw and McClellanville. No one can do a thing about it. Residents will be stranded without food or water for weeks on end.* Or so Bedon wished. Happy at the prospect, he decided to cozy up in his leather easy chair and pray for worse weather.

# 33.

# Larissa Afraid of a Storm, Who Would Have Guessed It?

Bedon had just sat down in his den armchair when a loud banging on the door that was blocked by the cedar chest scared him in a way no lightning bolt ever could. He vaulted to his feet and clutched his throat. When his heartbeat slowed, he tiptoed across the carpet still damp from the rain water he'd tracked in.

Before he could get to the door, whoever was banging on it began yelling unintelligible demands. Bedon knew who wouldn't mind creating such a ruckus. He shoved the cedar chest aside and unlocked the door, making it possible for Larissa to push her way into the room in a swirl of wind and water. Clutching the Build-A-Bear in both hands, she said through shivers, "Everything went black out in the building. And there was this terrible flash and an explosion. I thought the world was coming to an end."

Another flash and bang chose that moment to rip through the air outside, sending the frightened intruder flying across the den in a screeching tizzy. She jumped onto the sofa to safety and thrust her face into a throw pillow. The now-calm owner of the house closed the door against the stormy night and turned to watch his "guest" as she squashed the poor teddy bear under her full weight on the couch. How could it be this sobbing waif was the same tough customer who'd suffered maulings from her mom's boyfriend and unspeakable jabs into open wounds with Bedon's horse needle, all without a flinch?

"It's just a storm," he said. "Stop bawling. You almost gave me a heart attack beating on that door, and me without my Bayer."

Not only did she not stop bawling, she ratcheted it up to hysteria, yelling phrases in some foreign tongue deep into the pillow. Her host backed away as one might back away from an injured wild animal. "It'll be over soon," he said. "Already pretty much played out."

And as it did play out, Larissa quieted and fell asleep. But peace in Bedon's den did not produce peace in his mind or heart. He remained standing in the same spot for ten minutes while Larissa slept and the candles burned low. Not knowing what else to do, he went over and poked around on the bottom bookshelf looking for the battery powered portable DVD player Buddy had brought over a while back. It was for watching movies when the electricity went off, although Bedon owned only three DVDs. He pressed the on button and watched the middle part of *Casablanca*, the movie already in the player. Oh, that gorgeous Ingrid Bergman. Oh, that ugly Humphrey Bogart.

Thomas Turner, being sophisticated enough not to have to depend on the power company's slow progress, struck twelve. Larissa sat up on the last strike. Her host turned *Casablanca* off. The disoriented girl heard the faint click of the player button and squinted her eyes in the candlelight in an effort to figure out what Bedon was doing. "Is it over?" she said in a voice hoarse from yelling.

"The movie? No, but I'm tired of it. Seen it a hundred times."

She squinted harder. "What is that thing, not a DVD player. I can't believe you've got something like that. I don't have one. I don't even have a cell phone or a laptop or an I-Pad or Nook or Kindle or nothing. And I meant was the storm over, not whatever old people's movie you were watching."

"Sounds like it might be," he said.

"What about the power?"

He turned on the floor lamp beside his chair, and when the bulb lit up, he put a hand over his heart in surprise. "I stand amazed," he said. "Last time it took 'em all night to get the power going again."

She shielded her eyes from the lamp's glare. "It's hot in here, and my clothes are wet."

"You can go upstairs and find something of my late wife, Hildie's, to put on if you want."

Larissa snorted a laugh, no humor involved. "Yeah, right. Your late *old* wife. You got a flashlight? I'd rather go back out to the storage building and change into my own stuff. I stuck some jeans and things in the chest when you first fixed the room up for me. That was when I thought it was going to be more mine than it really is."

"It's yours all right, every square inch."

"Yeah, 'til you get mad at me about something else and take the key again. You're a nice man, Bedon, but let's face it, the building is yours, the house is yours. I got into a stupid habit of dreaming a little bit of it was mine, that's all. Dumb. Double dumb."

"Whatever," he said.

She bent over and giggled into the pillow. Still giggling, she sat up again. "*Whatever*," she said in a perfect mimic of her host. "You don't know how ridiculous that sounds when old people say it. Next you'll be trying to do a vocal fry like some lame pop star singer."

Bedon wasn't sure how to take any of this, whether to be insulted, so he ignored it. "Go change clothes and meet me at the front gate," he said. "We might see a heat lightning show over the water now that the storm is over. You aren't scared anymore, are you?"

"I wasn't ever scared. I…uh…was just worried about you being in here by yourself."

He started to say whatever again, but decided against punishing himself more. "Get going then. Put on your glad rags. There's not much better than a lightning show."

"Glad rags?" she said as she pushed the cedar chest aside and giggled her way out into the sultry night.

# 34.

# Moonbow Magic

Holding the forgotten bear by its arm, Bedon waited for Larissa at the gate. He smiled when she came around the house leaping like a gazelle. "What're you doing, puddle duck?" he said.

On her last leap, she landed by his side and took the bear out of his hand. Wrinkling her nose and looking up into her protector's face, she asked him a silly question. "Don't you hate it when you run through wet grass in flip-flops and get your toes all slimy?" She hugged and kissed the bear, and then hugged and kissed him again.

"I don't own any flip-flops," Bedon said. "Buddy, my grandson, and his girlfriend wear them everywhere. I've never been too fashionable."

Larissa reached down and plucked strings of wet grass from between her toes. "You must be the only person in the whole town who doesn't have about a hundred pairs."

"I reckon." He unlatched the gate and stepped onto the sidewalk, then turned to see she wasn't following. "Move out," he said. "You aren't going to believe what's in the sky tonight. And trust me, it won't last long."

"Move out? Do you talk funny all the time or just when I'm around?"

They walked together across the street to the battery wall overlooking the harbor. Bedon leaned far out over the railing and looked up at the night sky. Larissa copied his every move.

"Can you see it?" he said. "Look there, to the left."

"I don't see anything but sky."

He stepped behind her and put a hand on each side of her head. "That way," he said, adjusting her noggin to the correct angle. "It's a moonbow all the way across the clouds. Hardly ever happens here, but when it does…wow."

"Oh my gosh, I see it. A moonbow. What does that mean, a nighttime rainbow?"

"Yep." He moved back beside her at the rail. "A moonbow over Charleston. And you and I are probably the only two people in town who've spotted it. Everybody else is either asleep or watching late-night TV."

"I can't believe it," she said, enthralled. "Why hasn't anybody ever told me about this before? We never study anything worth a toot in school. I'm changing my name right now from Rainbow in the Mist to Moonbow in the Mist."

Bedon tried to take his sudden rise in stock to another level by stating in ho-hum manner, "Check it out on the Internet. You can see pictures that'll knock your eyes out."

Larissa, mouth open like a codfish, stared at the glorious lighted arch until a freshening wind disturbed the perfect conditions between mist and moonlight, and the bow faded away.

She looked at Bedon, whose chin now had an angle of pride to it. "Nobody will ever believe I saw that," she said. "I'll bet not a single one of my teachers knows such a thing exists."

"Be careful. You don't want people to think you're off your rocker. Another moonbow might not show up in these parts for years."

She leaned on the railing and laughed in the same lighthearted way she'd been laughing since she recovered from her fear of the storm. "Off my rocker? You kill me with that stuff. What am I, if I'm off my rocker?"

"Let's see. Loony tunes, soft in the head, one card short of a deck."

Her hair blew across her face in a way that would have enchanted any man of any age. "Thanks," she said.

He grinned. "For the moonbow? Don't thank me. Thank God."

"Whoever," she responded, then giggled again.

Bedon pressed his back against the rail so he could see her face full on. Her happy mood changed to irritation. "What?" she said.

Without sugar coating the problem, the good doctor stated what was necessary. "Larissa, you know we have to talk about your baby."

She turned and trudged back toward the house, away from the only person in her life who knew or cared about what terrible trouble she was in.

# 35.
# Ping Pong and Daniel's Law

Bedon sat on the top piazza step puffing his pipe and gazing down at Larissa two steps below. She played with her teddy bear while humming "Happy Birthday." Bedon said through his front teeth that were gripping the Mark Tinskey pipe stem so hard they set up a whistle as he spoke, "It's time to tell somebody, your mother, school nurse, somebody who'll help you get a plan together for your baby."

"It's a long way off."

Bedon took the pipe out of his mouth. "I can't tell exactly, but not as long as you think."

"You're a doctor. Can't you do something?"

"And you're sixteen, at least that's one of the ages you told me. I can't take care of you that way without a nurse present."

"Sixteen and three quarters now."

"Will you make an appointment with the school nurse tomorrow? I figure there's not much point in asking about the father."

"It isn't Jake, if that's what you think. I had my own boyfriend, but we broke up. He got himself another girl the next day."

"And you never told him you were pregnant?"

Larissa threw the stuffed bear down the rest of the steps and put her hands over her ears. "I don't want to talk about it anymore. I feel like killing myself."

Bedon alerted to such dangerous words, especially since he'd heard her make the disturbing threat before. "All right, all right," he said. "We'll deal with it later. Uhmm...let's do something else, something fun. How about table tennis? Buddy keeps everything set up in the garage."

"Table what?"

"Ping pong. I'm a champ at it. So's Buddy."

"I don't know how to play that."

"Good, I'll win."

The only time Larissa could hit the ball was on her serve. When Bedon hit it back to her, all she could do was swing and miss, then spend minutes chasing the maddening little devil-sphere as it bounced around the garage. Bedon tried to tap the ball over the net gently so that she could make contact, but no tap was gentle enough. The girl had zilch eye-hand coordination. He wondered, with no scientific basis for thinking it, if the pregnancy hormones flooding her system might be the cause.

After a while, he begged for a break, though she was the one who was tired. They sat down on the wooden church pew Hildie had salvaged at great price from an antique shop on King Street. Hildie had informed her reluctant husband on the day she'd bought the thing that cost should not be a factor, though Bedon and Buddy would rather have had a cushioned futon for their rec room than this hard-on-the-backside bench, even if it did have cherubim carved on both armrests.

"Did this come from your church?" Larissa said.

"Not our church. Someone's, though. Bud says it must have come from up north somewhere it's so uncomfortable. Hildie bought it downtown and had it delivered here."

"But..."

"Don't ask. It was her idea of decorating. She probably saw one like it in one of those symphony designer houses they floss up every year. Buddy detests it."

120

"I think I kind of like it," Larissa said, turning to look at the carvings of pomegranates on its back. Bedon took the moment of silence as an opportunity to revisit his main worry. "I want you to promise me you'll go see the school nurse tomorrow and ask her to tell you about Daniel's Law. Will you do that, for the baby's sake?"

"I get sick of never knowing what you're talking about. What's Daniel's Law?"

"It's a state code making it okay for a girl to take her baby to a safe haven and leave it to be adopted, no questions asked."

"Safe haven?"

"Yes, some hospitals, fire stations. I don't know where else, but the nurse will."

"Okay, tomorrow morning. Daniel's Law. But you don't have to worry so much about me. I'll survive." She stood up and tried to balance the ping pong ball on her paddle. "Want to play another game?"

Bedon grabbed the ball and put it in his pocket. "Game over. You lose again. And it's not enough to survive, Larissa. You have to prevail."

She sat back down beside him and stared at her own dirty sneakers. Snuffling like a puppy, she wiped her nose on her jacket sleeve the way she always did. "I wish my mother had known about Daniel's Law when I was born."

# 36.

# A Cake and a Promise

Said Bedon to his little patient, "You scared the dickens out of me, bursting in like a wild child during the storm. That and all this strenuous ping pong has made me hungry. I need some chocolate cake to settle my nerves."

The mention of cake cheered her. "I need some chocolate cake to settle my nerves, too," she said. "I haven't eaten since my sausage Hot Pocket at suppertime."

"Come on then, let's ease over to the kitchen while we talk. Maybe I can scrounge up something more than sweets. There's leftover spaghetti and meatballs and a huge homemade cake."

"Where would you get a huge homemade cake with your wife... gone?"

"Widows from the church bring me things like that all the time. I'm one of two eligible bachelors in our age range still kicking in the congregation, and the other guy's a hundred and three."

"And they bring you food, because...?"

"It's their way of courting me. Whoever's the best cook would make the best new wife. It's like a contest."

"Who's winning?"

"My dear, I'm a lost cause. Too lazy to put up with another woman's girdles and hair rollers. Hildie spoiled me for other women. She was my only sweetheart, the love of my life."

"Girdles?"

"The concept of girdles is one I would not know how to explain to anybody. Something to do with fat displacement. A higher math formula."

"You keep letting those idiotic women bring food over here even though you have no intention of marrying any of 'em?"

"I like chocolate cake."

"It's a scam, a cake scam."

"Whatever," he said and opened the kitchen door with a deep bow to usher her inside.

Larissa tucked a dish towel into the neck of her tee and dug into the spaghetti. She spiked a meatball with a fork and ate it like a candy apple.

"First time I ever had spaghetti that didn't come out of a Chef Boyardee can," she said. "And first time I ever saw a stove lit with a match. Didn't know they made 'em, like I didn't know they made moonbows. Why don't teachers tell us interesting stuff like that in our classes instead of all the time talking about junk like trigonometry and calculus?"

Bedon smiled as he watched her spear another meatball. "How old did you say you were? What grade are they teaching calculus now?"

"Technically, I'm not old enough to take calculus, but they always put me in the smart classes, 'cause I'm smart. I mean really smart. I'll be seventeen soon. Gonna be a nurse."

"Seems like you've been sixteen an awfully long time."

"That's because when I first told you I was sixteen, I was really fifteen. So I've sort of been sixteen a couple of years now."

"Uh-huh. Do me a favor and don't explain that again. Why do you lie about it so much?"

"I'm afraid some do-gooder like you will make a call and have me taken away from my mom again."

"I probably should've done that very thing the very first night."

"You know what, now that I'm so much older, I think you're right. Jake could'a killed me eighteen ways to the middle."

"But it's been only a few weeks. How can you say you're so much older?"

"When you're almost seventeen, it's way older than almost sixteen, even if you're really still fifteen. I'm graduating a year early, I'm so smart and all. And there ain't one thing the school people can do about it. I've got all my credits, more than I need, and I made good on the SAT. Going to summer school every year was better than hanging out at arcades. Can't beat free tuition, not free for everybody, but for kids like me. They probably thought it would be cheaper to keep me in school all summer than to have to paint over all the graffiti I'd spray on public buildings if I didn't have anything else to do. People get ideas like that about you once you've been in foster care. Anyhow, I went to school free every summer, got straight A's, and one session they gave me a check for forty-two dollars every Friday just for showing up."

"How old are you again?"

"I'll be sixteen my birthday."

"You just said you'd be seventeen."

"I was lying, and you knew I was before I got it out of my mouth."

Bedon scratched his head in genuine confusion. "I can't keep up, and I'm willing to bet your teachers can't, either. What about college?"

"Kids like me don't go to college. They go to fast food, except I'm going to Trident Tech to be a nurse, if I can figure out the bus system to the end of Rivers Avenue. That'll be the only hard part. The college is like...a hundred miles away."

"Street wise, aren't you."

"If you're saying what I think you're saying, I'll punch you in the face. You can't treat me like you treat those women at your church, not and get away with it."

He scratched his head again and took another swallow of milk. "I honest-to-God think I should have called someone that first night. I know I should have."

"Yes, sir, you should'a. You should'a called anyone you could have thought of to call, including the President of the U.S. of A. But you didn't. And now I have a pile of stuffed animals in the carriage house that I could sell on E-bay for about a million dollars, if I could ever get hold of a computer. Set myself up for the rest of my life."

"I made the carriage house available to you for safety purposes. I felt sorry for you, and for your mother, and you stopped me from calling DSS with all that talk about the thing I don't want you to talk about anymore."

Larissa cluck, cluck, clucked. "I can't believe you let me get away with telling you what to do. There's more to it than that. I think you sort of got a crush on me or something, and you didn't want anyone to know about it, especially your precious grandson. You were probably embarrassed, me being project trash, and you knew I was way too young for you to be crushing on. Some people would say it was el creepo."

Bedon's face flushed as she chattered away between bites of meatball. He got up and went to the sink, where he slammed down the marinara-stained casserole dish and ran water into it to soak. Drops of the sauce splashed onto his face and shirtfront making small red dots that matched his complexion.

"Are you mad at me again?" she said. "I was only kidding. Can't you take a joke?"

"You weren't kidding. I've tried so hard to help you with no expectation of your ever being able to pay me back. But I never dreamed you'd be so cruel. I don't want anything but for you to be safe. I swear it before God."

"I saw a preacher on TV the other day," she said, "one of those guys who have wives with great big bleached-blond hair sitting beside them on a couch asking people to send in money, and he said some missionaries went overseas and spent their whole lives helping some natives in the jungle, and the next thing they knew, the natives killed'em and ate'em."

Bedon dropped his head and looked at his Rockports. "Well, sirree," he said. "I'm grateful for small blessings. At least, you didn't eat me."

At that, he allowed his eyes to meet hers again, and they laughed together like old bar pals well into their second bottle of Grand Estates. "Ready for cake?" he said, his facial color having faded from crimson to a less startling shade of mauve.

"Somehow I don't think the old lady who brought that cake over here meant for someone like me to be eating any of it."

"What she doesn't know won't hurt her." Instead of slicing off wedges and serving them on plates, Bedon got two clean forks out of the silverware drawer, and he and his guest proceeded to eat the cake straight from its plastic carrier. He had to refill their milk glasses twice...no, thrice.

"I'm done," she said when the three-layer dessert before them had shrunk to half its original size. She pushed the carrier toward Bedon. "First time I ever ate all the chocolate cake I wanted to. I bet you do it every night."

"Sure, only sometimes it's coconut, sometimes rum or apple cinnamon, or on a most excellent day, fresh strawberry with real whipped cream between the layers."

"First time I ever drank three glasses of milk all at once, too," she said. "I feel sick. Can I use the bathroom in here or do I have to go back out to the storage building?"

"It's not a storage building. It's a carriage house. No, a safe house."

"If you say so, but I know better. You were definitely using it as a storage building before you..."

"You can go to the bathroom in here if you promise you'll talk to that nurse in the morning. What school did you say it was?"

"No way I'm telling you what school I go to, so you can call over there and tattle on me. I'll go see her. I promise. Now tell me where the bathroom is before I..."

"Up the hallway toward the front of the house, second door on the left. Better hurry if it's an emergency."

She sprang from her chair and ran out of the kitchen, yelling all the way up the hall, "It is, it is, it is an emergency."

Bedon heard the door to the bathroom slam and the sink taps start running full blast to create privacy. "It's my humble opinion," he said to the mutilated cake, "that women defy understanding."

# 37.

## What Is a Compact Disk?

Clarissa stuck her head out of the bathroom, peeked right, peeked left, then tiptoed toward the front of the house where the parlor was located. She could hear Bedon still banging around in the kitchen as he cleaned up the spaghetti and cake things. She, being a nosey teen of the most normal variety, seized the chance to explore a little, maybe even plunder if the opportunity presented itself. Slinking into the parlor, the curious little cat flattened herself against the wall next to the archway and looked around. It was dark, but she didn't reach out to turn on the nearby table lamp. Snooping in the murky gloom was too much fun to spoil it with light. She crept across the rug to check out a piece of furniture the likes of which she had never seen before. Lifting the lid to the old phonograph, she put her face deep inside it to try to get a look at the works. That was the moment Bedon stepped into the room and clicked on another of Hildie's prized possessions, her Meyda Tiffany lamp with reversed-painted, rose-colored fringe.

Larissa jerked her head out of the phonograph and let the hinged top fall closed with a clonk. "I'm sorry," she said. "I didn't know what it was. Just trying to see."

Bedon smiled at catching her up to something and walked over in as fake-casual a manner as an actor feigning irritation at being recognized in public. "It plays vinyl albums," he said. "That's all we had before eight tracks and cassettes and compact disks."

"What are compact disks?"

He smiled again while flipping through a stack of LP's (long-playing albums). "A smart girl your age would call a compact disk a CD. These big things were their forerunners." He held up a Tony Bennett album still in its cardboard cover. "Used to be the latest thing in technology," he said. Turning back to continue his search, he found another album of interest and paused to read part of the cover promo aloud. "Judy Garland...the torch singer my Hildie was most jealous of."

"That's not what it says. What does it really say?"

"Who cares? Let's don't play it. I associate it with too much female pouting."

He slipped the cardboard jacket back into its place and pulled out a different one. Satisfied with his new choice, the self-styled, living room DJ took the black vinyl album out of its jacket, lifted the lid on the phonograph, and placed the thirty-three-and-a-third record on the turntable, the apparatus Larissa had not been able to see in the dark. She watched, amazed, as Bedon turned on the power knob and lowered the needle to the spinning record. Andy Williams began crooning his schmaltzy sixties interpretation of Johnny Mercer's "Moon River."

"Woh," Larissa said. "Sounds like he's right here in the room with us, him and his whole band. Wonder why he didn't get some drums for the background. I like drums. I think drums should be in the background for everything."

"Even ballads?" Bedon said. He hummed along with Andy a moment before going on. "Do you know what I like best? Not the dreamy stuff this guy sings. I like the guitar C-Major baseline riff that starts 'My Girl' by The Temptations. Motown at its best."

"Never heard of 'My Girl.' Never heard of Motown. Must be some of that antique stuff baby boomers are always slobbering about."

"Well, thoroughly modern Millie, I'd bet a million dollars here and now that you wouldn't be able to stop a goofy grin from creeping across your goofy face if you ever got to hear those boys sing 'My Girl.' David Ruffin beats any vocalist today senseless."

# 38.
# Waltzing In The Parlor

Bedon turned Andy Williams up louder. "It's a waltz," he said. "Listen to the beat. One, two, three. One, two, three." He bowed to her. "Dance, my lady?"

Larissa stared at him. "I don't know how to do that kind of dance. I like heavy metal...Twisted Sister."

"Hush and listen. One, two, three."

He went through the steps as he chanted the rhythm so she could see how it was done. She watched for a moment, then began moving her head in time. "One, two, three," she whispered.

"That's right. Now your feet. One, two, three. One, two, three."

He took her hands in his and pulled her along as they counted. She tripped and stumbled over her own left foot before getting the hang of it. But when she did, what fun. What wholesome, apple-pie, old-fashioned, one-two-three fun."

After Andy finished singing, Larissa kept waltzing and counting aloud, for to her the steps had little to do with the music. Bedon let go of her hands and watched. "I'll start it over if you'll stop looking at your feet," he said. "You have to relax and let the accent on beat one do the work. He restarted the album. "Now this time look up, not at your flip-flops."

She complied, and after two false tries, their feet somehow moved in rhythm. Bedon led. Larissa followed. An excellent dancer all his life (don't tell his good Baptist brothers and sisters over at the church), Bedon was able with little effort to make her look and feel like a star.

"I got it," she shouted. "I'm doing it."

"Don't look down. That's the main thing. Don't...look...down."

She forced her eyes to stay glued to the tip of her instructor's nose, making herself a bit cross-eyed, and counted with him. "One, two, three. Step, two, three. Turn, two, three. Dip."

The deepest point of the dip was precisely when Buddy and his girlfriend, Caroline, appeared in the parlor archway. Bedon and Larissa sprang apart. With round eyes they stared at their visitors. With rounder eyes their visitors stared back.

Buddy broke the silence. "What in tarnation is going on in here, Pop? It's two o'clock in the morning."

His grandfather stepped over to the phonograph and lifted the needle off "Moon River" just as Andy Williams was "bringing it" for his second grand finale of the evening. (Good-bye sixties. Good-bye ballroom. Good-bye every other thing that made life worth living for the night.)

"Nothing is going on," Bedon said, his voice shattering the brittle vacuum in the room that had replaced the comfort of the waltz. Then he added in his most polite style, "Buddy, this is my friend, Larissa."

The exceedingly offended Buddy, though he could not have explained to himself or anyone else exactly why he was offended, pulled his chin back into his neck like a Summerall Guard at The Citadel, or, not to put too fine a point on it, like an arrogant turkey gobbler. He blinked authentic shock at his grandfather's introduction, then responded with an ill mannered, *"La-who!?"*

Bedon, ever the gentleman, turned to his friend. "Larissa, this is my grandson, Buddy, the one I've told you so much about, and his girlfriend, Caroline."

The party crashers who'd been so politely introduced managed not to let a smidgen of Bedon's finely tuned courtesy rub off on them. They looked their new acquaintance up and down with rude eyes, though not with rude eyes in the same galaxy with which their new acquaintance looked back. Bedon, uncomfortable now, yet still the courteous host of this hostile gathering, attempted to redirect everyone's attention to a less incendiary discussion. He began with his own kin. "What did y'all come by for, Buddy? Kind of late for lunch, or early, whichever way you want to look at it."

Buddy kept his eyes fixed on Larissa as he answered his grandfather's question. "To borrow some money. We got a chance to go to a Folly Beach house party this weekend." The brilliant law student paused long enough in his explanation to engage in another episode of rapid blinking, after which, he said, "Who is she, Pop? I don't get this."

"She's a friend. Am I not allowed to have friends now?"

"But it's two in the morning."

At that, Larissa took a scary step toward the "brilliant law student" and his loyal girlfriend, whose clown eyes expanded to the size of case-quarters when Larissa began to swivel her neck and signify in her project street voice. "It's none of your business who I am, prep boy," she said to Buddy. "You and Olive Oil there better get out of my way." She took two more giant steps forward, forcing Bud and "Olive Oil" to take two more giant steps back. Their cowardly retreat caused the project bully to smile a crooked smile. Said she with another neck swivel, "If you're scared, say you're scared." And when neither Buddy nor Caroline could utter a word, could do nothing but gape open-mouthed at their intimidator, their intimidator turned back to her silver-haloed benefactor and smiled at him as beguilingly as a silkie from a Scottish legend would smile at the handsome young fisherman with whom she'd just fallen in love. "Thanks for the chocolate cake, sweet prince," she said to Bedon. "See ya when I see ya."

On the second "see ya," she looked back at Buddy with knives shooting out of her eyes. Tilting her chin high, she approached the parlor archway for her triumphal exit. Buddy and Caroline split apart to make a clear, wide passageway for her to parade through. Then they watched, hypnotized, as she sashayed up the hallway toward the kitchen, the cheeks of her bottom pumping up and down like a well-oiled coffee grinder, and they heard as she let herself out the back door with a mighty slam.

Following a deafening silence, Buddy spoke again, this time to vacant air space, "Knows her way around the house pretty good."

Bedon, the sweetest of sweet princes, who had already started the process of sliding Andy Williams back into his album cover and shutting down the phonograph – which effectively shut down every vestige of fun for the evening – agreed with his grandson's observation. "Matter of fact, she does."

Caroline could not resist making a certain comment a truly well-bred young woman would have left unsaid. "She looks pregnant."

"I wouldn't know," Caroline's hoped-for, future pop-in-law (Bedon) replied.

Suffering from paralysis, Buddy continued staring down the empty hall. Said he after a low whistle, "Wait 'til Bo Gaillard hears about this."

Bedon tried to wipe the thick layer of dust off the top of the phonograph with his shirt cuff, but all he managed to do was disturb it. Something about the lamplight caused the magical cloud of fine dust motes to explode in the air all around him, sparkling and twinkling as they dispersed. Fairy dust? Sylphie dust? And did Larissa really consider him her prince? A mysterious smile softened the timbre of his voice as he spoke a last word to Buddy. "Be careful how you spin it, son. After all, I'm your grandfather."

# 30.

## Labor Pains

Bedon was dozing in bed when a feeling like a needle prick to the sole of his left foot made him bolt upright. Normally not intuitive, he did not know what to make of the way the fine hairs on his forearms were standing at attention. He got out of bed and moved to the window, rubbing his arms as he went. If he leaned way to the right, he could see the carriage house partially through the limbs of the giant grand oak that connected his and Sol's back yards. A seam of light shone from underneath the door.

Clad in pajamas and nothing else, he hurried down the wide curving staircase of his mansion, ran out to the carriage house, and flung open the door without knocking. When his eyes adjusted to the light, he saw Larissa, red-faced and sweaty, lying in a huddle on the daybed. She had the unmistakable look of a woman in labor.

"It hurts...help me," she said between pants.

Bedon kicked the door shut behind him and raced to her side. "How far apart are the pains?"

"Not any time apart. Hurts all the time in my back. I thought I could do it by myself, but it's gotten so bad, I don't know." She moaned and hugged a pillow. Bo Bo Newsome, her Build-A-Bear, lay abandoned on the rug.

"Have you had to push yet?" Bedon said, shifting gears to physician mode. "If not, we might make it to the hospital in time."

Larissa looked into his eyes and began pushing with all her might. The aging doctor changed course. "Okay, we'll stay here, but you have to do exactly what I tell you. Will you try?"

She nodded, though her eyes glittered wild and brilliant with fear. He nodded back. "Then don't push so hard next time. Save your strength for blast-off."

Squeezing a pillow to her chest, she pushed again harder than before.

# 40.

## Baby Boy

Qarissa lay back with her eyes closed. Bedon sat at the foot of the daybed holding her newborn and smiling. The little squirmer, whom Bedon had swaddled in a soft white bath towel, made kitten sounds and angel faces.

The proud doctor glanced at the baby's mother, whose own face told him she had traded her all-out fear for all-out exhaustion. He congratulated her success. "You did great, honey. Five pushes and, voila, a brand new baby boy."

"I thought I was dying."

Bedon smiled love and said to the new mom, "Want to hold him?"

Mom tried to sit up. Doc held the baby in one arm and stuffed a pillow behind Mom's back with the other. She reached for her infant. Bedon, now in a role somewhere between physician and grandpa, settled him in her arms.

"My own baby," she said. "My very own baby."

Bedon was taken aback. "Didn't you talk to that nurse at school?"

"No, I knew you'd help me."

"You aren't going to try to keep him..."

"I want to do Daniel's Law. I don't want him to have to grow up like I did."

"Tonight? You want to do that...tonight?"

"When I can walk. I'll wait a little while and try. Will you drive me to a hospital?"

Bedon gestured toward the door. "I'm going inside to get dressed and make you a sandwich. Will you be all right holding him?"

Larissa pressed her baby to her cheek and fell asleep before she could answer. The tired doctor slipped him out of her arms and wrapped him a bit tighter in his towel for the short journey to the main house.

———— ❧ ————

Bedon, now in regular clothes, stood at his kitchen counter layering ham and cheese onto a sandwich for Larissa. The baby, still happily swaddled, lay sleeping in a basket on the floor. He mewed when someone knocked with a heavy hand at the locked back door.

"Open up, Pop. You don't have anybody in there, do you?"

It took two seconds for Bedon to scoop up the basket and stash it in the shadows of the hallway, and two more to hurry back to the door and unlock it. Bud, as he entered the kitchen, made a point of looking all around the room with narrowed eyes. He halted his wandering gaze when it bumped against the half-made sandwich on the counter. Bedon spoke without revealing a hint of nerves. "You got lucky, sport," he said. "Just in time for a midnight snack. Hungry?"

As cagey as a TV detective, Buddy made an astute remark. "I see you're making only one sandwich there."

"Uh-huh, one sandwich for one guy...me. But I can throw another one together if you like. Speak while I've got all this stuff out of the fridge."

"No, no," said the cagey Bud. "I was just driving by on my way home and saw your lights on."

"Driving by?"

"You can't fault me for checking on my grandpaw. My old grandpaw, who stays alone at night...most nights, anyway...who has headaches."

Bedon closed one eye and zeroed in on his grandson's suspicious face. "Your senile old grandpaw?" he said. "The one you found waltzing with a young woman in the parlor?"

"You can't fault me, Pop. See you tomorrow." After a few more "cagey" glances around the kitchen and one extremely "cagey" move toward the doorway to the dark hall – a serous heartstopper for Bedon – Buddy, the one man surveillance team, vacated the area.

Bedon waited for the roar of Bud's Super Bee to grow faint before rescuing the basket from the hall. He set it down on the kitchen table and checked its contents. "Hey there, squirtimer," he said and adjusted the towel away from squirtimer's face. "Thanks for not crying out. Buddy would have had a cardiac arrest and without an aspirin on him."

# 41.

# Nothing Can Be Easy

When Bedon got back to the carriage house, he found Larissa sitting on the side of the bed dressed in jeans and a tee, though she was not her usual spunky self. She had that wrung out look women get after birthing a baby.

Bedon went over and set the basket on the rug at her feet. He had to make a second trip to the house to get the grocery bag full of food he'd made. As he spread a red checkered table cloth on the daybed and laid out the picnic, he reported his close call with Buddy.

Larissa picked up her baby and snuggled him. "A little late for family visits, don't you think? Was that skanky girl with him?"

"Caroline? Naah. Bud was concerned about his pop, that's all."

"Bud was nosey, that's all. I can walk now. Not great, but I can do it. Why do you think I feel so rough?"

Bedon took the lid off the thermos of iced tea and filled a plastic cup. "Drink this. It'll make you feel better. Not great, but better. And I've got some bananas and a sandwich. Eat up."

Bedon and his patient, who was holding her baby closer than she needed to, entered the automatic double doors of Roper Hospital in downtown Charleston. Larissa, her face pale and devoid of expression, walked on silent feet to the reception desk behind which

sat a receptionist/nurse, her bleary eyes glued to a computer monitor.
"Clara Barton" held up a forefinger to Larissa, her unwanted patron,
to signal she couldn't be interrupted from her important computer
task: that of conducting a desperate search for an all-night pizza
joint magnanimous enough to throw in free delivery if one ordered
an eighteen-inch with three toppings. The young woman kept
Larissa waiting long enough to make Bedon angry. He was about to
intervene when the paid employee, expert that she was at timing the
outer limits of how long she could get away with not doing her job
without getting fired, raised her eyes from the monitor long enough
to burn away with a condescending look the last shreds of Larissa's
strength.

"May I help you?" she said in a superior manner, still not realizing
the girl standing before her was holding a baby in her arms. When
Larissa was unable to respond quickly enough, the busy employee
became impatient. "Look, sweetie, unless you have chest pains, it's
going to be a while before you can be seen."

For the first time in her life, Larissa was too spent to defend
herself with a snappy comeback. In a raspy voice, she said, "I'm here...
about Daniel's Law. This is my baby. He was born tonight."

The receptionist gasped as tears began trickling down
Larissa's chalky cheeks. Bedon also gasped, as heretofore his
special patient's face had shown so little emotion. He reached
over the reception counter and picked up the box of Kleenex
belonging to the receptionist, snatched out a few tissues, and
handed them to Larissa. Then he thawed the hospital employee's
frosty attitude with his best professional glare, the effect of which
caused her to rise above her personal feelings and refocus with a
transformed attitude upon her new patient. "Daniel's Law?" she
said. "I've never done one of those. Uhhh...let me get Mrs. Miller,
my supervisor."

Bedon's icy blue eyes declared war on the whole hospital. "While
you're at it, 'sweetie,'" he said to the stunned receptionist, "tell Mrs.

Miller this young lady needs to be taken care of by an emergency room MD. She's been through a great deal this evening."

As Bedon spoke, Larissa's strength ebbed away. He had to hold her up as she slumped against the counter. And the receptionist? Well, she ran off like a scalded cat to ruin Mrs. Miller's coffee break.

# 42.

# Larissa...Sick and Sad, Lost and Lonely, Yet Still Capable of Violence

Still in the clothes she had worn to the hospital and still in a daze, Larissa lay resting on the daybed. Bo Bo Newsome had taken the place of the baby in her arms.

Bedon, her touchstone, busied himself tasking on the other side of the room. Larissa watched his every move. The last task he completed was to stuff a wad of cash into an envelope and place it inside the top drawer of the chest. He sneaked a look at Larissa to see if she might be showing signs of returning to the land of the living. "I've decided," he said as he crossed the room to talk to her in closer proximity, "to start leaving the kitchen door unlocked in case you need something from inside the house."

He tried to stand still, but was too agitated. He began pacing again, looking for something else helpful to do. "And don't dare get on that bicycle. Use the cash in the drawer for busses, cabs, whatever. I'll lay in more money from time to time. The last thing I want is for you to run short at a time like this." He stopped his nervous prattle and movement long enough to give his patient another diagnostic stare. "Are you going to be all right out here, Larissa? You could come inside. I kind of wish you would 'til you feel better."

The weary girl placed the teddy bear on the pillow beside her head with the utmost of care. As she gazed into its black plastic eyes, tears welled in her own and rolled sideways onto the pillowcase. She didn't bother to wipe them away, just closed her eyes and slept.

In the wee hours of the morning, Bedon continued a losing battle he'd been engaging in all night with his bed sheets. The tortuous click-clicking of the ceiling fan assured him there would be no rest for an old man on this cruel night. Harsh realities attending the birth of Larissa's baby, accompanied by details associated with her surrendering him to the nurses at the hospital, goose-stepped through his mind in appalling parade. Several times he wiped tears from his eyes, remembering with a heavy heart that the new young mother hadn't had the strength to wipe her own. She would never see her baby again. And when Bedon had left her sleeping in the carriage house, she was lying so close to the ridiculous rock star teddy bear, it was a pitiful sight. Was she dreaming it would come to life? How bad was this thing going to get? And what could one man past his prime do about any of it?

In such a deep study about how the trauma of it all might affect his young patient, Bedon missed hearing the initial cues that all was not well on his front piazza. In degrees he became aware that someone, a hostile someone from the gravelly sound of his voice, was out there grumbling and knocking things over with bumps-in-the-night so loud, no responsible homeowner could ignore them.

Bedon got out of bed and stood in the darkness of his bedroom, head cocked, ears pricked, waiting for the other shoe to fall. He didn't move until the unknown caller began pounding on his front door. Remembering his last encounter with Jake, the only intruder he'd ever had to contend with in his sheltered life – not counting the foundling now recovering in his carriage house – the unnerved

Bedon opened the bedside table drawer and took out the Smith & Wesson Airweight .38 Revolver, a double-action "Saturday night special" according to Buddy, its owner, who had insisted a year ago that his grandfather keep it in the house "for protection against boogers."

Since the front door lock seemed to be holding, Bedon took a moment to don his robe and slippers before heading downstairs to face his foe. Halfway down, he realized he'd neglected a small detail, ammo, and had to go back up to his room to get his "protection against boogers" squared away, the accomplishment of which was made more difficult by an uncharacteristic jumpiness in the small muscles of his hands, jumpiness that was escalating at the same rate as the pounding on the door. When he reached the bottom of the staircase, he hunched over and crossed the foyer, holding the gun vertical to his leg like he'd seen police actors do on TV when they were sneaking up on bad guys.

A body-length from the locked door, Bedon repositioned the loaded weapon behind his back and shouted at the trespasser on the piazza – who was Jake, for sure – in the manliest voice he could muster, "Cease and desist. Get off my property."

Jake understood the "get off my property" part, but the meaning of "cease and desist" was nowhere to be found in his limited knowledge base, even more limited at the moment due to alcohol consumption.

"Where is she?" Jake shouted back at the brave proprietor of the house through the solid walnut door.

"Where's who?" the brave proprietor said, though he knew very well who. He'd recognized Jake's voice, no matter it was twice as slurred as last time he had paid a call.

"Don't play dumb, old man," Jake said. "I've followed her here twice already."

"You've got the wrong house. I'm alone."

"Well then, I'll go around back and check your storage building. I'll..."

Bedon kept the revolver behind his back as he opened the door to the surprised thug. Sneering, the thug said, "That's more like it, old man." Then he executed a push-in so successful it could have been argued by any rookie police officer that Jake, a repeat offender ex-con, had perfected the move by practicing it many times on other elderly folk.

Bedon lost his balance and fell. On his way down, the gun flew out of his hand and bounced through the archway into the darkness of the parlor. Where a small delicate hand with small delicate fingers reached down and picked it up. A cat with its nocturnal eyes would have been able to detect it was Larissa, but Bedon could see nothing from his prone position on the floor except four slender fingers and a slender thumb as they closed around the grip of the revolver. Though it made no difference he couldn't see. He knew whose fingers they were. He understood in an instant the exhausted Larissa, who'd just given birth a few short hours before, and, more crushingly, put her newborn under the protection of Daniel's Law, had, on will alone, made the trek from the carriage house, through the unlocked back door of the kitchen, and up the long hallway to the parlor. It was also clear to Bedon she had accomplished this feat with the precious intention of protecting her protector.

Bedon squinted harder to bring Larissa into focus. She stood in the dim, a teddy bear in one hand and a loaded gun in the other, waiting for Jake to make his inevitable wrong move. Jake, boring in his predictability, did that and more. As his young observer kept watch from the other side of the archway, the wicked interloper stepped over Bedon, who was still scrabbling about on the foyer floor in failed attempts to regain his footing.

From the blackness of the parlor, Larissa, the brave, was invisible to Jake, the stupid. But she could see him plainly as he stumbled from place to place in the large foyer, a space that would have been unfamiliar to him even in daylight. He did not realize Larissa was close enough to smell his liquory breath. She coughed in the darkness of her hiding place, cueing him of her presence and precisely where she was standing. He stopped moving, except for swaying a bit from the effects of too much Jack Daniels, then turned in her direction in pretense he could see her.

"I heard you," he said, "and I heard the old man's gun hit the floor. Where is it, you little smart-tail? I know you're in there...and I know the gun is, too."

Larissa let Bo Bo Newsome drop to the floor. She switched on Hildie's Tyffany lamp. When Jake realized what he was looking at, he swallowed harder than normal, for the girl he was used to batting around was now using both her dainty hands to point a .38 revolver directly at him. "Hello, Jake," she said as friendly as apple pie. "Does Mom know where you are?"

"Mom don't know nothin' about nothing,' not even you're pregnant, or it was me got you that way."

Bedon, spurred by the fear Larissa might do something irreversible, scrambled to his feet on adrenaline and yelled at Jake. "You'd better get out of here, you monster. She's too weak to be slapped around tonight."

"She don't look weak to me. She looks pretty danged strong with that cannon pointed at me. And who are you tellin' what to do anyway, you crusty waste of skin? You don't have no idea what kind of tiger you got by the tail here, not when you're messing with a hellcat like Larissa." Jake had to turn less than half-way around to knock Bedon down again. Pleased with himself, he gave a hoot into the air to celebrate his prowess as a fighter, albeit with a contender twice his age and half his weight. "Dirty old man," he said to the defeated Bedon now immobilized on the floor.

While Jake was still congratulating himself on knocking down a senior citizen, Larissa moved closer until she was standing within an arm's length of the intruder. He jerked back around and growled at her, then reached out to grab for the gun. She shot him in the upper chest, twice. For two heartbeats he stood there without moving, silent, holding her gaze with his own astonished eyes, then fell on top of Bedon.

Larissa dropped the gun and sank to her knees next to the two men. As fragile as she was from her earlier ordeals, she pushed hard at Jake's body, barely making enough headway to allow her protector to slide from underneath. Doctor to the end, Bedon got to his knees and began searching for a pulse at his attacker's neck. Finding none, he looked at Larissa with panic in his eyes.

"He's dead. You've killed him. Go out to the carriage house and get the money I left for you in the chest. You have to leave here and not come back unless you need more cash. And don't say a word to anyone. No one can ever know about this."

Larissa, on her knees on the other side of the body, trembled inside and out. She stared at Bedon, unblinking, but could not see his face in the shadowland of the foyer. He could not see hers, either, and hoped to God she wasn't in medical shock. For certain, he knew she was out of touch with reality to be capable of doing what she had just done.

"Larissa, listen to me," he said. "You have to go home and rest for several days, maybe more. Tell your mother you have the flu or something. Tell her anything. Just don't come back here unless you need money, and when you do, come at night like always. I'll keep the envelope filled. Now go and do the best you can to take care of yourself. Postpartum can make a woman feel like she's losing her mind. And now you have this..." He gestured toward Jake's body. "I don't want you to do something stupid to yourself."

He looked down at Jake again, trying to think of some last thing he could do to revive him. Larissa wasted no more time. She got up, stepped into the parlor to retrieve Bo Bo Newsome, and hurried back down the familiar hall to the kitchen. Bedon closed his eyes in relief when he heard the back door slam, the trademark sound of most of her departures. Now all he had left was a prayer that she'd have the restraint to keep her mouth shut and give herself time to recover, or, at the least, find a hidden vault somewhere in her young brain where she could lock away every memory of this terrible night. Having a baby was normal and natural. Feminine. Giving a baby up had to be heartbreaking and more heartbreaking. Bedon knew all that. But killing a man? And keeping it a secret for the rest of your life? This was into the far reaches of abnormal. Was it possible to seal something like that over with scar tissue? Bedon, though a medical professional, had not a suggestion of an answer to that question. And the next agonizing twenty-four hours he spent fretting about it proved he never would.

# 43.
# How Did a Dead Man Wind Up in Bedon's Foyer? Buddy and Two Homicide Detectives Want to Know.

Though every light and lamp in Bedon's house blazed, their brilliance failed to expose the truth, the whole truth, and nothing but the truth. Buddy sat on the sofa beside his grandfather and, without realizing it, copied every detail of his posture – upper body leaning forward, feet wide apart, elbows resting on knees. Three uniformed police officers and two blue-gowned crime scene technicians bustled about in the foyer taking photos of Jake's body. Two plainclothed officers sat in wingbacks across the coffee table from Bedon and Buddy. The grandfather and grandson had already been identified by the two plainclothesmen informally as "persons of interest," reason being there was no one else around to identify as such, except the corpse, who, if the attention being paid to it by the technicians with cameras was any indication, could very well have been the most interesting person in all of downtown Charleston.

Bud said in a way that sounded like he thought the two officers questioning him could have somehow prevented the disaster, "That dirt bag could've killed my grandfather. Shoving him down on the floor. Two times." And then a half-second later to Bedon, "Good grief, Pop. Why did you unlock the door? You promised you'd never do such a thing."

Bedon didn't lift his eyes from Hildie's Anjou area rug that harmonized with her coffee table just so. Plainclothesman Number One filled the silence with a gem from his vast mental storehouse of information. "In the profession, we call it a 'push-in.' Happening more and more these days, mostly to old people. Lots of times somebody'll get shot from it, but it's usually the guy who owns the house, not the intruder."

Buddy clamped his eyelids shut in exasperation. "Is this going to take much longer?" he said and cracked his eyes back open to find out he was now seeing double. Four plainclothesmen instead of two. "My grandfather gets bad headaches," he said to one of the hazy men in front of him. He hoped he was talking to a real officer and not a hologram. "I'm telling you, my pop is exhausted. The guy had him on the floor..."

Bedon took advantage of Bud's correct diagnosis of his condition. He kept his eyes on the golden Anjou to avoid being asked more questions by the officers.

Plainclothesman Number Two weighed in on the matter with a keen scrutiny of the obvious. "Yeah, hadn't have been the guy was dead drunk, I don't know if he could'a gotten the best of your old grandpaw. I s'pose your pop's the victim if you look at it one way, or the perp if you look at it another. Anyhow, I'm Detective Walker and this is my partner, Detective Brock." Then, with a peculiar abruptness, the heavyset Walker addressed Bedon directly. "How did you do that again, sir? Get the best of him?"

Bedon didn't move for a moment. In no hurry, he brought his head up and looked Detective Walker in the eye. "I told you. He knocked me down. I dropped the gun, but he didn't see which way it went. Neither did I. So I got back up, and he knocked me down again, and that time he didn't know it, but I fell right on top of the gun and was able to get hold of it again. I sat up on the floor, and when he came at me the third time, I shot him in the chest....two shots."

Detective Walker nodded. "I understand," he said, "and the guy fell and didn't get up. Self defense, open and shut. You can go on upstairs to bed, sir. We'll take care of everything down here. And you're not the perp. You're the victim. I don't know why I was doing all that foolish talking before. Nervous, I guess. We don't get many shootings in this part of town."

Afraid the detective might change his mind, Buddy began helping his grandfather up off the sofa. "Thanks," he said to both of the men-not-in-blue. "This is one wore-out old guy."

"Yeah, he is," said Detective Brock, "but I would'a wanted him on my side at the OK Corral."

# 44.
# Mrs. Flynn/She-Devil

Morning dawned bright and clear after the dark night of death by firearm. Bedon and Buddy sat at the kitchen table drinking coffee. Remains of their scrambled-egg breakfast hardened on plates before them. Buddy took a slurp of Joe and plowed forward with information he knew his pop would consider dreadful.

"Listen here, gray man, I know how you feel about Mrs. Harris, so I canned her by phone. The Senior Help Services people are sending a different lady over this afternoon. This new one'll have the same hours Mrs. Harris had, strictly daytime, but I'm thinking of hiring somebody else for the night shift. If you can't stand the thought of that, though, I guess I'll have to move back in myself."

Bedon pushed his plate to the middle of the table and screwed the top back onto the Smucker's jelly jar. Old fashioned blackberry. "You're young," he said to Buddy with the purest of intentions, not because he was trying to deceive him. "You need your own place. It's why you moved out to start with."

"But, Pop, that maniac could've killed you. We gotta have some help in here from now on. Me or somebody else...Aunt Pauline, Uncle Lawrence, somebody."

Bedon bit deep into his bottom lip before answering. "All right, if it'll make you feel better, I'll go along with help during the day. And I want you to know, Buddy, I'm aware I'll eventually need help at night, as well. Eventually, but not yet."

Buddy dropped the subject without giving in. Sad for his pop's loss of independence, he lowered his gaze to the tabletop and began studying the scribble of notes he'd made about the new med helper on a legal pad next to his plate. "Great," he said in his best take-charge voice, though his heart was breaking for his grandfather. "Here's how we're gonna approach it. When this new gal shows up for her interview today – Mrs. Flynn," he read carefully from his notes – "you and I are going to keep it on the down-low that she's getting hired to help me, not you. Trust me, she'll never know the difference, or care, as long as she gets paid on time." He consulted his wrist watch. "Twelve thirty," he said. "Her appointment's at two. And please don't fire her before Thomas Turner strikes three. We're having to pay her by the hour even for the interview. Can you believe Senior Health Services gets away with that? No wonder they love them some Medicare."

He stole a look at Bedon to see if his grandfather's pride had been shattered to Kingdom Come never to return. "Don't worry, Pop. She'll be an employee, not a jailer. If you hate her, she's history. I swear I won't bulldoze you on this, okay?"

Bedon answered neither yes nor no. Instead, he made a forthright announcement. "I'm going to the den to take my nap, as usual."

"Why don't you go upstairs. You'll get better rest on your bed. It was a long night, longest one I ever spent in my life, excluding unnatural disasters I lived through with Bo Gaillard."

Bedon ignored Buddy's suggestion. He pushed his chair back from the table and got up to leave for the den, not the master bedroom upstairs. Buddy, faltering now, summoned the courage to ask his pop a touchy question he'd been wanting to ask all morning. "Don't go quite yet, Pop. There's something I want to know, and don't take it personal or anything. It's only to relieve my mind. That girl you were dancing with in the parlor the other night, she didn't have anything to do with the shooting, did she?"

Bedon hit the top of the table with his fist, a move totally, completely, wholly out of character for the mild mannered physician.

It startled Buddy so much his legal pad went flying out of his hands and landed with a slap on the linoleum. With remorse, the normally respectful Bud remembered his proper place, that of obedient, considerate grandson. Giving in to the case of nerves he'd been suffering from since the night before, he began a jittery stammer. "Oh...uh...okay, sorry. Forget I asked, none of my business. It's just... ever since I saw the two of you together, well, the whole scene keeps rolling around in my head like a roulette ball. I can't stop it. And Caroline won't shut-up about it, either. I've got to break up with her. What a pain in the pa-toot. I don't care if her daddy is loaded."

Bedon, his anger flying away as quickly as it had alighted, chuckled at the various predicaments his grandson had gotten himself into. To lift the atmosphere in the room from horrible to bearable, he said to the nervous Buddy, "Maybe Caroline ought to get herself some med helper training. If the shoe fits..."

Bud lay snoring on the couch in his grandfather's den taking the after-lunch nap Bedon should have been taking himself. The weary, though sleepless grandfather extricated himself from his leather chair and slipped out of the room in his sock feet, although there was no real need for him to be quiet. Buddy was more weary than he. The young man could've slept through a reenactment of the bombing of Fort Sumter. His grandfather knew this, but he didn't want to risk involving his much-loved grandson in a sensitive task that had to be completed before he, protector and blame-taker for the real shooter, could allow himself rest of any sort.

Bedon unlocked the carriage house door, walked straight to the undersized chest, and opened the top drawer. He found the cash envelope empty – thank goodness – and refilled it with a fistful of twenties. When he'd closed the envelope back inside the drawer, his face took on the same drained look Buddy's had. It was a look not unlike someone being ravaged by a terminal illness. Feeling faint and dizzy, he wondered if he had the strength to make it back to his easy chair. No use calling out to his sleeping grandson for help, not when Bud had already sunk into a near coma as a result of the all-nighter he'd been forced to pull due to gunplay and bloodshed in his pop's foyer. The stressed Buddy had every right to be dog tired. Therefore, Bedon, central character in this outrageous drama, would have to get back to Mr. Easy Chair under his own steam.

Bedon's journey to the main house was touch and go the whole way, but at long last he was able to flop down in his chair in the den and join Buddy in a snoring contest. Bud had no notion that his adored pop, the pop he was supposed to be seeing after, had eluded him for a full twenty minutes while making a shifty roundtrip to the carriage house.

When the two Calhoun men awoke, they faced with matching misery their destiny with Mrs. Flynn. Sitting unbusinesslike at the kitchen table, they both stared at the prospective med helper while she held forth on the subject of her advanced degrees in medical something or another.

With a tortured grind upon his late grandma's red linoleum, Buddy scraped his chair closer to the table and tried to make sense of the paperwork the interviewee had brought with her, all glowing documentation of the worthiness of her own self. Under the table, he crossed and re-crossed his legs to keep them from falling asleep and sang the national anthem inside his head to keep his brain and body from doing the same.

Bedon, however, remained as poised as a copperhead ready to strike. His controlled gaze hovered six inches above Mrs. Flynn's head, focusing with chilling concentration on the pot rack hanging from the nine-foot ceiling above the stove, where dangled ten copper-colored pots that could be used at any moment as weapons to silence evil med helpers. The more Mrs. Flynn droned on, the more entrenched became the offended look on Bedon's face, the same look people get upon entering the air space of Kraft Paper Mill in North Charleston. Sulfur fumes have a way of making folks sit up and take notice and not in a good way.

But tooting her own horn too long wasn't the worst mistake Mrs. Flynn made. Her worst mistake was planting her ample backside in the ladderback chair that had been Hildie's regular seat, which, in Bedon's estimation, was the most rotten faux pas the woman could have ever committed, making her rotten interview even more rancid. Never mind the hopeful job applicant had no way of knowing Bedon's darling Hildie had ever drawn the breath of the living, much less where she'd sat every day for breakfast, lunch, and dinner.

Thus, into Hildie's chair the unwanted outsider had let down her considerable weight. Belly and boob fat swallowed up her skeletal frame. Her starched-and-ironed white uniform, that was supposed to be as crisp as a sacramental wafer, wilted in stinky perspiration. The very sight of her offended Dr. Calhoun to the limit of his Christian patience, a monumental occurrence considering the respected doctor had the distinction of being the most devout Southern Baptist who lived on the Charleston peninsula, although one didn't have to be excessively devout to hold this honor downtown.

But now, with no remorse, he was shedding his lifelong religion bucketful by bucketful with every syllable Mrs. Flynn spoke across Hildie's table, that hallowed surface whereupon the faithful wife had snapped her green beans and served her home cooked meals. Bedon knew Hildie wouldn't have put up with the likes of an overbearing shrew like Mrs. Flynn for longer than a match strike. She'd have run her out of there faster than Bo's Nana would have.

Was there no end to the information this "nurse" was determined to impart? Buddy's eyes spun in blue spirals; the "nurse's" eyes glowed yellow and goat-like. And Bedon's? Well, have you ever heard of the Vatican City Borgia family daggers? Those bloody blades were tame compared to the single dagger protruding from Bedon's left eye that had drawn a bead on Mrs. Flynn's left tittie.

Yet, on and on she rattled about her skills and competencies. "...and I'm more than qualified to administer medications to include injections, and I do light housework, prepare light food, keep written documentation and..."

Bedon hit the table with his fist...again. And Buddy, still shell-shocked from the first time his grandfather had done the very same thing earlier on the very same morning, and from the shooting incident of the night before, jumped hard enough to lose a whole other set of paperwork. It sailed down to the floor in separate sheets, and down to the floor Buddy chased them.

When he'd collected most (two had slipped under the refrigerator never to be seen again), and collected himself, he sat back down and watched in horror as Bedon stretched his upper body over the kitchen table and thrust his snowy head into Mrs. Flynn's personal space. "Flatulence," the old man said to the she-devil, nose to beaky nose.

"What?" she croaked.

"You heard me. Flatulence. Will you be documenting that, too?"

# 45.
# Bedon and Jake Make the News

After they'd hired Mrs. Flynn on a probationary basis – actually, Buddy had had to lower himself to begging her not to leave when she'd threatened to do just that following Bedon's foray into talk of natural gas – the responsible grandson considered it would be worthwhile to have a conversation with his pop about how to proceed to give the relationship with the new med helper a fair chance of working out. But about this consideration the responsible grandson had been wrong.

The split-second Bud breathed Mrs. Flynn's name, his pop developed such an interest in the evening news on TV, he became deaf and blind to anything else. He watched as Bill Blatt, the news commentator, put on his most serious face while describing the "frightening, dreadful push-in last night in Charleston peninsula's high-end neighborhood South of Broad Street..." (Imagine at this point a photo of Bedon's Murray Boulevard home projected in a small insert box next to the male news anchor's intricately coiffured head.) "...a violent crime that turned more violent when shots were fired, resulting in the death of the intruder caused by bullet wounds to the chest."

As the commentator closed out his account of the "frightening" incident, right before he moved on to a lengthy story on the negligence of downtown dog owners who refused belligerently to clean up their pets' poop from public curbing – Miss Posey and Hamp weren't mentioned by name in this story, though they should have been – another set of photos relating to the deplorable "push-in" flashed up, this time filling the whole screen. There they were, Bedon and Jake, both looking pretty rough around the edges. Where do news people get photos like these? And who in the world could tell from the grainy quality of the images which was the victim and which was the criminal? Bedon had been on the news only one other time in his life, back in the sixties when the Chamber of Commerce had named him Citizen of the Year and given him a wooden plaque they'd ordered from Creative Carving Company in South Bend, Indiana, the company with the famous motto: Awards That Last a Lifetime, Unless There Is a Fire.

Thus, being on TV per se was not new to Bedon, but the last time they hadn't shown a picture of his house or referred to him as "a resident in his golden years trying to survive in his own home." What happened to Citizen of the Year? What happened to the title of "Dr." before his name?

Buddy walked over and turned the TV off. Standing squarely in front of the widescreen and the floor model television supporting it, he took his time mobilizing his strength. But mobilize it he did. Choking down a gallon of trepidation, he forged forward into the battle his grandfather was trying to avoid – a discussion about Mrs. Flynn.

"We need to talk, Pop," Bud said and moved with bogus confidence to sit down on the sofa next to his sulking namesake. "I know you don't want this new woman or any other woman aggravating you twenty-four seven. So, like I offered before, if you want me to come stay with you at night for a while... That way you won't have to put up with another hired hand. It's me, or Aunt Pauline and Uncle Lawrence, or a Mrs. Flynn look-alike. Take your pick."

Bedon, irritated beyond belief that Buddy not only had the gall to turn off the nightly news while he, Bedon, was still watching it, but was now suggesting again he might move back in after Bedon himself had already nixed that idea unequivocally, shouted out a frightful *"No!"* Then, turning his head so slowly toward the culprit beside him on the sofa that the very deliberateness of the motion struck fear into the heart of Buddy Calhoun, Bedon shone the two powerful spotlights that had become his eyes straight onto his grandson's face. In abject fear, Buddy jumped off the sofa and fled his pop's mansion, coattails a'flying, without presenting a single syllable of his closing argument.

# 46.

## Larissa, All Grown Up?

All of the above sadly explains how it came to be that Bedon spent the next four months of his life enduring Mrs. Flynn in the daytime to keep Buddy from hiring another one just like her for nights, or worse, moving back in himself. It was the fortuitous reason the aging king of the castle, who was currently hanging onto the last vestiges of his sovereign rule, was alone in the house when Larissa dropped by one random morning in the teeniest, tiniest hours for a casual visit at her usual casual time of somewhere between three and four a.m.

Naturally, it had to be raining and cold outside. Bedon smiled, frowned, and smiled again when he saw her, shivering in the glow of his back porch light. "Hey," he said on opening the door. "How are you? I've missed you. But you shouldn't be here. The police... Come in. Let me get you a blanket. You're shaking." He tugged her through the kitchen door, continuing to gabble on as he hurried off to the den to fetch a blanket. "Seems like every time you come around it's storming. Why do you suppose that is?"

She didn't speak, remained standing in the middle of the kitchen, shivering, hair plastered to face, rain water puddling around soaked sneakers.

Bedon came back in and gave her the blanket he'd promised. "You're going to get sick. There's a terrible cold going around. Buddy's had it. Terrible."

She didn't do anything with the blanket, though her lips looked bluish. He took it from her and threw it around her shoulders. "Some chamomile tea'll warm you up, just like Peter Rabbit..."

Still, she didn't speak, though her teeth chattered intermittently. Bedon went to the sink to fill a huge mug with water and pop it into the microwave. He stood there looking at her, the tea bag dangling from his fingers. When the microwave dinged, he retrieved the mug and dropped the little net bag into it. "Want some honey to sweeten it up? Lots of antioxidants."

"No," she said, taking the mug and warming her hands around it.

"Well, good. You can still talk. I was beginning to think the cat had gotten your tongue..."

"Stop it, Bedon," she said and wiped rain water from the tip of her nose with her same old hoodie sleeve. She made a face to force back tears. Now it was Bedon who didn't speak.

When able to get control of herself, she said, "Look at me, Bedon. I'm not a child anymore."

But he couldn't let go of treating her like one. "By Jove, I think you're right. Drinking tea instead of Mello Yellow, wearing athletic shoes instead of flip-flops..."

"I said stop. I really am older now. But there're some things I can't handle on my own."

Bedon dragged a chair away from the table and sat down, facing her. Looking upward into her dull eyes, he said from the depths of his heart, "Larissa...Moonbow in the Mist...I don't know a soul who could have handled any of the things you've been through."

"I need your help, Bedon. I need it tonight."

"What kind of help? If it's anything illegal..."

"No, I wouldn't ask if it were wrong. Come with me to the carriage house. It'll be easier to understand if you see it with your own eyes."

Holding the warm mug to her croupy chest with one hand, she took hold of his arm with the other and pulled him out of the chair and toward the back door. She stopped at the entrance to the pantry and said, "Get your umbrella and wellies out of there. We can't have you coming down with that terrible cold, not at your age."

# 47.
# New Girl, New Problem

Larissa, still gripping the mug of tea, stepped inside the carriage house. Bedon followed and closed the door behind him. Larissa moved to the side so he could see the problem. The gentle doctor stood staring at a petite girl sitting on the edge of the daybed. Larissa waited a moment for the shock to wear off before walking over to the girl and handing her the mug. "Drink this," she said to the sweet, heart-shaped face. "It'll warm you up, make you feel better. My friend, Bedon, made it for you." She pointed toward her old benefactor still standing in the middle of the room.

Larissa left the girl and re-joined Bedon, who was barely hanging onto enough calm to speak. He used his quietest voice to keep the new visitor from hearing. "I don't know what your thinking is here, Larissa, but I can't take in every kid in Charleston who's hard up. It's not smart. Could be trouble, already been trouble. I'll take her to the authorities, but there's no way she can stay here."

"Why not? You let me stay."

"Yes, a mistake that's been blowing up in my face ever since. Don't get me wrong. I'm not abandoning you at this late date, certainly not when it comes to funding your education, but I can't take on... Suffice it to say my own life isn't a bed of roses anymore."

Bedon didn't realize he'd gotten louder. The girl on the bed began whimpering. He looked at her in horror, at her pale, pitiful face. Larissa took his arm again. "At least come meet her," she said and drew her good angel to the one place in the room he did not want to go. He balked three feet from the bed and refused to be moved a step closer. Larissa didn't try to force him. She slipped around to the end of the daybed, leaned down to the rug and lifted a bundle out of an infant seat that Bedon had not yet spied.

When she straightened up, and he saw she was holding a baby in her arms, he lurched backward. Larissa chuckled in spite of the seriousness of the matter. "For Pete's sake, a baby won't bite you," she said. "You're supposed to be a doctor."

Bedon looked back and forth between the girl holding the infant and the girl sitting on the bed. "Whose baby is that?" he said to Larissa. "Not yours, I hope. You didn't go back and get him." And then to both girls, "What's going on here? What...?"

Larissa, now holding the sleeping baby on her shoulder like an expert, sucked her teeth at Bedon's muddled reaction. "Don't go ballistic," she said. "We have to talk about what to do."

# 48.
## Kind of a Long Story

Bedon's legs were so wobbly he had to sit down on the daybed next to the girl, who edged away from him like he might smell funny. Larissa cuddled the baby closer and stood before the old man and the new young patient. "Bedon," she said, "meet Michelle. Michelle, meet Bedon. Michelle isn't her real name, but it's good enough for now." She then held the swaddled infant forward and made Bedon take a look. "This is Michelle's baby girl. Cute, huh."

At the sight of the infant's tiny pink face, Bedon's mind kicked back into working order. "How old?" he said to Larissa with renewed confidence.

She blinked at the change in his demeanor. "Two days."

"No, I mean her." He gestured at the girl beside him.

"Oh, fourteen. I thought you were talking about..."

"Fourteen? I can't manage this. Where's her mother?"

Annoyed, Larissa said, "She *is* the baby's mother."

Now it was Bedon's turn to be annoyed. "If you start that round and round talk of yours, I'm going back in the house."

"Okay, okay. But I can't tell you everything at once. Bonnie, I mean Michelle, lives next door to us in the project. And when I was asleep a couple of nights ago, she woke me up crying from inside her apartment. Her mom had already gone to work. She helps make pies for a bakery downtown on King Street, and they start doing that in the middle of the night. I knew her mother wasn't home. Mine wasn't, either. Don't ask where she went. I don't know, and wherever it was, she's been gone a week and still is. So, I went next door by myself and found Bonnie having a baby right there in her bedroom. I helped her and stayed with her 'til it was over. What was so weird was nobody even knew she was pregnant, like nobody knew I was pregnant, not her mother, not my mother. Weird."

Bedon's eyes registered panic. "And who cut the cord?" he said, white-faced. "And who took care of the placenta?"

"I did," said Larissa. "I tied two strings around the cord and left a space between the strings like I saw a midwife do on TV one time, and then cut it in two in the little space between the knots. I really had to lay into that thing. It was tougher than it looked. After, I poured some of the peroxide you gave me on the baby's tummy and wrapped her up in a doll blanket. I didn't know what to do about the other thing, the pla-centa. I guess that was what Bonnie pushed out not long after the baby. I put it in a plastic trash bag and threw it in the green box outside. Bonnie seemed all right after a while. You're all right now, aren't you, Bonn?"

The pallid girl nodded yes, though she didn't look like she meant it. Bedon stared at her from a doctor's perspective while Larissa chattered on. "Then I gave the baby to Bonnie and cut up the blanket from her bed to make some little blankets, and then called a cab and brought'em both over here. That was a day and a half ago. We've been staying really quiet out here like Bonnie was Ann Frank or somebody. She spent the whole first day sleeping with the baby, while I went around on my bike and got this infant carrier at Good Will, and some Pampers, and a case of disposable bottles of formula from a pharmacy, and a binky and three little shirts from a dollar store. You wouldn't believe how tiny a baby is with no clothes on.

"The thing is, Bonnie has gotten some sleep, but I haven't. I've been up night and day taking care of everything. Had to go out on my bike every other minute to get us food and stuff. Finally, after riding down to that all night gas station by the marina in this rain to get us some crackers and drinks, and getting soaked to the skin and half freezing to death, I got up the nerve to tell Bonnie we had to discuss getting somebody to help us, to help her, and I told her how you knew all about Daniel's Law and everything, and she said it sounded good. And that's about it."

Bedon closed his eyes and tried to think. After a moment, he popped them open again and assumed the role of responsible adult. "You have to tell her mother, both your mothers. Why haven't they reported you missing? How is it the two of you can be gone for days at a time and nobody reports it to the police?"

"Didn't you hear me say my mother has taken off? And don't you know mothers like mine and Bonnie's don't report anything to the police? My mother wouldn't report it if aliens landed in a flying saucer and blew up the whole project apartment complex. She doesn't want me to have to go back into foster care anymore than I do. Neither does Bonnie's mom. Get a brain, Bedon. Bonnie wants to put her baby under the protection of Daniel's Law, like I did, like you helped me do. She has no other choice."

"Stop being rude," he said to Larissa, but the lack of vigor in his voice made his words sound weak, like an ineffective reprimand directed at Buddy for talking with his mouth full, not like a stall to give himself time to think about how to fix the fractured life of a fourteen-year-old girl with a newborn.

Larissa waited ten long seconds before speaking again. "Bedon, please," she said. "All you have to do is drive us. I don't have another dime for Uber fare, and I don't want Bonnie to have to go do this in an Uber. You helped me, and you can help her. I promise you it'll make her feel less miserable about the whole thing if you go with us. I know I couldn't have done it without you. Don't just give us money for a ride and blow us off. It looks to me like, you being a doctor and all, you'd be glad she wants to do it this way instead of putting the baby in a dumpster..."

"*Stop it!*" Bedon yelled at Larissa, and the harshness of his voice woke the baby. Bonnie began whimpering again. "Oh, that's just great," the old doctor said, the old doctor who had never experienced anything like this in his forty-two years of practicing medicine. "I'm going back to the house to clear my head. Listen here, Larissa, you said this girl is fourteen, and I believe you after getting a close look at her. But now I want you to tell me the truth about yourself. How old are you?"

She shrugged a shoulder. "Twenty-one."

Bedon looked away from her. "You little liar," he said.

"Why ask me if you knew I was gonna lie again? I've told you so many stories about how old I am, I can't remember myself."

Bedon shuddered. "I'm going inside to think."

"Don't think too long. It'll be daybreak soon, and don't come back out here without your truck keys. We'll be ready."

When the good doctor returned, he was no longer wearing his pajamas and robe. Larissa, relieved to see he'd changed into street clothes, began scurrying around the room getting her two patients ready to go. Bedon stopped her. "Be still a minute," he said. "There's something I have to tell you. And don't interrupt. I can't have you talking in circles and making me lose my train of thought." He sat back down on the bed and rested a moment before continuing. "Larissa, you have to listen to me closely."

She nodded at him from across the room where she was standing by the chest of drawers. He nodded back. "All right then," he said. "Here's how it is with me these days. I've been having mini-strokes for a long time, months, and for all I know they've affected my ability to think rationally, to make good decisions. My doctor says I'm okay in that department, but I gotta tell you, I'm not so sure he knows what he's talking about. I don't see how those things couldn't affect a man's mental abilities, and the T.I.A.'s, mini-strokes, are getting worse all the time. I've studied the literature, and research says they have a cumulative effect on thinking, a detrimental cumulative effect. At any rate, I want you to know all that, and I also want you to know I'm not afraid of causing problems for myself. I'm really not. In fact, it makes me feel good to think I might be of some help to this little girl here. But I am afraid of making a bad decision and causing problems for her or anyone else, problems that might surface later and go on into adulthood. Are you following me?"

Larissa readjusted the baby girl on her shoulder and patted her darling back. "I guess so. I didn't know you were sick. How bad is it? I'm gonna be a nurse soon. I can take care of you."

Bedon smiled in spite of himself. "I know you're going to be a nurse, but I'm all right for now. I try hard to keep my life simple, avoid pressure."

"So do I," she said. "I guess my life's pretty simple most of the time. You, though... Bedon, you can't just sit around and do nothing in that big old house the rest of your life. You'll dry up like a raisin. You have to keep doing things, like you did for me, like you're doing for her... and her." She cocked her head once to indicate the girl sitting on the bed, and a second time to indicate the baby on her own shoulder.

Bedon wrinkled up one side of his face in amazement and amusement. "So you think your life is simple. I'd hate to see what you'd call complicated."

"What's complicated about a girl with a baby she can't support? It's the oldest problem in the world."

"But, Larissa...you of all people know that what she's thinking of doing could have psychological repercussions."

"Oh, please. You're making it complicated when it doesn't have to be. She's scared out of her mind. She could do something stupid, try to get rid of the baby. Are you gonna help her or not? If you aren't, go ahead and give us the money for a ride, and I'll do the rest by myself."

Bedon quashed all his hesitation in one brave instant. "Take her and the baby out to the truck," he said. "And when we get back, the two of you can camp out here a couple more nights, until Bonnie or Michelle, or whoever she is, is back on her feet. After that, she goes home for good. No coming back. Agreed?"

"Agreed," Larissa said, "but believe me, after she gets her baby taken care of, she won't ever want to see this place again."

"If I do this for you, Larissa, and for her, it has to be the last time. I'm not able to be involved in heavy problems anymore. My mind isn't clear enough. Do you believe me?"

"No, I don't. You're a good man, Bedon, and I think you'd go on trying to help girls like Bonnie and me for as long as you could figure out how. But I won't ask you again. Now that I know you're sick, I'll leave you alone."

# 49.
## More Fine Dining

Buddy and Bo sat on benches in Washington Park eating hotdogs and drinking lemonade. Bo shook a few peanuts from the overpriced bag he'd bought from a peddler on a bicycle and tossed them one by one to the greedy park dwellers – a flock of cooing pigeons and a dray of barking squirrels. It was the only thing saving him from dying of boredom from his conversation with lifelong pal, Buddy C.

To "lifelong pal," said Bo, "Don't you just love eating out in downtown Charleston?" Taking another bite of his hotdog, he made a second inquiry between chews. "How'd you slip away for a Saturday lunch anyhow? Is your pop over being mad at you?"

"Still barely speaking to me. Despises Mrs. Flynn. Calls her a Nazi."

Bo stomped his foot at an aggressive pigeon before tossing it another peanut. "Your pop is an ace of a fellow. He'll come around. And don't waste your time thinking about what happened to that other guy he got mad at, the one he shot deader than a doornail. I'm pretty sure he was madder at him than he is at you. Anyway, that was a whole different thing…I hope." Pause. "You're all your pop's got in the world."

"Apparently not. I never told you about catching him in the front room with a babe. A month or so ago in the middle of the night, slow dancing. She ran off mad as a hornet when Caroline and I came in and busted up the party. Pop's been out of sorts ever since."

"Your pop...has got himself a babe? Well, well, well. That explains a bushel of things. And all this time I thought he was upset on account of a simple little thing like shooting somebody."

Bo stomped at the bully pigeon again while Buddy munched without appetite on the hotdog his best pal had forced him to buy. Bo, sensitive guy and more sensitive friend, leaned back on the hard slats of the park bench and gazed with pride at the bronze bust of Henry Timrod, poet laureate of the Confederacy. He quoted aloud the only line he could remember of Timrod's poem, "Ethnogenisis": "Thank Him who placed us here, Beneath so kind a sky..."

"Henry T. is right," he said to Buddy with nostalgia, "that thing he wrote about all us South Carolinians living out our lives 'beneath so kind a sky.' Even so, I get depressed about things." He twisted about in pain on the hard bench before sharing his most recent gloomy realization. "Bud, man...here I am married with four kids, and you half engaged to a department store manikin, whose only redeeming quality is her daddy's got a freight car full of dough. Our machismo is deader than roadkill. Why don't you ask your pop if his hot girlfriend's got any hot girlfriends for a couple of loser beta-dudes like us?"

# 50.
## Return of Detective Walker and Detective Brock

Buddy drove his Super Bee along Murray Boulevard toward home, home to Bud being wherever Pop Bedon hung his fedora. The picnic in the park with his best friend was over to the dismay of the squirrel and pigeon population. Bo was now taking up space in the passenger seat of Buddy's muscle car, his mind engrossed in the contemplation of important matters, such as what his wife, Susannah May Eleanor, might be cooking up for supper, and why he was already hungry again though he'd just scarfed down two jumbo slaw dogs, and why in the world some gal would be dancing with Buddy's pop in his parlor late one night?

Preoccupied by these critical considerations, Bo didn't notice two squad cars, one parked behind the other, in Pop Calhoun's driveway. "Describe her to me, man," he said to the distracted Buddy, who *had* noticed the two black-and-whites. "I want to know what kind of taste Bedon has in women. Roxie Hart or Joan of Arc?"

Buddy studied the police cars, but had gotten so used to odd goings-on at his pop's place that he saw no need in pointing them out to Bo, who would spot them on his own soon enough. Instead, he continued carrying on his inane conversation with his best pal like nothing out of the ordinary was up.

To Bo's inappropriate question about Bedon's taste in women, he replied, "I already told you all I know. The whole thing happened too fast to get her measurements. Main thing, she was young."

"How young? Fifty? Forty? Thirty?"

"I'd say twenty, less than twenty."

"*Woh,* " Bo breathed. "Those church ladies have so been wasting their time."

He sat up straighter and looked all around to see why Buddy had put on brakes so far from the house. As they approached the drive, Bo woke up to the fact that two police prowlers had rolled up for a visit and brought two officers in blue along with them. The officers were wasting their time lolling about on the end of the piazza where the joggling board was the chief point of interest. Bo couldn't keep his mouth shut as he and Bud gawked at the police presence interfering with the Southern charm of Bedon's luxury dwelling.

"I for one am proud to know your pop," he said to Buddy, who reacted by snatching the Super Bee to the right and bumping its front wheels onto the curb. Then, like Bo and Luke of "Dukes of Hazard," Bo and Bud of "South of Broad" vaulted out of the convertible and ran like two deer toward Pop Bedon's front gate.

The same two detectives who had questioned Bedon the night of the shooting sat next to each other in the same wingback chairs. But this time they were not looking across the coffee table at Bedon and Buddy. This time they were looking across it at Bedon and Mrs. Flynn, the two of whom made an odd couple if there ever was one, considering how far apart from each other they were trying to sit, a difficult endeavor taking into account the abbreviated length of the love seat.

Buddy and Bo burst in with no invitation on this intimate get-together. "What's going on here?" Bud said to the seated group.

"Hey there, son," his grandfather said. The old doctor seemed relieved someone had shown up who might take his side, and just as happy to see Bo for the same reason. "Hey there, my man," he said to Buddy's best friend. "How did y'all get here so fast? Did someone call you? These police officers here have been asking me some peculiar questions. I've never been at such a loss."

After Bedon's strange greetings to Buddy and Bo, and his stranger explanation as to "what was going on," he sank into immediate silence, closed his eyes, and slumped back against the sofa.

Buddy attacked Detective Brock in staccato. "Why are you over here again harassing him? Can't you see he's not well?"

The detective maintained a cool demeanor, though it took a fair amount of effort. "We're here, sir, because your grandpa's med helper requested us to come. She has grave concerns about Mr. Calhoun. Very grave concerns."

Buddy got down on one knee in front of his grandfather and looked intently at the aging gentleman's slack face. His pop's eyes remained closed, his mouth drooped. Upset by how weak Bedon looked, Buddy stood up again and made quick eye contact with the calm-as-a-green-meadow Detective Brock. He spoke to the officer with exaggerated slowness. "Don't call him Mr. Calhoun, Detective Whatever-your-name-is. To you, he's *Dr.* Calhoun. And to her, too." He jerked his head toward Mrs. Flynn before continuing. "Who, by the way, is nothing but hired help."

After putting Detective Brock and Mrs. Flynn in their places, the overwrought Buddy dragged an ottoman close to Bedon and sat down next to him. Bo, who was monitoring the situation from the periphery, flinched as Buddy directed his laser eyes at the bridge of Mrs. Flynn's pointy nose. It was a terrible thing to see and to hear as Buddy began spraying noxious words at the lady in white. "Who do you think you are, woman? Calling the police over here...for what?"

Detective Brock spoke up before Mrs. Flynn could get organized enough to defend herself. Brock: "It's not about the shooting, sir. The problem today is...different."

Buddy checked his grandfather again to make sure he was still alive. "Are you all right, Pop?" he said to the quiet man who looked like he might be losing consciousness. "Maybe you ought to go upstairs and lie down."

Bedon roused and gestured at a glass of water on the coffee table. Buddy, thankful for something useful to do, picked it up and handed it to his grandfather. Everyone in the room watched as the "person of interest," a senior citizen whose hands and arms were trembling so much that water escaped his drinking glass and dribbled onto his pant legs, took a few sloppy sips.

Detective Walker broke the sympathetic mood and said to Buddy with police crispness. "Are you his closest kin, sir?"

"You know I am from when you questioned me the other night. I'm his only grandson. My parents are deceased."

The detective seemed satisfied with Bud's answer, since he already knew what it was going to be. "Well, son, your grandpa's nurse here, Mrs. Flynn, called the station a little while ago and said the police needed to come over here and see something in connection with those two little girls who went missing in Georgia a few months ago."

Buddy looked confused, but not for long. In less than a second, he rose from the ottoman and bore down on Detective Walker as if to do him bodily harm. Bo lunged forward and caught his pal by the arm, which allowed both detectives time enough to get to their feet and scramble around to the back side of the upholstered chairs that their twin sets of buttocks had been warming for the last half hour.

Detective Walker appeared discombobulated, but not Detective Brock. He maintained his status as the perfect model for how-to-keep-a-cool-head-in-a-situation-on-its-way-from-bad-to-worse. Said he to Buddy in the irritating polite style police officers use when their real intention is to be rude, "We know this is hard on you, sir, but Mrs. Flynn here found some odd things in the carriage house, things she thought we...ought to know about."

Right before the phrase "ought to know about," the cool detective milked the meaningful pause he had inserted into his statement, during which time he looked at his partner with covert meaning and back at Buddy with overt condescension. Then he added as though talking to someone exceedingly dumb, "Well, son, if you don't understand, maybe we should all go out to the carriage house and let you see things for yourself. It's strange as heck out there, I grant you, but there's probably an explanation for it. Usually is."

The detectives, Walker and Brock, stood by with Buddy, Bo, and Bedon. Mrs. Flynn unlocked the carriage house door. Thrilled to be center stage, the heavyweight med helper blessed everyone in her audience with a running commentary: "The other helper, Mrs. Harris, wrote in her exit statement that he was real funny about this building from the start. Made me suspicious right away, but I left it alone. Seemed trivial at the time. And I certainly didn't want it ever said of me that I don't know how to respect a client's privacy." She paused a moment to sneeze a bullhorn sneeze, then jabbered on, "...but when I read about those missing girls, a bad taste like bile boiled up in my throat. I knew right then I had to do something. So...soon as he went down for his nap today, I made it my business to find out what the big secret was out here. I called the other med helper – Mrs. Harris, the one they fired for no good reason right before they hired me – and asked if she knew where the key was. She said to look in the pantry closet, that he kept it on the same nail holding up a wild animal wall calendar. And I did, and there it was, big as you please."

She gave the carriage house door a push forceful enough to swing it open. Crooking her dimpled elbow inside the room, she turned on the overhead dolphin light, then made a production of getting out of the way to allow Buddy and Bo unhindered entry. Once inside, the two young men spent a few moments in unspeakable shock as they gazed around. Buddy was the first to find the weakest echo of his own voice. "I swear, I am losing my mind," he whispered to no one.

Bo, the quicker thinker for one shining moment in his lifetime, came up with the best line he could, given the limited time he had to sift through his gray matter. With illogical logic, he tried to save the day. "Hey, man," he said to Buddy. "Y'all got a renter? I didn't know y'all had a renter. Why didn't you tell me y'all had a renter?"

Mrs. Flynn snorted up her nasal drip, and, with enormous disapproval of Bo's ridiculousness, said to the detectives, "The other med helper, Mrs. Harris, was a day person like me. Or she was before they fired her. That's why neither one of us knows what in high Heaven goes on out here at night."

She cut her eyes at Bedon, whose facial color was exceeded in palor only by Buddy's and Bo's. Detective Walker and Detective Brock tried to peer around Mrs. Flynn's bulk as the two younger men continued their visual inspection of the building's interior. Detective Walker said to the back of Buddy's head, "You can see why she was concerned, sir. Peculiar..."

Bud whipped around and glared at the detective with eyes so hot they melted the hoarfrost off the veteran officer's Frosty-the-Snowman persona. "No...I *can't* see why she was so concerned," he said to the arrogant officer.

Then Buddy turned back and gave Bo an unkind fist between his shoulder blades to divert his attention away from the plethora of stuffed animals lying this way and that on the pink daybed. "Come on, Bo," he said. "Show's over."

Bo allowed himself to be ushered out of what appeared to him to be a sissy's bedroom, more sissy than the suite of rooms his wife had decorated for their pre-school daughters, a room with no rhyme or reason for existing in the masculine world of Bedon and Buddy Calhoun. Nevertheless, out of loyalty to a pal, no matter what insane situation the pal found himself in, Bo made no more comments as Buddy drew him out of the carriage house with a rough hand, switched off the dolphin light, slammed the door shut, and locked it from the outside with the key he had snatched without asking from the hand of Mrs. Flynn, the worst med helper in all the world. The insult of which caused the battle-axe/whistleblower to blurt out, "But it's a young girl's room. That can't be right."

Buddy screwed up his face at her, pocketed the key, and trod across the yard toward the main house. "You're fired," he said without looking back. "Pack up your rectal thermometer and leave."

Incensed, she showered a flurry of words upon Detective Walker, her supposed ally. "Don't be fooled by him, Officer. Something shameful is going on around here, and he...." She pointed a pudgy forefinger at Bud's receding back, "...is trying to hide it."

Buddy whirled back around. His eyes burned red, the ghastly sight of which silenced the whole group, including his devious, conniving, deceitful pop. In frustration, the grandson shouted at Mrs. Flynn again to avoid shouting at his grandfather. "Leave the premises right now, madam, or I'll call the police."

Detective Brock sniggered. He was the "police," after all, and already present in official capacity, though he never expected the guy he was sniggering at to charge back across the yard and get all up in his face, greasy forehead to greasy forehead. Again, Bo had to intervene to prevent his lifelong pal, Buddy, from committing felonious assault on a policeman. "No, man. Going after a cop isn't the answer. Aren't they teaching you anything in law school?"

# 51.

# What Has Been Going On?

Later in the evening - a few hours after the drama-charged departure of Mrs. Flynn - Bo Gaillard, the most loyal pal Buddy could ever want, sat alone with his knees under the Calhoun kitchen table, pretending to read one of Bedon's South Carolina history books. Buddy re-joined Bo just as he was finishing up a selection on the proper technique of sitting down in a hoop skirt. Fascinating.

Bud collapsed in a ladderback across the table from his loyal pal and rested his head on his forearms reminiscent of student days in high school study hall. Said he to Bo in a voice muffled by his own shirt sleeve, "Finally got Pop to go to sleep up there. Geezol-pete, have I got a belly full of role reversal." He waited in silence for Bo to ask him if he were hungry, which Bo had no intention of doing, since he'd already polished off the leftovers in the fridge while Buddy was dealing with his pop upstairs.

Buddy raised his head from the table and continued his unproductive analysis of recent events. "What I can't figure out is why the Flynn woman thought she had to call the police. If that doesn't overstep the bounds of an employee, I don't know what does. Could be a legal thing. Yeah, a legal thing."

Bo, having lost interest in hoop skirts, floated an unfortunate comment. "A minor point considering your grandpaw has cooked up something resembling a teenage girl's boudoir out behind the big house."

Buddy's face went taut. He thrust his weight across the table and unseated Bo. Gripping his loyal pal's shirt front with both hands, Bud somehow managed to make them both lose their balance and fall to the linoleum floor. Bo, caught off guard, had to work harder than usual to get his good friend into a full Nelson.

"Why do you want to fight me, Calhoun? I'm not the one playing Barbie doll around here."

Bud struggled against Bo to no avail. He yelled at his best friend, "I'm not gonna let you make fun of Pop. It's your family who's whacked, not mine. Pop's a straight arrow."

Bo took liberties with his words since he had Bud contained in the most powerhouse wrestling hold in his repertoire, the expert execution of which had made him a jock celebrity at The Citadel four years running. "Not quite a straight arrow, dude, but don't let that worry you. Look on the bright side. I like stuffed animals, and I turned out great."

Buddy relaxed and tried to catch his breath. Bo, realizing he was victorious, let go of his beaten opponent and leaned back against the wooden cabinets below the sink. He looked with pity at Buddy now sprawled out on the red-black linoleum with his eyes rolled back in his head.

Bedon entered the kitchen and looked down at the two best friends with disgust. "What in Sam Hill are y'all doing?"

Buddy and Bo got to their feet and shook around in their twisted clothing like a couple of Bo Jangles hobos gearing up for a jig. The conquered Buddy did not want to admit he'd been "whupped," so he talked fast to keep Bo from jumping in and admitting it for him. "Why did you come down here again, Pop? You're supposed to be asleep."

The unintimidated Bedon said, "With all this noise?"

Buddy ha-rumped like an old man instead of the young man he was. "Okay, boss," he said, "I see how it is. You came back down to prove you ain't gonna be ordered around by the likes of me. Fair enough. Is your headache any better?"

Bedon sat down at the table. Buddy and Bo sat down with him as though nothing had happened between them in the way of fisticuffs. The tired old man regarded the two with a look akin to loathing, but asked no more questions about the recent fight scene for the good reason that he knew he'd never get a straight answer. He'd been dealing with Buddy and Bo all their worthless lives. That in mind, he stared at them in defiance and said, "I think some food would help my aching head and my empty stomach, if anyone's interested in fixing me any."

Buddy backed off being a smart-mouth and nodded to his grandfather like a good grandson. "Can we talk a minute first, Pop? About this thing today and the carriage house?"

"No, no, and no," said Bedon. "This thing today was every bit that gall-blasted med helper's fault. Now, for once in your no-account life, *you make the ham sandwiches*."

"Yeah," said Bo. "For once in your no-account life. Except you'll have to make PB&J's, 'cause I ate the rest of the ham while y'all were upstairs doing all that male bonding."

# 52.

# Buddy Goes to the Slammer

uddy strode into the police station like he owned the place. The attendant on duty, unimpressed and unafraid due to the bullet proof glass window between her and the wretched refuse yearning to be locked up who paraded through the golden doors of her kingdom every day, did not bother to raise her hawk eyes from the body-building rag she was reading. Bud knocked on her window with sharp report and said into the crackly microphone embedded in the window glass, "Is Detective Brock in?"

After a period of time sufficient to establish who was boss, the attendant lifted her chin and fixed Buddy with a heavy-lidded gaze no one could mistake for friendly. "And you are...?" she said.

"Bedon Calhoun, Jr.," Buddy answered. "Tell Detective Brock on that high-tech, two-way shoulder radio you got there I've come down here to discuss my grandfather's rights."

The female officer's raptor gaze wavered not. "How 'bout you tell him yourself," she said. "Left hallway, third door on the right." Satisfied that Buddy almost had sense enough to follow her simple directions, she settled back into her 'roid-rage' magazine and proceeded to blow a big pink bubble-gum bubble that popped with a major explosion all over her bird-of-prey face.

Detective Brock was sitting behind his own desk, minding his own business, when Buddy strode into his office. The officer looked up, then stood and extended his hand to Bud for a shake, a waste of courtesy, for Buddy rebuffed it like a gangsta. Brock, who hadn't lost his TV-cop cool, went ahead and wasted some more fake courtesy on Buddy, since he'd been issued an endless supply of it when he was a cadet at the police academy twenty-five years ago.

"Have a seat, Mr. Calhoun," he said. "What can I do for you on this beautiful Charleston morning?"

Buddy, still playing tough guy, snubbed the veteran officer again by refusing to sit down. Whereupon – bored as he was by his visitor's silly posturing – Detective Brock sighed, stuck his hands in his pockets, and remained standing, also.

Buddy began this impromptu meeting with the opening statement he had prepared in his mind on the way over. "Nobody may have told you, Walker, I mean Brock, but I'm a law student, so I know a thing or two about the load of bunk y'all have been trying to put over on my grandfather. Which means, if you don't suspect him of a crime, you have to leave him alone. And that's what I came over here to demand."

"Mr. Calhoun, sir, we were following up on a lead called in by a law abiding citizen, nothing more. The way that nurse was talking on the phone about your grandpaw, funny business was going on over at his house day and night. She told me out of her own mouth he was an eccentric kind of a guy."

"He's not eccentric. He's an ace."

"That's not what she said, sir, sitting right there in that same chair you won't sit down in."

"Are you telling me she came over here in person?"

"Yes, sir. First she called, then she came over to beat the point. Said it looked like Mr. Calhoun...*Dr.* Calhoun...might be keeping young girls locked up in his carriage house, and she was scared to death he might try it on her. We didn't pay much attention to that last part. Serial killers generally have excellent taste in women. Have you ever noticed that, when they show the photos on those crime TV shows?"

Buddy, so thrown off by the detective's monstrous remark, was a bit slow on the uptake. He blinked back tears of anger and said with a break in his voice, "The woman is a lunatic. You knew that the second she showed up here. Why did you let her string you along?"

"I admit, she's been here before with stories, but this one was too strange. And, bless me, when we got there, the room looked exactly like she described it. My partner and me, we didn't know what to make of it. Frankly, Mr. Calhoun...looked like you didn't, either."

Worn down and depleted of adrenaline, Buddy sank into the chair that had been offered to him when he'd first arrived. He dug the heels of his palms into his eye sockets and rubbed at them. Detective Brock eased into his own chair, but didn't let his guard down. Who knew what handle the confused young man sitting across from him might fly off next?

The "confused young man," who was trying to digest such a large serving of indigestible information about his grandfather that his mind was about to explode, spoke again, this time from behind his hands. "The point is, Brock, my pop doesn't deserve this onslaught on his character. I don't think he can bear up much longer."

"I understand, Mr. Calhoun...sir...and we won't be back over to his house. Got word this morning a suspect picked up in Georgia a while back is being indicted for what he did to those two little girls. DNA matches don't lie. Believe me, your grandfather's mental problems are small potatoes compared to a serial killer's profile. Yep, your grandpaw's just one-little-ole-piece-of-bread-short-of-a-sandwich, that's all."

Bud dropped his head for a moment to let his loathing for Brock wash through his body like a purgative. Then he reached over the plainclothesman's plain metal desk, grabbed the lapels of his plain sports jacket, and snatched his gone-to-fat body right across the plain piece of government issued furniture. It took him only a moment to wrestle the stout detective to the floor and pin him down onto his beer belly with his arms crossed shamefully behind his back.

"Listen," the detective's attacker (Buddy C.) hissed into his victim's hairy ear. "I won't have you or anyone else besmirching my grandfather's name. Do you understand me?"

Detective Brock would have answered his aggressor's question if he could have, but when he tried, he found he could do no more than make a humiliating peep. His aggressor had the upper hand and maintained it with little effort until Brock's partner, Detective Walker, along with two other sides-of-beef uniformed officers, one of whom was a female with a dirty-blond braid sticking out the back of her cap, rushed into the office and subdued Buddy. *And* took him into custody, *and* arrested him, *and*, eventually, threw him into a holding cell. What else are "hats and bats" for?

While all this was going on, Detective Brock managed to crawl over to the wall beside his desk and lean back on it to be nauseous in peace, at the same time that Buddy was being mauled by more back-up than was necessary. The fallen detective decided there was nothing left to do but abandon fake courtesy altogether and trot out sincere meanness, fake courtesy's evil twin, born to do nothing but romp and stomp.

"Lock the hairball up," he rasped from the floor. His voice had changed into the horrible snarl that rage alone can produce, except in Brock's case it came out, well, comical, what with his position of authority being so recently wrested from him by an unarmed citizen and splattered all over the foul smelling floor of his own office. *Fee-urious* is what he was, along with *em-barrassed*. In an effort to use hatefulness to take the edge off his humiliation, the detective addressed his underlings again, this time with the venom of a red-and-yellow/kill-a-fellow coral snake. "Cuff him and throw him in lock-up. We'll worry about what to charge him with later."

When "later" rolled around, and the brawl and brawlers had settled down, Bo and Buddy sat next to each other on a holding cell drop-down cot, hands in laps, staring straight ahead without speaking. Bo considered it was time to share a personal opinion with his lifelong pal, Buddy, an opinion that he (Bo) had formulated after a period of deep thought lasting two full minutes' worth.

Bo to Buddy: "Man, you're gonna have to change your ways, if you expect to practice law in this town. Even I haven't decked a cop in his own office, not with hot-and-cold running blue-shirts hiding in every grubby corner of this police palace."

Since he'd stated his brilliant observation so eloquently, Bo expected a response of thanks from his pal for offering up such wise counsel free of charge. Instead, Buddy scratched his own sweat-wet head and snorted a few times to dislodge the clot of blood in his left nostril that had leaked out and jelled there during the scuffle. He never did thank Bo for his gift of wisdom, but Bo forgave him, since he knew what bad shape his best pal was in. Attempting to approach Bud with a little more sensitivity, Bo spoke again with deeper feeling, "You don't talk much after a throw-down, do you, pal. It's okay, though, I don't mind. I'm big like that. And I promise when I get you out of here, I'm gonna take you down to Wet Willie's Bar where they know our names and buy you a Hairy Eyeball Ale, if you can spot me the twenty dollars."

After ten minutes of trying to cheer Buddy up with cheerful remarks, all of which were met with sweeping ingratitude, Bo grew tired of his friend's unwillingness to chat away the hours they were clearly going to be lolling about in the jail cell together, for Bo would never leave a chum alone in such a place unless some guard shook the keys in his face and actually ordered him out. He looked around at the walls and ceiling and again made a stab at small talk. "Hey, Bud. If you want to hear another of my well-thought-out opinions, this place could use a makeover. Every time I end up here it's the same vomit green."

Buddy, appearing to have gone deaf (a third opinion of Bo's), sniffed energetically once more and touched the bridge of his nose as tenderly as a lover might in a sad attempt to discern if it were broken. Of course, it was broken. It had to be. What other miserable outcome could there be to such a miserable afternoon? Thankful he still had a nose at all, Bud got up and began pacing the cell like Bo wasn't there.

Weary of trying to behave compassionately, Bo pulled out his wallet and began counting what little cash he had left after his wife had raided it that morning for the girls' lunch money. Since his pal, Buddy, appeared to have drifted off all mental radar for the moment, Bo conversed with nothing but the rank air of the jail cell while he counted his last few greenbacks. "Sixteen, seventeen, eighteen," he said. "Wouldn't cover bail for a parking ticket. Maybe I can get some money out of Nana. She always did like Bud." He decided then and there the best thing to do in a situation like this was to focus on the positive. Trying one more time to make contact with the AWOL brain of Buddy's, he called out in a loud voice, "If you can hear me in there, friend, it's my opinion," (his fourth for the day), "that Dr. Bedon Calhoun, Sr., affectionately known around here as Pop, is the best-of-the-west, I mean the best-of-the-east, and I wouldn't blame any grandson of his for not putting up with some flatfoot detective goon saying malicious things about him. Or any "Murder, She Wrote" med helper, either. We'll sue her first. She's the one started it."

The familiar vibrations of his best friend's voice aided Bud in his return to the atmosphere of terra firma. He relaxed and enjoyed his slow parachute ride from way out in thermosphere, down through mesosphere and stratosphere, all the way to troposphere, where he was finally able to tune in to and make half-sense of whatever it was Bo was trying to tell him. He turned and looked at his partner-in-crime as if it were perfectly normal for the two of them to be spending quality time together in a vomit green jail cell, talking over how to proceed with litigation. He said to Bo in guttural syllables, "Well, I don't know about you, but I'm suing the whole police department."

Bo, surprised by his friend's return to planet Earth, agreed with him. "Yeah, that'll fix 'em. Frankly, though...don't you think from here on out the less said the better?"

Bud, the newly arrived space cadet from the unfriendly outer fringes, trained unfriendly eyes on his pal's face, the same pal who was still sitting with eighteen one-dollar bills fanned out before him like a losing poker hand. Space cadet, Buddy, said to big time roller, Bo, in the same rage snarl Detective Brock had taught him how to use not too long ago, "What do you mean, *the less said the better?* Are you implying my pop has some kind of problem?"

Bo put his money away, stood up, and shoved his wallet deep into his back pocket in the off-chance he might need to have both hands free for combat. He gave Buddy a confused look, rage-snarling being a new addition to his friend's quarrelling style. "Listen," he said to his pal in a low voice, "will you *puh-leeze* calm down. It is my humble opinion," (his fifth for the day), "that it's not in your best interest to start a fight right here in this holding cell with the guy who's gonna have to borrow money from his nana to post bail for you. Frowned on is what I think it would be, so sit down and shut-up, like you were doing before you came back to the planet with that roaring case of diarrhea of the mouth."

Bo then took the small precaution of moving to the opposite end of the cell as far away from his friend as he could get, the friend who'd always professed to love and appreciate the unvarnished truth above all else, though, historically, Bud's emotional reactions to the unvarnished truth had left Bo thinking this particular conviction of his was a truckload of unvarnished horse manure.

Buddy, completely at ease now in the land of odd, took a couple of strides toward Bo, who'd taken to warming up the wall on the other side of the cell with the flat of his perspiring back. He'd seen it coming, this unwarranted possibility of attack. Buddy didn't hold back on spewing out stupid-certainty rhetoric in Bo's face. "Are you saying I ought to keep something hush-hush about my pop? This is Pop we're talking about. The guy who keeps half the charities in Charleston from going belly up. I'm gonna beat the breath out of you, Bo Gaillard."

Bo gave a single shot at diffusing the lighted human fuse standing before him. "Will you slow down and listen a minute? You know as well as I do the carriage house thing ain't right. Girl stuff? Pink frilly stuff? I'm telling you the less said the better. And I stand by that opinion like I stand by the respectability of the American flag."

Buddy, unable to comprehend the point Bo was attempting to make, made a point of his own. "When we get out of here, I'm going to teach you a lesson you won't forget." With great care, Bo slipped by his attacker and over to the bars of the cell. He craned his neck to look between them as best he could, up and down the dark corridor to see if some guard might be accidentally awake. Grabbing hold of a bar with each hand, he continued the testosterone-laced conversation he'd somehow gotten himself involved in with Buddy, while standing with his back to Bud-the-jailbird, which, for a refreshing change, wasn't Bo-the-jailbird, since he himself was currently fulfilling the role of concerned visitor, and not the role of unconcerned incarcerated.

"That's gratitude for you," he said to Buddy without looking away from the corridor. His hot breath made a tiny spot of condensation on the cold iron bar closest to his mouth. "You're the prisoner, Calhoun. I'm the loyal friend who rode up on my white horse to help. About now I'm wishing I hadn't ever let them lock me up in here with you. I'm on your side, dude, the guy who talked that square-jaw detective you whipped up on in his office into letting you off with no felony charges due to your extreme emotional upset over your pop's mental problems."

At that, Bud-the-prisoner balled up his fists, lowered his head and snarled again, which made Bo take a fleeting look backward to see if someone had let a pit bull into the cell through a false floor he'd somehow missed when he so innocently entered. Next time, he thought, I won't be so quick to do the Christian thing and visit folks in prison.

Buddy, more aggressive by the second, kept a'comin.' "I'm going to beat the breath out of you right now, Bo Gaillard," he said to his victim. But he didn't get the chance to, because his victim had, thankfully, found himself mingling bad breath with an ugly corrections officer, who was staring him down with one straight eye and one wandering eye through the bars of the jail cell, the cell Buddy was well on his way to turning into a cage fight arena.

The frantic Bo began beating on the iron bars with both fists. His erratic behavior did not match up with the smelly reality that the guard's face was so close to his own that he could identify the sauerkraut salad dressing from East Bay Deli that the officer was still digesting from lunch. "Sir, sir," Bo yelled at his deliverer, whose doughy jowls and bulbous schnoz (alcohol ravaged) looked more gorgeous than the face of a real angel with a real halo. Bo loved this guard, this kindhearted man who was about to deliver him from a sure butt-kicking if he got left in that jail cell much longer. "Please, let me out, sir," he yelled in falsetto at the baton wielding officer, a falsetto neither Bo nor the guard had ever before heard a grown man produce. "We're through with our little visit in here."

# 53.

## Bedon Falls Ill

Buddy, a free man now thanks to an interest-free loan floated him by Bo's nana – which Buddy had agreed to take, because he was too disgruntled at his pop to honor him by asking for financial help – continued sweating from his ordeal at the police station and his worse ordeal with Bo in the holding cell.

He lay limp in his favorite Westport Plank Adirondack in his pop's backyard, for he wasn't mad enough at him to stop hanging out at his house and partaking of free food and beverages. Bud's damp shirt grew stinkier by the second as he stared with the concentration of a cobra in full hood at the closed door of the carriage house. The Addie chair beside him was empty. Perhaps Jay Gatsby had excused himself and gone inside for a moment to make sure the caterers for the evening's wild party were making good progress with the hors d'ouvres.

"How're you doing, old sport," Bedon said to Buddy on returning from the kitchen with two tall tea glasses in hand. He gave one to Buddy and sat down beside him. Bedon followed the line of his grandson's vision to the carriage house and concluded he hadn't gotten over the trauma of it yet.

He tried in vain to lighten Buddy's funk with a dose of benign banter. "Story is the clay bricks in that old building were made by slaves who used to live out at Boone Hall Plantation."

Bud's mood lifted not a devil's teardrop. Bedon tried again. "Been thinking about changing the color of the trim," he said, pretending the appearance of the building was Bud's big concern. "Something that would go nicer with old brick. But that would mean going before the Board of Architectural Review, the notorious B.A.R., and mixing it up with the Charleston Zoning Board. Sol, next door, tore down an old garden shack behind his house the other year, and those old blue-hairs on the Architectural Board made him build it back exactly like it was, rusty nails and all."

Bedon transferred his gaze from the calm of the carriage house door to the turbulence of Bud's face. "What's the matter, son?" he said, though he knew full well what the matter was. But not everything, since no one had told him about his grandson's side trip to the police station earlier in the afternoon. Had he known about that, his own angst would have been vibrating at a higher pitch.

Bud set his glass down in the grass beside the Addie and laced his fingers together across his lap. "I don't know what the matter is, Pop. You tell me."

"If this is about those police officers coming over here again, 'cause if it is…"

"It's more than the police officers. Police officers are a dime a dozen. It's *that*." He pointed to the carriage house. Bedon took a long drink of his tea to buy time. "Come on, Buddy. I don't have a clue why that buffalo cow med helper called the cops. I haven't committed any crime."

"The police know you haven't. The buffalo cow – when did you start talking like that, anyway, Pop? – the 'cow' calls them on a regular basis with idiotic complaints. Detective Brock told me they don't pay any attention to her most of the time. But when she mentioned those missing girls…"

"Stop right there, Bud. I've officially had enough…"

"No, sir, I've officially had enough. You have to tell me what's been going on. I know you, Pop. There's got to be some good reason…"

Bedon ignored the demands of his interrogator and finished his own sentence with emphasis. "…officially had enough of people poking into my privacy." Then he winced and put a hand to his temple. The half-full tea glass in his other hand dropped to the ground at the same instant. Bedon made an effort to climb out of the awkward Addie and almost made it before beginning a slow fall forward. Buddy was able to wiggle and twist out of his own chair in time to break his grandfather's tumble to the flagstones.

"Pop...Pop...open your eyes," he said to his fallen hero.

Bedon could not respond. He let the hand at his temple drop away, and Buddy, helpless to help the one person in the world he wanted to, stroked his grandfather's craggy face and wept.

# 54.

# More Than a Mini-Stroke

Bedon lay motionless on the hospital bed, oxygen mask over his face, IV needle taped to his forearm. Bud gripped the side bedrail and stared at his pop's white forehead, the only facial skin visible beyond the mask. Bo gripped the other side rail and stared at Buddy's white forehead. "How bad is it?" he said to his distraught friend.

"Doctor said to notify the family."

"If that means Lawrence and Pauline, don't do it. They're lethal."

"I already called them. They're on their way up here from Florida."

"In that antique motor home? Towing that antique Camry?"

"Got a Ford Fusion now, gold kryptonite with metallic flame graphics. Uncle Lawrence told me about it on the phone."

Bo snickered, but stifled it when Bud gave him a stink eye. Buddy signaled with his thumb they should move to the foot of the bed. He picked up two Styrofoam cups of water from the bedside table and handed one to Bo, thinking it would be nice for the two of them to have something to sip on while they discussed things. Bo drank his water down without taking a breath, tossed the cup in the trash can, and asked the logical question. "Where in the world did Lawrence get enough money to buy a Ford Fusion?"

"Well," Bud said, "Aunt Pauline slipped and fell in one of those shopping malls in Florida, sprained her ankle pretty good. She and

Lawrence collected a fat insurance check. They bought the Camry same way ten years ago."

Bo snickered again. Bud gave him a stink eye again, which he pretended not to notice. Biting into the saltine cracker he'd snagged from Bedon's bedside table, he lisped through crumbs, "What did she have to sprain to get the motor home?"

"Long story. Their house in Sarasota caught on fire. They didn't own it or anything, just renting. But the renters' insurance for contents paid a so-so claim. That, combined with the check Aunt Pauline got for pain and suffering, plus the twenty thousand Pop threw in just to keep'em from moving in with him was more than enough to pay for the motor home outright. It was pre-owned, pre-rusted."

Bo stuck the rest of the saltine into his mouth and crunched away. "See there," he said. "And that radio finance dude, Donald What's-his-name, says Americans don't know how to plan for retirement."

# 55.

# Dr. Long and His Transcriptist

uddy stood at the nurse's hall-station counter with Dr. Long, Bedon's neurologist and friend, who'd been practicing medicine at the Medical University of South Carolina Teaching Hospital longer than anyone could remember. Bud watched the dignified doc as he scribbled on Bedon's medical chart. To write and speak, and on occasion chew Juicy Fruit at the same time, was a multi-task set of abilities that had to be mastered by all medical students of Dr. Long's era before any respectable institution would award them diplomas. Dr. Long had received high honors in every area of study with the exception of bedside manner. "If this thing hasn't killed your pop by now," he said while scratching illegibly on the chart with his Sharpie retractable, "it ain't gonna kill him, not right now, anyways. He can go home today if y'all want, but he'll need assistance when he gets there."

"I can do whatever's necessary," Bo said with the idealism of the young.

"What's necessary, Buddy, my boy, is twenty-four-hour-a-day care. And I don't mean the kind dispensed by those two C-rated actors who've been parading in and out of here since Bedon got admitted. What are their names? Lawrence and Patsy?"

"Pauline…Great Aunt Pauline." Buddy had figured out the hot little number of a nurse standing behind Dr. Long was flirting with him, distracting him big time with her augmented chest.

"Yesirree, bobtail t," Doc Long said, "you can give your Aunt Patsy full credit for Bedon perking up so fast. She and that husband of hers made him mad enough every day to get his blood doing water-beetle loops around his circulatory system."

Dr. Long signed his name at the bottom of the chart with exaggerated flair and snapped the metal cover closed. "Won't have these things around much longer," he said, patting the aluminum cover with nostalgia. "Everything's going to computers now. In fact, Crystal here..." He pointed to Miss-Flirty-Bird-In-White at his side. "...is a special transcriptist the hospital Board of Directors hired especially for moi. She follows me around and lets me write whatever I want to on my metal-bound patient charts, and later, when I'm already at home sipping my evening toddy, she transcribes everything I wrote and puts it all on the hospital computer. Medicare is a true blessing to pay for a service like that."

Speechless in the face of such blatant rule-bending by the hospital powers-that-be concerning Medicare (fraught with legal ramifications), Buddy, the "iffy" law student decided to make out like he didn't understand what kind of beans Dr. Long was spilling. He watched with interest as the old timer handed the chart to the transcriptist.

Dr. Long grew anxious when he realized he'd caught the little vixen up to something more than taking care of the sick. But no matter, she disarmed the doctor's anxiety as easily with her two-peaked mountain range as she always disarmed any man's anxiety who wandered too close to her spider web. At the same time, she kept on smiling and posing for Buddy like the Las Vegas showgirl she used to be before her mother made her start taking nursing classes at MUSC in the slim hope she'd meet-a-doctor-and-get-married-and-have-a-couple-of-crumb-crunchers-of-her-own and stop embarrassing the family by strutting around nearly naked on a dusty stage in Vegas.

Dr. Long thought, mistakenly, he might have a little more advice that would be of interest to Buddy. "I know those two sorry relatives of yours, Lawrence and Patsy, have been jacked up in y'all's house

the whole time Bedon's been here at the hospital. He knows it, too."
Doc Long, trained to be observant, slowly understood Bud had been
hypnotized by the siren of a transcriptist. He came to the conclusion
there was no alternative but to lance the spell with a precision cut,
drain off the deadly aphrodisiac elixir that had crippled many a man,
and cauterize the incision. He knew it would be the most humane
way to handle the development, since he himself had experienced the
same debilitating reaction to the girl on first meeting her. Turning to
the transcriptist, he said with dignified professionalism, "Miss Baker,
honey, don't you have a bed pan to empty in 401?"

Spell mitigated but not broken, Buddy now enjoyed the view of
Miss Baker from the back as she swished her way down the hall past
398, 399 and 400 on her bouncy journey toward 401. She took one
more peek back at him before going into the patient's room, waving
from afar with her acrylic-nail-tipped fingers that were polished
in OPI's Las Vegas Collection shade entitled "Royal Flush-Blush
Shimmer."

"Earth to Buddy Calhoun. Earth to Buddy Calhoun," Dr. Long
called, and Bud, after the siren had disappeared, turned and looked
glassy-eyed at the venerable brain surgeon. "Son," the doc said, "don't
let that little gal get up in your head. She's dating the CEO here at
MUSC, Dr. Malachi Maloney, Mac for short, and his wife's mad as
fire about it. But back to who's gonna take care of your pop when
he gets home. You have to promise me it's not going to be those two
relatives. There's still the Christian hope in America for what's known
as quality of life for old people."

# 56.
## Breakfast at the Barbadoes Room

Buddy kicked open the screened door on his way out of the kitchen and pushed Bedon in his wheelchair onto the stoop, where he paused and got organized before rolling the chair down a wooden ramp so new it still smelled like treated lumber from Lowe's Millworks Department.

Said Aunt Pauline as she minced along behind her great nephew with the daintiest of steps, "You shouldn't be doing this, Buddy. Two weeks home from the hospital isn't time enough for a stroke victim to be going out." She turned her upper body back toward the kitchen door when it slammed shut with the force of an evil spirit in search of someone to indwell. "Lawrence. Lawrence," she called toward the door, "come out here right now and help me with Buddy. He's acting the fool again."

Buddy continued acting the fool with greater relish. "We're going, Aunt P, and that's the end of it. Go back to the kitchen and make a cherry pie or something."

He pushed the wheelchair in a trot toward the driveway where his Super Bee sat gleaming in Heavenly sunshine. Pauline re-trained her attention from her absent husband back to her great nephew and brother-in-law and recommenced trying to catch up with the two fugitives as they hurried across the yard toward freedom, which caused her to miss seeing Lawrence as he stumbled out the back door to follow her, and hearing him as he cackled in glee at her inability to control Buddy. Nevertheless, the great aunt, like Winston Churchill of old, would "...never give in except to convictions of honour and good sense." The thing was that Winston Churchill had never had to contend with Bedon Calhoun, Jr. (Buddy), who'd learned his own "convictions of honour and good sense" at the feet of the master, Bedon Calhoun, Sr. (Pop).

Undeterred, Auntie P kept trying to get Buddy to see reason. "I know if our poor dear Bedon could talk, he'd stop you from doing this harebrained thing. Why would he want to go to a restaurant for breakfast when I can make him a perfectly good asparagus omelette right here at home?"

Buddy defended his mute pop's taste in breakfast fare. "If he could talk, he'd tell you he hates asparagus omelettes worse than caviar. Who knows? Maybe he can talk. Maybe he quit on purpose to keep from having to talk about stupid stuff like asparagus omelettes."

Buddy opened the passenger door of the Super Bee and jostled his pop from the wheelchair onto the front seat. As he buckled him in, Aunt Pauline stood by wringing her hands and punching her husband in his ribs with her elbow. "Do something, Lawrence. Stop them."

Lawrence did something all right. He brushed his wife's hand away and grinned like he was the happy attendee at a dancing monkey show, about the same caliber of entertainment as the real show he was now watching. Bedon grinned back at Lawrence through the Super Bee window glass and stuck his right thumb up. Lawrence grinned harder at his older brother's joy. Buddy, unaware of the pleasure he was bringing to the lives of his grandfather and his great uncle by "acting the fool again," ran around the hood of his pet Dodge, jumped into the driver's seat, and prepared for take-off. "There, ready to roll," he said to Bedon upon starting the vintage engine. "What did you say, gray man?" He stretched over to his grandfather and made-believe the old man was whispering something.

"Yeah," Bud said, "I will tell'em." Then to Pauline and Lawrence still outside the car, he yelled with a thrill-of-victory smile, "Pop wants y'all to know if you need us, we'll be over at the Mills House Hotel in the Barbadoes Room woofing down sweet potato pancakes and knocking back mimosas."

Pauline looked stricken. She covered her mouth with her hankie and semi-collapsed against her hubby's chest. Buddy raced his star-car's motor with the bravado of a NASCAR driver, after which he put his sweet ride in reverse and allowed her to drift backward. During the drift, he couldn't resist hollering out one last taunt at his great aunt and uncle. "Pop also said to tell y'all to kiss his big old wrinkled behind."

Beaming delight as he backed his fabulous car out of the driveway and into the river of tourist traffic flowing ever faithful along Murray Boulevard toward East Bay Street, Buddy waved to his Florida relatives in the professional style of a newly crowned Miss Teenage America.

Uncle Lawrence cheesed hard and waved back in imitation, an act that got his wife's goat and promptly turned it loose. Her humiliation was awful enough in scope to drive any Southern lady to crocodile tears so abundant they reminded Lawrence of the fructification of some horrible pathogenic fungus. Cryptoccus, perhaps, or Candida. It had been so long since Lawrence had spent the best years of his life teaching biology at Florida State University in Tallahassee, he'd forgotten the names of all the other grim possibilities. Way too fructified long.

# 57.
# Good Help Is Hard to Find

Buddy and Bedon sat at the Barbadoes Room's premier table next to the restroom, eating pancakes soaked in Old Plantation Syrup milled by the Russ family in Cowards, South Carolina. Thank you, God, for sugar cane. Thank you for the entire Russ family.

As the Calhoun men ate in the non-tranquility of the roaring noise inside Charleston's most elegant restaurant, Larissa, dressed in waitress attire and balancing a tray loaded with the breakfast orders of a four-person table, rushed past Bedon and Buddy on her way to the other side of the dining room. Bedon, the only wheelchair-bound patron in the place, had been about to take a sip of his coffee when he saw her zip by. He became so agitated his hands began to shake. Coffee escaped the rim of its china cup and dripped Jackson-Pollock-style upon the white tablecloth. Buddy rubbed at the brown splash sites with his napkin, ruining their abstract genius. As he tried to keep up with the ever widening puddles, he said to the coffee artist, "What the devil is the matter with you, Pop?"

Larissa, still not realizing Bedon's presence, hustled back toward his and Buddy's table. As she did so, her old healer/benefactor reached out and grabbed her skirttail. Buddy saw his grandfather do this cuckoo thing and stood up to try to deal with a circumstance of which he had no understanding. As far as he could see in terms of choices, there were no roads but bad roads to go down. Other patrons stretched their necks to enjoy the free diversion, although they'd have paid extra for it given the option.

Larissa thought Buddy, not Bedon, neither of whom she recognized out of context, was the troublemaker who'd almost caused her to fall down by grabbing her skirt. "Hey..." she snapped at Bud, "this isn't a bar. Keep your grubby paws to yourself."

The innocent Buddy had no time to defend himself. He was too busy trying with all his might to force the guilty Bedon to let go of this unknown waitress' skirt, an endeavor not entirely new to him since he'd had so much experience navigating the downtown bar scene alongside bar-star, Bo Gaillard, who, after the click that always occurred in his left frontal lobe after the witching hour, had a tendency to fall in love with any skirttail that happened by.

"Let go, Pop. I mean it. Let go." (How many times had he said that very same thing to Bo? A hundred? A thousand?)

After a struggle and a threat, Larissa succeeded in accomplishing what Buddy could not. She gave her own skirt a yank, then spun around and held up a karate-chop-hand in Bud's face, her other hand being encumbered by the large round tray. Teeth clamped, she said, "What are you, a rabid tourist? You want me to call the manager on you?"

"No," Buddy said, "please, don't call anybody. Just get our check."

But something about the old man in the wheelchair prevented her from hearing Bud's request. Her attention, now fully arrested by the older gentleman, had no more room for the younger bozo. She set her tray down on the table and knelt in front of him. "Bedon? Is it you? What...?"

Buddy flipped up both brake levers on his grandfather's wheelchair and tried to back it away. "Do you mind?" he said to the angry grouse-of-a-waitress whose feathers didn't seem quite so ruffled anymore. Again, he said, "Do you mind?" Adding when she continued to ignore him, "Listen, miss, I have to get him out of here. I'll come back later to pay."

Larissa, still kneeling before Bedon, stayed on her knees and held onto the wheelchair arms to keep Buddy from jerking it to and fro. She wrinkled her brow in concern as she spoke softly to her old friend. "It's me, Bedon...Larissa. What's happened to you? Was it one of those strokes you were telling me about?"

Buddy kept trying to dislodge the chair from the grouse's grip. "Will you please let go?" he said. "You can see he's having trouble."

Larissa stood up and used her eyes to shoot V-Max varmint bullets at the sweet spot in the middle of Buddy's forehead. "Now I know who you are," she said. "I remember, you're the snotty grandson. What's wrong with him? Has he had a worse stroke?"

"Yes..." Buddy paused while multi-squadrons of neurons in his brain skipped about in search of the specific group of synapses where the memory of her pretty face had taken up residence one extraordinary evening at his pop's house. "You're the girl," he said, "dancing with him in the parlor. *You're her!*"

"Who's taking care of him?"

"I am."

"Oh, yeah? Well, you're not doing a very good job of it. Look at his hair. Why didn't you brush it before you brought him out?"

Bedon interrupted the conversation by pulling at Larissa's skirt pocket. He managed to snag her ballpoint pen and begin scrawling something on the tablecloth.

Moonbow in the Mist, will you come
take care of me? I'll pay you.

He beat on the table with his fist to make her see he had written something. She read his request, then smiled and pointed it out to Buddy. While the law student was trying to decipher this newly introduced piece of evidence, Larissa snatched off her apron, slammed her order book onto the table, and began pushing Bedon in his wheelchair toward the exit. Buddy followed her like a little red caboose.

"Open the door," she said. Bud obeyed, then watched with worried eyes as she maneuvered the wheelchair over the raised metal threshold that led outside to the uneven sidewalk. While working with the chair, Larissa barked a command back at the hostess, a bottle-blond mumbling to herself something about it being her first day there, and her nerves were shot all to pieces, and she felt like she was going to barf up her breakfast of three doughnuts and a five-hour energy drink. Larissa, after running over the poor woman's naked toes with the left wheel of Bedon's chair, said to the hostess-minus-the-mostess, "Stop that complaining right now, Trixie, and go tell Dwayne I quit. And make sure he gives my tips to the busboys."

She directed a quick glance at the red caboose behind her to let him know he, too, was about to receive a communique from the top brass (herself), and not the kind that would have anything to do with whether he wanted more coffee. "You," she said to the caboose (Buddy), "get my purse from behind the counter, the big silver one with red sequins."

# 58.

# Stud Puppy

Larissa pushed Bedon in his wheelchair back up the ramp to his own kitchen door. Buddy chug-a-chugged along behind them, faithfully, obediently. He carried Larissa's gigantic purse in one hand and Bedon's felt fedora in the other. Pauline held the door open before she realized she was letting an enemy into the camp. Lawrence positioned himself in the best spot he could find in the kitchen to watch the morning's second show, upon which his sixth sense told him the curtain was about to rise.

Pauline looked Larissa up and down before delivering the scene's opening lines. "Is that a waitress uniform? It looks like a waitress uniform."

"No," said Larissa. "It's a new kind of nurse's uniform. We wear orange mini-skirts now with white spandex tops and little white aprons that have big sashes tied up in bows in the back. That's 'cause big bows set off our beautiful hineys so nice, 'specially when we lean way over the bed to take care of our patients."

She wheeled her newest patient through the kitchen doorway past the opening to the pantry, former dwelling place of the twin carriage house keys and wildlife calendar. Once in the kitchen, she situated the rolling chair in the middle of the room, so its occupant could have an unobstructed view of everyone present. Bedon, the patient, shone sunshine and gladness over the expanse of spectators…Pauline, Buddy, Larissa, and Lawrence (happiest spectator of all).

Pauline arched her eyebrows higher than a surgical brow lift and fired a question at Buddy. "And who is this?" She tossed a queenly hand-flick in the general direction of the orange-mini-skirted, white-bow-sashed visitor, who clearly hailed from somewhere far across the tracks. Buddy dropped the visitor's red sequined bag on the table, glad to be rid of the scratchy thing, and spoke his own lines badly.

"Her name is La-something-or-another. That's all I know, except Pop acts like he's going to have a cardiac arrest every time I try to tell him she can't work here."

Larissa piped up on that note to inject more oomph into the scene. "I'm Bedon's new caretaker," she said to Pauline. "That's who I am. And y'all two are fired."

It came to Pauline in a blinding flash of insight that the self-proclaimed new "caretaker" was talking about her and Lawrence. "Buddy...do something," she said. "This is an outrage. I'm so outraged I feel dizzy-headed."

Bedon frowned and started breathing hard. Everyone looked at him, frightened he was on his way to a bout of dizzy-headedness of his own. "Pop?" Bud said to the old man.

Bedon didn't give Bud an answer, but the orange mini-skirt did, sort of, but not really. What she really did was to lump Buddy in with Pauline and Lawrence and start issuing instructions to the three of them as a single subservient assemblage. "All y'all clear out of here so I can cook Bedon some breakfast. He hardly touched his pancakes at the restaurant."

"But we're family, the closest relatives," Pauline said. "We live here."

Larissa scooted around from behind the wheelchair and stooped in front of her new boss. "When did they move in, Bedon? Are they like...fixtures now?"

Bedon whispered something into her ear. When he finished, she nodded and smiled, then stood up to face Pauline. "He says you can stick around as long as you like, but that I'll be taking care of his personal needs from now on."

Pauline bristled. "You're too young to be taking care of his personal needs."

I'm twenty-one and six courses short of getting my practical nurse's certification from Trident Technical College on Rivers Avenue, the flagship campus of the Lowcountry's most powerful educational machine. That's what my high school guidance counselor called it, anyway."

"Never heard of it," Pauline said. "And you certainly don't look twenty-one."

"I know. A lot of people think I'm thirty-one."

"I meant you look younger than twenty-one."

"Bedon knows my qualifications. We go back a long time. Been friends for years and years."

"You should be calling him Dr. Calhoun."

Bedon pulled Larissa down to whisper something else. She smiled at him again before popping back up to deliver worse news to Pauline. "He said to tell you I'm not to call him Dr. Calhoun. I'm to call him Stud Puppy, and he doesn't care a monkey's butt if you don't like it."

# 50.

# Pop's Got a Nifty New Nurse

Buddy held an iced sweet tea in his hand as he rocked in the piazza swing. Nearby, Larissa sat in a wicker rocker facing Bedon in his wheelchair. Bud, audience for the happy twosome, scrutinized the new caretaker as she fed his grandfather from a tray on a side table. Bites of grilled cheese sandwich, fruit, tea through a straw.

"He can feed himself," he said to Larissa. "I don't know why you're doing that."

She turned to Buddy for a moment and shrugged a shoulder, then, refocusing her attention on her patient, asked, "Why am I doing this, Bedon?"

He pulled her close to answer in a whisper. She glanced back at Buddy. "He says I'm doing this for the fun of it." She held out a spoonful of apple sauce to Bedon and giggled as he slurped it down. Then, piercing Buddy with another sharp glance, she asked him a sharper question. "Is it possible you'd know something as simple as how long he naps after lunch?"

Buddy shrugged a shoulder of his own. Could it be he was mocking her? "An hour," he said. "Two. I don't know."

"You told me you were the one taking care of him."

"Aunt Pauline and Uncle Lawrence are here while I'm in class all day. I know he goes to sleep after lunch, but I don't know for how long."

Larissa gave him a scathing look. "What are you taking classes to be, an actor?"

"Worse than that. A lawyer."

Buddy waited a second for her to stick him with another prickly remark, but she let him off the hook. He decided this might be the moment to mention a problem that had to be addressed. "Guess you'll have to sleep in the bedroom next to his. That way you can hear him if he needs you in the night."

"I'll move in tomorrow. My mom won't care. She and her new boyfriend will be glad to have the apartment to themselves."

"The room is small."

"I don't have much stuff, and there's always the carriage house."

"What do you know about that?"

"Bedon fixed it up for me when one of my mother's old boyfriends was using me for a punching bag at home."

Buddy's mouth dropped open. At last...an explanation for the carriage house. He came close to shouting at his grandfather. "Is that true, Pop? Is she for real?"

Bedon nodded, took the tea glass from Larissa, handled it by himself with no problem, wiped his own mouth with a napkin... again, no problem.

Buddy stared hard at Larissa. "How old were you then?"

"Sixteenish."

"No way."

"I didn't stay there all the time. Haven't spent the night there in forever. Bedon's been leaving money for me in an envelope every now and then, so I could pick it up without bothering him. He started doing that after we had a...thing to happen, and I had to quit coming around so much. Hasn't left me any in a while. I thought he'd gotten tired of me being a mooch. Didn't know he was sick."

"What kind of a thing?"

Before she could answer, Bedon grabbed her arm and forced her to look into his eyes. She understood what he wanted to communicate. "Oh...nothing," she said with a quaver in her voice.

"Just a scare. I brought some other kids over in the middle of the night one time, and they got too loud."

Buddy clenched his jaw. "How much money has he given you?"

Bedon continued to force Larissa to lock eyes with him. "Enough for school," she said, more quavery. "Waitressing helps. But I haven't been old enough to do that for very long."

Buddy switched his attention to Bedon. "Why didn't you tell me any of this, Pop?"

Since no answers were forthcoming from the new questionee, Buddy shifted back to the initial questionee and imparted to her a disquieting piece of information. "The carriage house has caused Pop and me a pile of trouble. Police have been here half accusing him of having something to do with those two missing girls in the news."

Larissa jerked around and gave Buddy a shocked look minus any smarty-pants attitude. "But why?" she said. "Who called'em?"

"A med helper we hired. She unlocked the building and jumped to a bunch of gross conclusions. I think it's what brought on Pop's last bad stroke."

Larissa looked back at Bedon and took his hands into hers. "I'm so sorry," she said. "So...sorry."

The patient pulled his new caretaker close again, causing Buddy to lose his temper. He used a loafered foot to stop the swing from rocking. "What's he telling you now? And I don't want to hear some made-up junk you think is cute. What he's been through because of that carriage house is a far sight from cute."

Larissa started to cry in the same odd way she always cried, producing tears, but showing little emotion on her face. "He said it wasn't my fault and for me not to worry about the police or what people around here think." She paused, tears dripping off her chin. Wiping them away with an unconscious motion, she added a conviction of her own, "He took care of me when I needed help. I'd be dead or locked up by now if he hadn't. And now I'm going to take care of him."

# 60.
# Larissa, Exemplary Employee

Upon being summoned by Great Aunt Pauline to the parlor-of-the-midnight-waltz, Buddy found himself teetering on a ladder as he changed the miniature flame-shaped bulbs in the chandelier. Great Uncle Lawrence tried hard to hold the ladder steady, succeeding every other second. Aunt Pauline stood to one side using the rare moment Buddy couldn't get away from her to grind her axe of disgruntlement to a razor's edge. "She's a snippy little pill and you know it," she said about Larissa. "Treats Lawrence and me like we're outsiders instead of the closest relatives."

Bud lost his balance and came close to falling off the ladder. "Wohhhh... Hold her steady, Lawrence. I've got claustrophobia up here."

"No, you don't," Pauline said. "That's a fear of close places. What you've got is msyophobia."

"No," Lawrence said. "That's a fear of germs. What he's got is acrophobia, fear of heights." Every now and then a nugget like that poked its head up from Lawrence's long-term memory. He was, as mentioned before, a former science prof at Florida State, but for Heaven's sake, don't ask him what he had for breakfast.

Bud tried to get a grip on himself. "I don't care what you call it – claustrophobia? compost-phobia? – whatever it is, I got a bad case. And I don't want to hear any more about Pop's new helper. He likes her, and I can't do a thing about it."

Pauline looped back to her axe. "We came here to cook and clean and take care of poor Bedon, and now she won't let us near him. Always pushing him up and down the sidewalk in his wheelchair, reading to him out of that thick blue history book, playing checkers, mixing him those alcoholic drinks at night. I tell you she's making him miserable."

"I should be so miserable," said Buddy. "Cook all you want, Aunt P." And he sincerely meant that, since Pauline's smothered chicken and shrimp boudin were equally as delicious as the Southern fried everything the church ladies dropped off every few days. "But don't wear yourself out cleaning. Molly Maid sends people in twice a week."

"I'll cook all right, to keep those long-in-the-tooth Bethel Baptist biddies from running back and forth over here annoying our poor Bedon with their imitation Tupperware containers full of slop. Those sub-standard plastic tubs they buy from the gadget aisle at the Piggly Wiggly are a dis-grace to the modern art of homemaking, nothing but an excuse to keep coming over here to 'drop off and pick up' as they call it."

"Don't be getting after those ladies to their faces, Pauline. Ever since Grandma Hildie died, Pop and me have had a steady diet of tuna casseroles, chicken cooked every way you can think of, homemade coconut cake, and I don't remember what all else. We do not want you puncturing the pipeline."

Pauline snorted like Ferdinand the bull. "I can't get rid of 'em to save my life. Why yesterday I caught one making eyes at Lawrence."

Buddy climbed down the ladder and folded it for storage. Pauline drew her sharpening rod across the blade of her glinting axe one last time. "I suppose I could handle their interference, if I didn't have to put up with *her*."

Buddy took the burned-out bulbs from his pocket and handed them to Lawrence. As he hefted the folded ladder and walked toward the parlor archway, his male helper and female hindrance followed him like two lost ducklings. Bud spoke once more to his hindrance.

"What do you want me to do, Aunt P? Every time she leaves to go to one of her nursing classes, Pop cuts up so bad, I get scared he'll have another spell."

Uncle Lawrence, feeling a measure of safety with Buddy present, volunteered a sentiment he should not have. "And she is a pretty little thing."

Pauline glared at her husband with white heat. Poor Lawrence would have disintegrated on the spot if Buddy hadn't shoved him out of the way of the radioactive gamma waves discharging from his wife's eyes. Bud said to his great aunt in the soothing tone he'd learned hunting wild bore, "Get a grip, Aunt P. I'll talk to her today while Pop's taking his nap. And then I have to go to class myself. I'm so far behind, it's gonna take me eight years to get through law school instead of seven."

Pauline dialed her hate stare at Lawrence down to normal ranges and made a point of checking her watch. "It's already twelve thirty," she said. "Bedon's nap started at twelve. And, Buddy, darling...I don't want you to just talk to her. I want you to give her a talking to."

Larissa, dressed in shorts and a halter top, jogged in her athletic shoes from the side lawn of the main house around to the front, where she bent over to re-tie her laces. Buddy hurried out the front door and stopped on the top piazza step to watch this procedure – no use in squandering an opportunity like that – before hurrying down to speak to her. Unbeknownst to him, Pauline and Lawrence had slipped through the front door onto the piazza and were watching him as he watched Larissa. From the suspicious look on the female closest relative's face, anyone would have known she didn't trust Buddy to do what she had told him to do, which was dress the little culprit down to the very ground.

Buddy smiled at Larissa's jogging shorts, though he was trying as hard as he could to smile at her face. "Hi," he said to the shorts. "Can we chat before you go?"

"Shorts don't chat," the wearer of them said. "I'm up here if you've got anything to say to a person's face."

Buddy blushed scarlet and zoomed in with adoration on Larissa's charming, ski-slope nose. "Oh, hi," he said, noticing for the first time she even had a nose."

She nodded. "Hi yourself, and hi to y'all, too." The y'all she was referring to included Pauline and Lawrence, who were standing on either side of the front door on sentry duty. Aunt Pauline crinkled her snout as if she'd caught the smell of pluff mud. Uncle Lawrence crinkled his snout, too, and smiled goofily as if he'd caught the smell of lilacs.

Larissa dismissed all three Calhouns with a toss of her head and sauntered toward the lyre gate to leave for her jog. Buddy trotted after her like an adolescent Labradoodle. "Hold up there," he said. "We have to talk."

"Sorry, prep boy. Can't right now. The only chance I get to run is when Bedon is napping. You'll have to come up to my room tonight after he goes to sleep. We can talk a minute before I start my homework."

And with no further ado, she opened the gate and jogged down the sidewalk with the golden sun warming her golden shoulders.

# 61.

# Gossip, Southern Style

Buddy and Bo sat across from each other in the back booth of Pearl's Oyster Bar on East Bay Street, shucking Blue Points and drinking Rattlesnake Beer. "Everybody's talking about her," Bo said to his despondent friend. "She's a heck of a lot more interesting than that shooting thing your Pop was involved in."

"And what, pray tell, are they saying?"

"That she's your granddaddy's hot-thang from the project."

"Where did you hear a vicious rumor like that? Anybody who knows Pop knows it ain't true.'"

"My wife, my sisters, Nana, Miss Posey, all those other pure-hearted ladies from the church, all my teacher buddies at school, the guy who mows the lawn next door..."

Buddy pushed the giant bucket of oysters toward Bo. "You eat the rest," he said to the source of town news. "I'm sick on my stomach."

Bo grinned big and slid the galvanized bucket all the way to his own side of the table. Buddy, already depressed, descended to the depths of the ocean where nothing can survive but worms. He sank even deeper when he saw Mr. and Mrs. Johnson, an elderly couple from the church, staggering toward his and Bo's booth. Buddy and Bo made a clumsy effort to stand up in deference to Mrs. Johnson.

"Sit...sit," she said. "Bill and I saw y'all over here and had to come by to ask about Bedon before we left."

Buddy nodded like a bobble head. "Better every day, thank you, Mrs. Johnson."

This was not the report Mrs. Johnson was looking to hear. Terrible news would have been so much more gratifying. She fished deeper for a tastier tidbit. "All this has been so hard on him," she said. "First losing Hildie, then closing his practice down, and now... that dreadful shooting right in his own house, and a stroke. We heard from your closest relative, Pauline, that y'all got him a live-in companion..."

Mr. Johnson cut his wife off. "You boys tell Bedon to holler at us if there's anything we can do to help out. Been missing him at the men's prayer breakfast on Tuesdays."

Bo's limit on behaving himself skidded to a halt on the heels of Mr. Johnson's mention of the prayer breakfast. "He can't come to that anymore on account of he's having too big a time playing poker on Tuesday mornings now...with his live-in companion."

Bud, hoping to keep this side trip into water-moccasin-infested swamp territory from getting completely away from him, exhaled a puff of beer breath right into Mrs. Johnson's face. He couldn't help it. She was hard of hearing and had to get way up into his personal space to keep from missing out on any morsel of incorrect news. When she smelled the beer, she coughed like a smoker, which, indeed, she was, her and her whole ladies' Canasta club. Buddy attempted to reassure her. "What Bo meant was Pop and his caretaker play checkers, not poker. Why don't y'all stop by sometime? He'd love a visit."

Mrs. Johnson opened her mouth to say they'd "love a visit," too, but Mr. Johnson jumped in on her again. "We'll call before we come," he said, smiling like a deacon, "to make sure the old guy's not knee-deep in poker...I mean checkers."

The two oyster connoisseurs, for Buddy loved oysters as much as Bo when his stomach wasn't churning out battery acid, made a second effort at standing out of respect for Mrs. Johnson. After the bumbling old couple doddered away, Buddy took a long slug of his Rattlesnake beer, strangled on carbonation bubbles, and spent the next sixty seconds coughing and choking. Bo concentrated on cracking oyster shells without noticing his pal was on the precipice of death by suffocation. Said Buddy when his coughing eased off, "I'm going to have to move away from Charleston. No other option left open."

"Naw," said Bo, "people around here'll find something else to talk about soon enough. But a shooting, that involves a death? A thing like that does tend to stick in the mind. Not as much as your pop's live-in companion, though. What's her name again?"

"Larissa. I finally learned it. I've called her La-everything but the right thing since laying eyes on her."

"Yeah, La-her. And we won't even go into the prurient interest folks have in your pop's carriage house shenanigans."

Buddy winced. "I've been trying to protect his reputation for weeks, while all he does is laugh it up with...well, you-know-who."

"Listen, man, whatever else you do, don't stop her from jogging around the neighborhood in those short shorts. Talk about street credit."

"I can't stop her from doing anything. Aunt Pauline hates her living guts. When Grandma Hildie died, Pauline decided to dump Lawrence and go after Pop. Dollar marks got to dancing around in her head like sugar plums. Pop put a stop to it when he figured out what she was up to, but she's still lurking around in the background laying her black widow spider eggs all over the place. And she thinks this time she's being foiled by a tart. That's what she calls Larissa on the sly. It ain't easy being in the middle of a cat fight day in and day out."

Bo burbled a laugh into his beer mug, coming close to choking worse than Bud. "Man," he said, "you are what I call a tragic figure. A regular Tennessee Williams character."

"It ain't funny."

"Oh, yes, it is. Let's rewind to the short shorts. You do know that every old codger South of Broad Street makes it his business to be out sweeping his front walk between twelve-thirty and two these days."

"Leave me alone. I'm moving to Georgia, or somewhere worse. Hell Hole Swamp. Foggy Bottom."

Bo gestured at Buddy with his oyster shiv. "Your problem is you like her, a lot. Let's see...you like her, but she likes your grandpaw, who's madly in love with her from what I've seen. So is Uncle Lawrence. And Pauline is madly in love with Bedon. Seems like you and Pauline and Lawrence are the losers in your household. No one's got a crush on any of y'all." He paused for the length of time it took to slurp down a raw oyster, not long considering how slippery it was. "You know, Bud, I'm beginning to think you're right. You are gonna have  to move away."

# 62.
# Pills or Pauline; Buddy Chooses Pills

Bud entered the kitchen through the back door. He went straight to the cabinet where he knew Larissa had stored Pop's prescription meds and initiated an intel-gathering mission among the brown plastic containers. Pauline came in to see what he was doing, startling him into a headache worse than the one he already had. He knocked several child-proof-capped bottles of supporting evidence from the shelf to the floor, where they rolled about noisily. Bud felt justified in raising his voice. "You've gotta stop sneaking up on me like that, Aunt Pauline. I'm gonna have a stroke myself."

Pauline arranged her face in a hurt expression and said with the emotion of a soap opera maven, "Would it make you happy if Lawrence and I took the motor home out of storage and went on back to Florida, where we eke out a living every month on nothing but social security and Lawrence's pittance of a state retirement check?"

Buddy chased down the escaping medicine bottles and didn't wait to stand all the way up before starting to read their labels again. To his great aunt, he said, "Whatever you think is best, Aunt P. Have you seen any pain pills around here?"

If Pauline had seen any, she didn't tell Buddy. "I'm heartsick," she said with so much emotion that sitting down at the table was required before she could go on. "I can't believe you'd let poor dear Lawrence and me walk out the door and leave poor dear Bedon in the clutches of a...a...*a tart.*"

Buddy gave up on finding any labeled prescription-strength med for his headache and shook out two pills from a devil-red bottle that had no label at all. He didn't care what drug it was. He'd have taken anything to dull the sandpaper with which Pauline was scraping him. He tossed the pills into his mouth, filled a cupped hand from the cold water tap, and sucked up a mouthful of H2O to help him swallow he-knew-not-what. "You have to let up on her, Aunt Pauline. You're going to end up making yourself sick, like I am right now." He made a to-do of putting the conglomeration of bottles back on the cabinet shelf and closing them behind the set of warped doors. "She's a nice girl, really, a trained practical nurse almost."

Pauline effected a shuddering sigh as unconvincing as the one she'd seen effected that very afternoon by a Golden Globe winning screen actress whose career had taken a swan dive into the tasteless world of made-for-TV movies. Downcast, the great aunt forced herself out of the chair and took a stack of Hildie's Italian Countryside Mikasa dinner plates from the cabinet next to the one housing Bedon's meds. Buddy found a can of mixed nuts on the counter by the sink. He opened it and began picking out the cashews and eating them one by one.

Pauline, though disapproving, let him go ahead and ruin his appetite, since she hadn't finished addressing more important issues, and more important people, of which and of whom she disapproved worse. Honestly? She didn't care if her great nephew did ruin his dinner. She didn't care if he ruined it every night. Like Betty Davis in those old black and white pictures on Turner Classic Movies, Pauline sneered an award winning sneer. "Money is the reason that tramp came here to stay."

For a confusing second before he came to his senses, Buddy thought Pauline was talking about herself. (What was in those pills, anyway?) "Oh...no, no," he said when he figured out what his great aunt really meant. "Larissa doesn't take any pay. Nobody's probably told you this, Auntie P., but Pop helped her out of a jam a while back, and helping him now is how she's returning the favor."

"That's not what the neighbors are saying," Pauline sneer-r-r-ed Betty Davis style again.

Buddy looked longingly at the pharmaceutical cabinet. Would it be noticed if he went into it again? "Neighbors?" he said to Pauline, restraining himself from opening the cabinet doors and scrambling through the brown bottles like an addict. "What exactly are the neighbors saying?"

"That she's a cunning little schemer trying to take advantage of the elderly."

"Who said that? Was it Sol's wife, Rachel, from over there?" He pointed with his thumb in the direction of Sol's run-down mansion.

Pauline didn't know and didn't care who Sol and Rachel were. Ignoring Bud's mention of them, she hit the fast/forward button on her own theatrics. "Never you mind who said it. You and Lawrence are both wrong about that little hussy."

"So-o-o-o...Uncle Lawrence thinks she's fine and dandy?"

"Uncle Lawrence is soft in the head, worse off than Bedon. He wishes *he* had a live-in companion."

Buddy, feeling the effects of the pills, turned away from the cabinet and giggled at his "close relative" in an unmanly fashion. "I'm sorry, Aunt Pauline. Did anybody ever tell you that you have lovely green eyes? All I know at the moment is I'm hungry. You didn't happen to make Cajun shrimp boudin balls for supper, did you? I'd give a million dollars to smell some of them frying on the stove about now. And did anybody ever tell you that you have lovely green...eyes?"

Pauline used her lovely green eyes, that were in truth an atypical yellowy hazel, to give her great nephew a scornful look. "I see what

I'm good for," she said. "*Cooking.* And what about that little almost practical nurse? What's she good for?"

For the life of him, Buddy couldn't think of one thing Larissa was good for. The pills had made mush out of his brain. "Well," he said after considering Pauline's deep question deeply, "all I know is Pop likes her. She keeps him on an even keel somehow. And please don't tell anyone this, but..." He looked all around the kitchen to make sure he and his "close relative" were still alone, then he took her by the shoulders and confessed in a whisper, "I'm a little bit afraid of her." He would never have said such a thing, but for the pills.

Before Pauline could berate him for acting like his father's side of the family, male and female laughter erupted somewhere in the front part of the house, the parlor from the sound of it. Aunt Pauline pulled away from Bud and slammed the stack of plates she was holding onto the kitchen table. She tucked her first chin into her second chin and curled her upper lip into unladylike contempt. "What I'd like to know," she said more to herself than to the befuddled Buddy, "is what's so blasted funny about checkers?"

# 63.
## Buddy Reminds Larissa of Bedon

**B**ud leaned on the railing of the battery wall in a stance reminiscent of his grandfather. Larissa crossed Murray Boulevard from the house and joined him. "It's after eight," she said. "Why didn't you come upstairs to tell me whatever it was you wanted to this afternoon when I was going on my run. I've been dying of curiosity up there, not a good thing when you're trying to do your human anatomy homework."

"Didn't want to get in the way."

Larissa scanned the night sky with her luminous eyes. "Ever seen a moonbow?" she said to Bud, who, standing beside her in the reflection of moonlight off the water, reminded her of Bedon in a heartbreaking way.

"What's a moonbow?" he said and turned to stare at his companion's face, the pills still playing happy havoc with his inhibitions.

Larissa noticed something was off with his behavior, but decided not to get into it. She said in a quiet voice that sounded almost like an adult's, almost, but not quite, "Bedon showed me a moonbow out here one time when I first started coming around. He told me how light refraction formed it, like a rainbow, only at night." She paused in her speech, but not in her loveliness. In Buddy's eyes and heart, her beauty increased in intensity by the second. His gaze upon her face grew so concentrated she couldn't bear it, had to lower her eyes to the spot where her hands gripped the railing. "I wish I were older," she said and was telling the truth for a change. "But that's how it's always been for me, wishing I were older."

"Why is that?" the Bedon look-alike asked.

"So I could get away from home, foster homes, get my own apartment."

"Is there anything I can do to help?"

"Don't waste your time on me. Feel sorry for Bedon. You're the only person standing between him and Auntie Black Widow."

"You're probably right. Though…I happen to know that Auntie Black Widow made macadamia nut cookies this morning and sprinkled them with confectioner's sugar. I saw her hiding them in the pantry behind the oatmeal and cream of wheat boxes."

Larissa looked up at Buddy and grinned. They laughed together as they sprinted back across Murray Boulevard toward the house, giving a horn-tooting tourist from New York City a near heart attack.

# 64.
## Buddy Wants Answers

Bud and Larissa sat at the kitchen table finishing off the last of the cookies Pauline had made strictly for Bedon, and guzzling down the bottom half of a gallon of whole milk she'd purchased at the Piggly Wiggly strictly for herself. The two young people looked much like they were doing a re-play of the night Larissa and Bedon had eaten the chocolate cake together before waltzing to "Moon River" in the parlor.

Buddy, still courageous from the pills, skipped niceties and moved straight to blunt observations. "The way it looks to me, you're doing a pretty good job of defending Pop with no help. What do you need me for?"

"You're so dense. I need you to back me up. She's after me every day like Peg-Leg Pete on Mickey Mouse."

"You aren't as tough as you pretend. I'm getting that gradually. And who's Peg-Leg Pete?"

"A video game villain. Guess you're right. I'm not so tough. If Bedon hadn't come along, I'd be history. He stitched me up, let me hide out in his carriage house, and took care of plenty of other stuff you wouldn't believe, not if I swore it with my right hand on the *Holy Bible*. Main thing, he never told on me to a soul, which kept me from having to go back into the foster care system. Most of the time he didn't know when I was staying in the carriage house and when I wasn't. Gave me my own key. I've still got it."

"Bi-zarro. Pop is the most conservative man in the universe. Now something as outlandish as this."

"Another big help – I guess not as big as keeping me alive, but big enough – has been the money he's given me along the way. Nursing classes aren't free. Bedon doesn't know it, but he's the reason I'm sticking it out at Trident. I want to be like him, a medical person."

"Did you ever bring those other kids back? The ones who made all the noise?"

"Are you kidding me? I wasn't about to risk losing my sugar daddy to please a crowd of dummies."

Buddy assumed a knowing look and leaned so far back in his chair that its wooden legs dug two new holes into his grandmother's floor. "Sugar daddy. I suppose that might make sense if we weren't talking about Pop."

"That came out wrong. I didn't mean it the way it sounded. Sometimes I say stupid things, or say things stupid."

"Okay, not your sugar daddy. What then?"

"He's been...to me...somebody who knew I was pretty much a hopeless case, but tried to help me anyway. He loved me."

"Loved you how?"

Larissa stood up and snatched the cookie plate and milk glasses off the table. Bending over the still-seated Buddy, she sputtered into his face, "You better not be asking what I think you're asking, prepster."

"Stop calling me those mean names? Call me Buddy, or Bud. You're always trying to make me look shallow, like you think I've got some idea I'm better than you."

She went to the sink, rinsed the dishes off with the sprayer nozzle, thought about shooting cold water at the back of Buddy's head, reconsidered, and balanced the dripping plate and glasses upright in the dish drainer. After which she returned to the table and sat down again. "All right...*Buddy*," she said, "one time at the beginning, I asked Bedon if he were a rich perv. I hated so bad I said that after I saw how much it hurt him. You know what a softy he is."

"All right, all right, I get it," Bud said. "It's just Aunt Pauline..."

"Yeah, I know that female spider's itching to run me out of her territory. She wants a certain fly all to herself. But the decision of whether I stay or go is up to you, prep..., I mean, Buddy, not some toxic arachnid."

# 65.
## Sidewalk Antics

Larissa, in her fabled short shorts, smiled with Marilyn Monroe brilliance as she pushed Bedon in his wheelchair along the sidewalk of Murray Boulevard. Bedon also smiled big, like Joe DiMaggio or John Fitzgerald Kennedy in their respective glory days with Marilyn. Great Aunt Pauline was trying hard to follow Larissa and Bedon. She found herself having to dance a peculiar little quickstep to keep up, necessitating sharp-and-painful inhalations and exhalations of ragged puffs of air. Pauline did not smile. She could not. It was all the poor thing could do to keep from falling on her face. She had to forego even proud queen waves to the surprising number of jolly gentlemen out sweeping their front walks in the middle of the day. That was all right, though, because Larissa and Bedon waved to each and every jolly gentleman, and each and every jolly gentleman waved back.

Irritated by all this energetic waving and smiling, Pauline managed to shout out an order that was sure to be disobeyed. "Slow down, I say, slow down. I'm getting a catch in my hip from this slanted sidewalk."

———— & ————

From the opposite direction on the same battery walkway jogged Pastor Tradd Petigru, straight for Bedon in his wheelchair, Larissa in her Nikes, and Pauline in her Easy Spirits. Just as Auntie P was about to croak her last croak, Larissa brought Bedon's wheelchair to a jolting halt to allow her patient to shake the hand of the pastor.

"Dr. Calhoun," Petigru said. "Oops...sorry I'm sweaty." The pastor wiped his hand on the front of his shirt and stuck it out again in the self-conscious manner he was always plagued with when not buffered by the pulpit. "It's wonderful to see you out and about, sir. Won't be long before you'll be back in your old pew."

Pauline pushed past Larissa to get closer to the goodlooking preacher. "Oh, Pastor Petigru." she crooned. "How grand to see you. It's been such a long time."

The goodlooking preacher's face confirmed no recognition whatsoever. Larissa, unimpressed by Pauline's wild leap to center stage, tried in vain to get her patient's wheelchair rolling again. It took her a moment to figure out the patient himself was the impediment. He had kicked the foot pedals upright and was using his feet to brake against a three-inch rise in the sidewalk. Larissa stepped around front to find out what Bedon's malfunction was. Meanwhile, Pauline, though sweating like a farm mule, persevered in her sparkling performance for the pastor. The show, as they say, must go on. Never mind what Larissa, the lesser light on the stage, might be trying to accomplish.

Pauline gushed girlish. "How could you not remember me, Pastor, dear. I'm Pauline...Lawrence's wife. You know Lawrence, Bedon's only brother."

Up stage left: Larissa's patient, Bedon, continued balking at his cutie-pie nurse's every effort to get his wheelchair pedals back in place. "What's the matter with you, Bedon?" she said. "Will you give me some help here? You're working against me."

Down stage center: The pastor, jittery now from the pressure of being put on the spot by a terrifying unknown old woman with rivers of sweat running down her face, fell victim to a serious stutter. "Oh, oh. Yes, yes. You've been to church with...uhm...uhm...Dr. Calhoun. I think...yes, Dr. Calhoun, and you sat in his pew. Your name is Hildie, right?"

Pauline let out a piercing shriek at being confused with the love of Bedon's life, which caused her wheelchair-bound brother-in-law to step up his struggle with Larissa over the foot pedals.

"No, no, no…I'm Pauline. Hildie – God rest her soul – has been dead and gone for years. But that doesn't mean Bedon is alone. I'm here now to take care of him. Already a member of the household and a faithfully tithing (not!) watch-care member of the flock at Bethel Baptist, your dear church. Lawrence and I – Lawrence is my current husband, Bedon's brother, remember? We've visited Bethel for weeks at a time in the past, when here for extended visits as Bedon's guests. And now that he's ill, Buddy has asked us to stay on indefinitely."

When Bedon heard the word indefinitely, he lunged out of the wheelchair and stood over Larissa a full second before plopping back down. The surprised girl hung onto the foot pedals as hard as she could to keep the chair from rolling out from under her agitated patient. Pastor Petigru somehow had the presence of mind to grab the wheelchair's back handles to help steady it. After Bedon was safely seated again, Larissa addressed him no-nonsense. "It's time to go home. You've gotten upset for some reason."

Auntie P couldn't resist chastising Larissa. "I told you before we left the house it was bad for him to be out in this heat." Then she gave the pastor a quick phony smile and spoke directly to him in a tone revealing her low opinion of this tiresome girl. In her rancorous apology for Larissa, Pauline explained with false patience, "She's our new live-in maid. Good help is so hard to find these days."

Preacher Petigru never wavered from his perfect public persona. To the bitter end, he continued gifting all parties present with his impeccable pastoral manners. To Larissa he said with chivalry polished enough to please a visiting princess from a foreign realm, "I'm sorry, miss. I didn't catch your name."

To which she replied, "Oh…my name is Baby Doll. I'm just temping here. My real job is pole dancing at the Diamond Strip Club over in North Charleston. They've set me up with health insurance and a 401K plan. Now will you stop standing there like a cell phone tower and help me get this wheelchair going?"

The petrified Petigru hurried to obey the "new maid," while Pauline clawed her way back to center stage. Said she to Larissa, "You can't talk to the preacher like that. Who do you think you are?" And then to the preacher, "I apologize for her again, Pastor. You can be sure Buddy Calhoun will be hearing about this latest offense of hers, as soon as we get back to the house."

The pastor had no canned response for a single thing being said to him by these two clucking hens. He made an effort to calm his nerves by doing what seemed to him the righteous thing to do given all the variables. He knelt on his bare knees upon the unforgiving concrete and tried to help Larissa flip down the foot pedals of the wheelchair that her patient was determined to keep flipped up. Bedon kicked the pastor's hands away and motioned for Larissa to come close so he could say something into her ear. She complied, then straightened up and crossed her arms under her boobies. "No, Bedon," she said. "I've been telling you *no* to that for days. No means no."

Pastor Petigru, ever the gentleman his mama reared him to be, kept on trying to be of help to someone, anyone, in this impossible cluster of butt-heads. Out of desperation he asked Larissa and Bedon a question he should have had better sense than to ask. "Is it something I can help with?"

"Obviously not," Larissa said, then snatched the foot pedals back into their correct positions and placed Bedon's feet on them by herself. Bedon frowned, but let her have her way since not letting her have her way had become too taxing. Still on his knees upon the concrete, Pastor Petigru held up both hands in surrender to "Baby Doll" as she brushed by him on her way around to the back of the wheelchair, where she grabbed hold of the handles and twirled the chair around on its two left wheels so quickly that her uncooperative patient was surprised to find himself pointing in the direction of home instead of East Bay Street.

Larissa then said to the pastor, "Dr. Calhoun is acting out today." The good preacher was having a hard time getting up off his knees, but doing the best he could in case he might have to run for the hills. Larissa felt sorry for him and gave him a hand up. "I have to take this impossible ill man home," she said, "where he can go on being a brat on his own turf without an audience."

Pauline saw this as a perfect lead-in for a three-line scene stealer of her own, one she was certain would upstage Larissa once and for all. At the unsuspecting girl, she hissed, "Listen here, Miss Priss. You're an employee, not a close relative like me. You have to do whatever Bedon tells you, and you're not to call him a brat."

Pastor Petigru took several steps back from the main goings-on. He ran a hand through his hair and looked about wildly. Maybe a freight train would come along and run the whole crowd over, including himself. Anything would be better than being in the middle of this girl-fight.

Larissa bowed up at Pauline like a Halloween kitty. "What do you want me to do? Throw myself in front of a tractor trailer every time he belches?"

"Don't sass me, you little vixen. I'll fire you myself, and Buddy will back me up when he gets home."

"All right, you win. I'll do exactly what Bedon is telling me to do, and I'll do it right now."

The angry girl walked back around in front of her patient, who was no longer frowning, but grinning like a mule eating briars. She gave him a withering look. "Okay, Dr. Boss Man, are you sure you want me to do this? Your 'fraidy-cat preacher doesn't look to me like he can handle it."

Her ecstatic patient nodded and smiled like a naughty child getting his way after throwing a temper tantrum. Aunt Pauline stood at the ready to make sure the "employee" minded her "employer." The employee turned and faced the perspiring, though still amazingly goodlooking Preacher Petigru, whose expression communicated clearly he wanted no part of whatever debacle was about to get dropped at his feet. But Larissa didn't care what the "fraidy-cat" preacher wanted. Now *she* was in the position of attempting to do the righteous thing. She inhaled sharply and began a sentence she was unable to finish. "Pastor...Bedon wants me to ask you..." She hesitated.

"Ask me what?" Petigru said like a fool. Could this man not tell it was going to be something he'd be better off not knowing? Pauline used Larissa's second hesitation to sprinkle more Cayenne into the pot. "Go ahead, young lady. You're here for one reason... to do Bedon's bidding. Otherwise, I'll tell Buddy you're being insubordinate, abusive even."

Larissa hesitated a third time, but not because of Pauline's threats, because of her own wish to protect Bedon. Looking with kinder eyes at Pastor Petigru, whose own brown eyes had no more guile than a baby's, she said with newfound softness, "Bedon has been after me for days to call you, to ask you to conduct our wedding ceremony. He wants me to...marry him."

Aunt Pauline dropped to the sidewalk in a dead faint, legs sprawled spread eagle. Pastor Petigru choked on his own saliva and gave in to a coughing fit. Bedon slid forward in his wheelchair and laughed out loud, as Larissa beat the preacher on his back to help him catch his lost breath, though not his lost dignity, which had fled the scene never to return.

# 66.
# Pauline Tells the Tale

Buddy entered Dr. Mark Belton's medical suite waiting room from a carpeted hallway. No one in the room would have noticed him if it hadn't have been for the out-of-tune tinkle bell hanging from the doorknob. He glanced around the small space and spied Larissa and Pauline. They both sat locked in sourpuss mode with their sourpuss fannies warming the cushions of a faded sage green sofa. Bedon slept in his wheelchair, slumped over, making up for the nap he'd missed at midday by snoring extra loud to the consternation of other occupants of the close room who were already feeling poorly or they wouldn't have been there in the first place.

Lawrence napped also, but in a regular chair, joining his sibling in a brotherly snoring duet. Pauline and Larissa precision-pumped their crossed legs in tandem. Bud approached the prickly pair with caution. Said he with insufficient calm, "Are y'all two gals okay? Tradd Petigru called me..."

Pauline continued competing for the academy award she had been competing for all day, the one she well deserved. "Did our dutiful preacher tell you I fainted, almost died right there on the boulevard sidewalk. It was so precious of him to walk me home after I came to."

Horrified, not precious, would be the best word to describe what Buddy felt in response to his great aunt's testimony as to what had caused his entire family and his pop's new live-in companion to wind up in Dr. Belton's outer office. Tradd Petigru had neglected to mention in his phone call that Auntie Pauline had "almost died right there on the boulevard sidewalk." Dry-mouthed for some reason, Bud turned to the new live-in companion for reassurance. "Larissa?" he said, his voice cracking like a teenager's.

"Oh, yeah," she replied, nodding her head in exaggerated ups and downs. "She passed out like a party girl. Ker-plop, right on the concrete. Didn't wake up for five minutes, a heck of a long time when tourists get involved and want to call 911 for nothing. The preacher didn't tell you about it?"

"Not everything. He seemed nervous for some reason when we were chatting on the phone. Said it all turned out for the best, though, as disasters go. And he was already on his way back to the church to get down on his knees at the altar to give thanks in fervent prayer the whole thing was over."

"Seriously?" Larissa said. "If he does get down on his knees, it'll be the second time he's had to do it today. The dude needs to pray, and about more than gratitude. He ain't *no* help in an emergency."

Buddy swallowed the bitter lump of whatever it was that had formed in his throat. He knew for a fact Larissa was correct in her evaluation of the beleaguered preacher's coping skills. It was only in the last few years he'd stopped drinking, married Bo's sister, Logan, and started having kids, two girls and two boys. Bud flinched at the thought of any poor schmuck having to stop drinking, get married, and start having kids – two girls and two boys – just to keep his job, especially in the bosom of Bo Gaillard's dysfunctional family. He flinched again on having to turn back to Pauline. "Are you sure you're all right, Aunt P? Are we waiting for Dr. Belton to see you or Pop? He's a family practitioner, you know, not a neurologist."

Aunt P sniffed a disgusted sniff at her clueless nephew. "It's Bedon who needs to see a doctor, not me. But a psychiatrist in my opinion, not a neurologist or a family practitioner. Your grandfather is a sick man, Buddy. He's been talking out of his head in pure delirium."

"Pop's been talking? When did he start talking?"

"Not exactly out loud," Aunt P said. "*She*...." The accent Pauline put on the feminine pronoun, she, enhanced the appalling accusation she was about to make against Larissa. "*She*," the great aunt began again, "has been talking for him, making up things he isn't saying." As Pauline finished filing her indictment against the pretty suspect, she poked a forefinger repeatedly in her direction in an attempt to build strategic tension, emoting being a valuable skill for an actress.

Buddy, in an effort to lower the temperature in the room, said after a glance at his pop, "He looks all right to me."

"She's brainwashing him," Aunt P said. "It's elder abuse. I read about it in the *AARP Magazine*."

Buddy noticed the receptionist was sliding open her opaque window to the waiting room. She laid an open hand upon her own cleavage and looked sideways at Bud. Then in a gruffy whisper, she asked a string of stingray-barbed questions. "Sir? Is something going on out here we should know about? Do we need to make a call?"

Buddy waved both hands in the air to restore her confidence. "No, no," he said. "We're all good. Fine. Good."

She gave him a hate stare before sliding the window shut again, to which Bud responded with smiles and more smiles – the kind that hurt the cheeks because they're so bogus – first at the receptionist, then all around the room at his fellow travelers on the *Twilight Zone* bus who were also giving him looks. The question at the front of Bud's mind now was how everything that had transpired over the course of one horrific afternoon, in his total absence, had somehow gotten to be all his fault. When he dared to steal a glance at Auntie P, he knew from the sizzle in her eyes she had no intention of showing him any more mercy than the receptionist and his fellow *Twilight Zone* traveling companions.

Said his great aunt with the bitterest of spleen, "You are going to die, Buddy Calhoun, when you hear what this little tart said to the pastor."

Dismay was what Buddy Calhoun felt when he heard his aunt use the word tart right in front of Larissa instead of behind her back.

Continued the tirade of the sizzler, "...and all the time carrying on like Bedon was telling her to say it. But the pastor knew it was a lie the whole time. He's quick-witted like that."

Now Buddy knew from witnessing numerous early encounters Bo had experienced with Tradd Petigru that the pastor was not and never had been quick-witted, not even on his best day, but the discerning law student decided to let this particular misjudgment of Pauline's die away like it had never been made. He blew out a little breath to access what was left of his composure before inquiring of the group, "I'm afraid to ask how Petigru got mixed up in this circus in the first place."

Bud might have been hesitant about asking this question, but Pauline was not hesitant about answering it. "He was jogging in those close-fitting, modern athletic togs he wears every day," she said, "the ones I like so much. Anyway, she told the pastor that Bedon wanted him to conduct their wedding ceremony."

Bud blinked a few rapid times, his customary response to the absurd. "Whose wedding ceremony?"

"Hers and Bedon's," Aunt P said.

The stunned Buddy looked at Larissa, who gave him her finest one-shouldered shrug. Before he could untangle his thoughts enough to ask Pauline what she was talking about, the receptionist, whose job description included guarding the entrance to Dr. Belton's inner sanctuary, in addition to monitoring the frosted window to it, opened wide the pearly entry gate with formal pomp and circumstance. "Dr. Calhoun," she said to the sleeping Bedon, "you may come back now."

Dr. Calhoun woke up bewildered when he heard his name called. He checked out everyone in the room and did not crack a smile until he came to Larissa, whereupon he broke into a boyish grin, took her hand in his, and kissed it in the courtly manner King Arthur would use to kiss the hand of Lady Gwinevere.

King Arthur's grandson blinked a few more spasmodic times just as Uncle Lawrence sputtered awake to join in on the fun. "Is this a hospital?" Lawrence said in explosive syllables. "Am I in a hospital? Did Pauline try to finish me off?!"

# 67.
## Family Meeting to Address Family Problems

Buddy, Larissa, Aunt Pauline, and Uncle Lawrence sat in Bedon's den in a semi-circle around the wheelchair occupied by the homeowner himself. Bud took the lead in the intervention. "Pop, will you help me get to the bottom of this? Things around here aren't making sense."

Bedon held up his right thumb, and his grandson understood how the discussion was going to go. "Thumb up means yes?" he said.

His pop nodded and pointed a thumb down, a gesture Bud also understood. "And down means no. Okay, you're aware you passed your Alzheimer's test with flying colors today at Dr. Belton's office, right? You don't have Alzheimer's or anything like it, not even the earliest stages. Do you understand that?"

Pop gave a thumb-up and put his other hand in the air for a high-five with his grandson. Buddy complied, then plodded forward with the business at hand. "And you know Dr. Belton said it was the stroke that affected your speech and your ability to walk. He thinks the walking problem might be simple weakness. But the speech, well, he said it could come back, that it *would* come back. You know all this... right, Pop?"

Bedon went quickly through a thumb-up, a head-nod, and a finger-point to his own throat. Buddy went on. "What I can't figure out is how you can make Larissa understand you, but none of the rest of us."

Thumb-up, thumb-down, up, down. Bud tried to translate. "Is that an I-don't-know?

Thumb-up.

Bud put his own thumb up for good measure. Monkey see, monkey do. "All right then," he said, "here's the question of the day, of the year. Did you tell Larissa you wanted her to marry you?"

Bedon grinned his lopsided grin and put his right thumb higher and higher in the air with jerky movements. Aunt Pauline fanned herself in equally jerky movements with a Stuhr Funeral Home fan (*Funeral Chapels and Crematory; "We'll be with you all along the way…"*). "I told you he's lost it," she said to Buddy. "Needs to be institutionalized. Bull Street in Columbia is what I'm thinking."

Bedon scowled and held his thumb down as far as the arms of the wheelchair would allow, at which point Larissa jumped in to defend herself. "Bedon, you need to tell your nosey grandson you've been aggravating me about this ever since I came back here to take care of you, and I've been saying no-way-hombre from the beginning."

With a sad face, Bedon gave the whole group a weak thumb-up. Larissa drove home her point. "Have I one time said yes?"

As her patient gave a shakier thumb-down, his eyes began filling with tears. Buddy refused to let Larissa apply any more pressure. "Stop," he said, "I get it." And to his grandfather, "You know marrying her is impossible, Pop. What's the matter with you?"

Pauline took Bud's question as her cue for yet another improv performance. "I know what the matter is," she said. "He's gone soft in the head like Lawrence. They're brothers. Could be a weak gene pool."

Bedon used the armrests of his chair to brace himself and stand up, his plan being to go after Pauline, only to begin falling forward. He toppled onto his sister-in-law before Buddy could catch him.

Aunt Pauline caterwauled when the wheelchair turned over onto her lower legs and feet. "He's killing me. Get him off. Get him off."

It took the strength of Larissa and Buddy combined to right the wheelchair and get Bedon back into it. They checked him over for injuries, the process of which Uncle Lawrence interrupted. "He's not hurt. She is."

He pointed to an obtuse angled cut in the shin of Aunt Pauline's right leg. The whole party, including Pauline, gaped as blood began a slow trickle toward her fat kankle. She whimpered in pain without having to fake it. "I want to go to the hospital. Take me to the emergency room."

Larissa ran to the bookshelf to get Bedon's black bag. She sat down on the ottoman in front of Pauline and tried to tend her cut. "Get away from me," the injured Aunt P said to the almost nurse. "You don't know what you're doing."

Lawrence, having gotten over the initial shock of seeing blood, addressed the practical side of the matter. "May as well go ahead and let her fix you up, hon. No insurance to collect around here."

# 68.

## Bedon, Contented Patient

Bedon, ensconced in bed in his room, picked up Walter Edgar's massive history book and held it out to Buddy, who, in the process of backing away, tipped a potted plant off a table. "I'm not reading history or anything else to you tonight," he said as he scraped some, but not all of the dirt on the floor back into the pot. "Not even an article out of your ten-thousand-volume collection of *Black Powder Guns & Hunting Magazine*. Maybe you can get Larissa to do it."

Larissa, as though responding to the sound of her own name, came through the door with one arm behind her back. Her feminine presence warmed the room for both men, but she focused on only one of them, the gentleman propped against his pillows in bed. She spoke to him with a certain tenderness. "Had your toddy yet, Bedon?"

He gave her a thumb-down with a smile. She brought her hidden arm around and presented his drink to him in the showy style she'd learned waitressing at the Barbadoes Room. Bedon motioned her to come near. She obeyed after giving Buddy a firm shove to the side. "Don't mind me," he said. "I'm just another highboy chest-of-drawers in here."

"I'm *not* minding you. I'm minding my patient. But from the looks of those bloodshot eyes of yours," this after a glance in Buddy's direction, "somebody ought to be looking after you. Guess the troubles of life weighed down hard today."

"The troubles of life surely did." Buddy regarded his pop's cheerful face. "Dude, are you not tired? Everyone around you is exhausted."

Bedon sipped his drink and made believe he didn't hear Buddy's complaint. As Larissa walked around the bed straightening her patient's covers, he indicated he had something to tell her. She stretched over the bed to listen, then straightened up without letting him finish. "No," she said. "We're not talking about that anymore. I'm taking care of you, because I want to. You don't have to pay me back."

Buddy, out of fear approaching paranoia, felt compelled to find out what fresh hell was about to escape the lower regions and jump up in his face. "What is it?" he said.

Larissa kept working with the bed covers. She appeared confident she had already dealt with whatever it was. "Nothing important," she said. "He's just always telling me if he marries me, I'll have security after he's gone, whatever that means."

Buddy shut his eyes in an effort to sever reception of all other unnerving information for the day. As Bedon would say, he had "officially had enough." The tired grandson opened his eyelids to a slit to make sure the furniture was still in place, and the walls and ceiling. Sliding his gaze over to his pop, he checked also to see if the old man still had one head on his shoulders instead of two or three. When Bedon realized Buddy was studying him, he grinned a happy grin and gave his grandson a cheerful thumb-up.

# 69.

## Everybody Is Worried, Except for Bedon

Folly River. Buddy and Bo sat with their feet and legs dangling off Crosby's Seafood dock with no hope of catching a fish. Bo reeled in his line and changed his bait. He consoled Bud in the only way he knew how. "I thought my nana was awful, but your pop makes her look like a Sunday school teacher. How old is that live-in of his anyhow?"

Buddy lifted his line and saw that something had stolen his saltwater minnow. Not caring, he let the hook sink back into the current as bare as it was the day he first purchased it at Haddrell's Point Tackle on James Island. "I don't know," he said. "She takes nursing classes at Trident Tech. Gotta be out of high school to do that."

Bo gave his friend a fishy once-over to see if Pop Calhoun's misfiring mental acuity of late was somehow rubbing off. "High school," he said. "I guess that's better than say...middle school." He paused before casting his line farther out into the current. "And how old is your pop?"

"Funny, but I don't know that, either. Not exactly. Seventy-six, seventy-seven. Somewhere in there."

"And that's something, too, I suppose. Could be he was already seventy-eight or seventy-nine and too old for a gal fresh out of high school. Are you going to call her Grandmaw?"

Buddy squeezed one eye shut like Popeye the Sailor Man and restrained himself from socking Bo. "Look," he said, "I'm trying to think this thing through, and you're not helping."

"Oh, I know you're pre-occupied, oh-faithful-pal-of-mine. Not many Lowcountry boys try to fish without bait. That hand-fishing fad going around on the cable TV channels is a crock full of something or other, but not catfish."

Bo balanced his rod and reel safely on the dock and took Buddy's rod out of his hands. He reeled in his friend's line to attend to his bait issue, at the same time trying to clear up his pal's muddled thinking. "Listen here, Buddy boy, ain't nothing wrong with backing off for a while. Why not? Your pop is doing good. His live-in is doing good. Police don't come around much anymore."

"You don't understand anything about it," Bud said. "He's obsessed with her. Even *she* can barely keep it real."

Bo thought over the definition of "it" while he worked with Bud's hook and line. "H'mm," he said. "On a more serious note, maybe Petigru can talk some sense into him. He's the father of my sister's children, after all, and my personal pastor to boot. Yours, too. Clergy can be a big help sometimes, 'specially in the South."

Bo finished skewering a fat saltwater minnow onto Buddy's hook, cast the line, handed the rod and reel over to Buddy, and watched in dejection as his friend promptly lost the new minnow to a sneaky sea bass. Beyond dejection, Bo pulled up his own line and saw that the same bass had made off with his own minnow, leaving the barbed hook shining in the sun. "I give up," he said.

"So do I," Bud agreed, though he thought he was agreeing with Bo about the hopelessness of trying to solve his pop's problems, not the hopelessness of catching a fish. "You know as well as I do," he said in an attempt to block yet another infusion of Bo's wrong-headed thinking, "this thing with Pop is beyond the scope of a garden variety Baptist preacher."

"All the same," Bo said, "I think you should call him. He ain't busy. Only work he does is his twenty-minute sermon once a week. I know, 'cause he's my brother-in-law."

"Okay, I will. He can come over and add to the bedlam. Maybe he'll talk to Pop. Maybe Pop'll come to his senses, and Pauline and Lawrence will go back to Florida, and Larissa will go back to wherever it was she came from..."

"Let me know what day you're gonna try to get all that done," Bo said. "I want to make sure I'm offshore where I can actually catch a fish."

"No, really," Buddy said. "I think you're right. Petigru can get through to Pop. He'll use Scripture verses, counseling techniques. And he'll pray, *hard*. I've heard him do it in the pulpit...like Paul, the apostle...like Simon Peter. This really is the answer, Bo. You're a genius."

"Yeah, I'm a genius all right, like the time in college when I thought dating a girl who grew up in the middle of Bloody Bay Swamp was the '*answer*.' You remember that five-hundred-pound gator she called her pet? Named Cuddles? Petigru ain't no more the 'answer' to your Pop's problems than Sheba, the Swamp Woman, was the 'answer' to mine, whatever they were back then. I consider myself lucky I got out of that swamp alive or dead. And you were no help. You thought Sheba was a real looker. Sometimes I think your head is made out of a cypress knee. I don't know what would happen to you if you didn't have me around to help you. *Cuddles?*"

# 70.
## Pop on Attack

Pastor Petigru cowered behind the baby grand piano in Dr. Calhoun's parlor. He protected his head with the *Holy Bible* he'd brought along for Scriptural support during counseling. Bedon, the wheel-chaired counselee, was beating the pacifist pastor with a furled, University of South Carolina umbrella. Buddy and Larissa, followed by Aunt Pauline and Uncle Lawrence, rushed in to try to restrain the stroke victim.

Buddy, who found himself in an embarrassing tug-of-war with his grandfather over the umbrella, delivered a series of unobeyed suggestions. "*Stop it, Pop. I said stop. No, man...stop that right now.*"

Bedon wrested the umbrella from Buddy's grasp. Buddy had almost gotten control of it, but failed in the end, giving Bedon the opportunity to "get his racket back" (the umbrella) in such a professional tennis technique it was certain to cause injury if and when it made contact upside the preacher's salt-and-pepper head. Which, thank goodness, it did not do, since Larissa was able to somehow grab it in mid-swing and twist it out of the combatant's hands. "Let go, Bedon," she said. "You're gonna give yourself another one of those transient ischemic attacks I learned about in clinical class yesterday, a T.I.A."

Buddy made himself useful, finally, by taking hold of his pop's arms and forcing him to settle down. Bedon, tired out by all the exertion, gave in to his grandson, but continued glaring at Pastor

Petigru with the fierceness of a wildcat. When Buddy felt sure he'd subdued his pop sufficiently, he relaxed his grip and immediately got jostled out of the way once again by the angry, wheel-chaired assailant, who was now going after the pastor with his bare hands. Buddy restrained him again as Larissa wheeled the chair backward out of reach of the defenseless man-of-the-cloth.

The breathless Buddy yelled above the frey, "Get out of here while you can, Preacher. I'll handle this and call you later."

Petigru shot out of the room through the archway like a cannon ball gone wrong. The sound of the front door opening and closing, followed by the pastor's Italian-loafered feet clicking across the piazza and down the front steps (a bit like a girl's feet might click), let the occupants of the parlor know the preacher had made it out of harm's way, a positive outcome that provided the whole assembly with undeniable evidence that emergency prayers of a sincere man of God can elicit emergency answers.

When certain the pastor was safely on his way to wherever pastors spend their time on weekdays, Larissa parked Bedon's wheelchair in front of the sofa. She and Buddy sat down opposite him, and Larissa spoke first. "Bedon…you are killing me. I can't deal with much more of this. They haven't told me anything in my classes about how to handle the kinds of stunts you've been pulling. You had no right to get so mad at the preacher, just 'cause he said you ought not to be talking to me about getting married."

Bedon reached out and got a handful of her hair with the intent of yanking her near him to tell her something, something quite important judging from his disturbed behavior. She resisted, saying, "No, no. I'm worn out fighting with you. Don't ask me to do another thing today."

The patient let go of his nurse's hair and put a vice hold on her wrist. "All right, all right," she said. "I'll tell them whatever it is you want me to tell them. But after, you have to give me a break. I'm beat."

Buddy, who considered himself far more "beat" than the almost nurse, tensed up in anticipation of more bad-news-by-the-gallon about to rain down on his head. "Tell us what?" he said in a husky tone, "that he wants you to have his children now? Why the blankety-blank not?"

Larissa wasn't amused. "He's saying if you and Pauline and Lawrence and Tradd Petigru don't leave him alone, he's going to call the police."

Pauline, also, wasn't amused. "Well, I never," she said. "Am I the only one around here who knows what a mental patient acts like?"

Buddy glared at his great aunt with the eyes of a man who had bio-chemicals of rage flooding every cell of his body. "You're the mental patient," he said, "not Pop."

The accused Pauline stepped behind Great Uncle Lawrence and peeped around at her great nephew, who was now burning her up with a look she'd seen before upon the many faces of the many other folks she'd managed to enrage over the course of her long lifetime – total strangers even – on making some innocent remark they took the wrong way. "You better hush up, Buddy Calhoun," she said. "I'm a close relative, same as you, and my dear Lawrence won't have you talking to me like I'm an outsider."

That was when Bedon rolled his wheelchair around on a dime and got hold of the USC umbrella for the second time. He scooted close to Lawrence and Pauline and began swinging it at the two of them, whereupon Pauline screamed like a poltergeist and whooshed her way through the archway toward freedom faster than the pastor had done earlier, leaving, with no remorse whatsoever, poor Lawrence to perish alone.

Bedon, though newly mobile in his wheelchair, could not keep up with the fleeing Pauline, s-o-o-o he gave the closed umbrella his best wind-up and slung it after her, hurting her feelings more than her backside. She accidentally bumped Hildie's Tiffany lamp as she dashed by, causing it to crash to the parlor floor and shatter into a myriad of jewel-toned fragments that caught the sunlight like rubies and emeralds. Larissa jumped up from the sofa and walked over to where Lawrence was standing all watery-eyed and a'tremble. "Are you all right?" she said to him in the same sweet voice she usually saved for Bedon. "Did he hit you with that thing?"

"No, I dodged him pretty good. I'm fine, I think."

"Good, 'cause I'm not fine," and she pressed her forehead against Lawrence's chest and began sobbing. Uncle Lawrence smiled as dearly as an old man can smile and stroked her hair.

Bedon didn't appreciate Lawrence lending comfort of this nature to Larissa, but he couldn't do anything about it right then as he had a more pressing matter to attend. He spied Buddy's iPhone on the coffee table and rolled his chair near enough to make a grab for it. Buddy saw his own sorry future playing out before his own sorry eyes like a horror show nightmare, which would become a horror show reality if his grandfather were somehow able to snag that phone and get the police on the line. The possibility gave Bud the strength and accuracy to dive for the phone at the split second his grandfather's fingers were closing around it. With help from above, Buddy's own fingers bumped the phone out of Bedon's grasp – a bona fide miracle – and scooped it up with the finesse of a high-tech pooper scooper. "Oh, no, you don't," he said to his pop in a husky voice new to his vocal cords. "We aren't calling the police today. They'd lock every one of us up."

Bedon frowned and worked his mouth, trying to speak above a whisper. He made a few grunting sounds. Larissa, still enjoying her emotional breakdown upon the chest of lucky Lawrence, remained unaware of the marvel taking place right under her nose, that of a mute man regaining his speech. Uncle Lawrence and Buddy, however, were both fully aware and amazed at what was transpiring before them. They stared at Bedon with genetically pure love in their hearts as the old man grumbled out his first words since his speech-stealing stroke. If only those first words had been kind instead of cutting. With terrifying menace, the elderly grandfather said, "They're lots of other phones in this house, Buddy Calhoun. Either you let me follow my heart for the first time since Hildie died... Either you back off and let me marry Larissa and get my estate in order, so I can keep on being of some small help to her after I'm gone, or I *will* call the police over here and tell them I-don't-know-what-yet, but I'll call them and tell them...some awful thing."

# 71.

## All Y'all Are Cordially Invited

uddy's young hand turned on the phonograph and started Judy Garland's rendition of "Embraceable You" in the same delicate manner his grandfather's aging hand had turned it on so long ago and started Andy Williams' rendition of "Moon River." But the choice of song was not the only difference in the two lovely parlor tableaus. Whereas Bedon and Larissa were alone in the former scene, they were joined by dozens of guests in the latter, all of whom were dressed in smart afternoon wedding attire and frantically striking every Cole Porter party-pose in the Cole Porter party-pose handbook to look good in every photo the hired photographer shot.

Imagine the faultless Pastor Petigru – apparently back in good graces with Dr. Calhoun – square-shouldered and dignified in his black robe before a twin set of candelabra stands, each bearing twelve white flaming tapers wilting with their intense heat a funeral-sized arrangement of cream-colored, long-stemmed roses purchased at BI-LO Grocery Store, to which the bride and half the wedding guests were allergic. The pastor, looking fabulous despite how he felt (ridiculous approaching agony), held a *Bible* open with both hands and tried to force the tremor that had begun two inches above his elbows from creeping down both forearms and setting up dangerous vibrations in all ten of his digits. The last thing the preacher wanted was for the *Holy Book* to go flying across the room due to his inability to hang onto it. This irrational fear had something to do, no doubt, with his being beaten up the week before, in the very same room, by Bedon himself as he wielded his garnet-and-black umbrella. (Go Gamecocks!)

Imagine Judy Garland crooning in the background with her signature overkill of emotion as the current parlor scene unfolded shot by disturbing shot:

One – Pastor Petigru conducts Bedon and Larissa's wedding ceremony in the presence of a roomful of close relatives and confused guests;

Two – Bedon in his wheelchair and Larissa somewhat off balance in her high heels and fru-fru, second-hand wedding dress (already dirty around the hem from its previous owner's outdoor reception for which it rained a frog strangler) as they allow themselves to be led through their nuptials by a pastor who has endured worse than this, but not much worse;

Three – Buddy (with blank face), Caroline (with frown), Aunt Pauline (with frown) and Uncle Lawrence (with smile) huddle together and watch the ceremony unfold like the petals of a white Southern gardenia, or, to be more accurate, the petals of a white Southern kudzu blossom;

Four – Buddy stares entranced at Larissa for the entire ceremony, behavior to which Caroline reacts with flashing evil-eyes as she snatches her boyfriend back to reality with an unkind jerk to his upper arm and a more unkind demand he pretend the only purpose of the peculiar ceremony at hand is that it is forerunner to the one Caroline hopes will soon join the two of them together in holy matrimony.

(Close the wedding shot series here and return to the gripping narrative.)

At the conclusion of the ceremony, Larissa leaned over, and, smiling wanly and with little enthusiasm, allowed Bedon to kiss her on the cheek. Pastor Petigru and Buddy congratulated her, after which she thrust her bouquet of three-day-old, brown-at-the-edges tea roses (also from BI-LO's sale table) toward Caroline, who blinked in surprise and came close to smiling.

# 72.

# Candles, Cake…and Catastrophe

Still trapped in the lunacy of her own wedding celebration, Larissa discovered her main role in the proceeding was to find a way to defend herself and Bedon from being congratulated until death did them part right there in the parlor. She did this by pushing her patient's wheelchair into the dining room and trying to hide in a nook at the end of the massive china cabinet where she thought, incorrectly, traffic flow would consist solely of members of the catering staff. She sat down in an antique occasional chair next to her groom, who by this time was so tired he could hardly eat the small bites of wedding cake his bride was determined to feed him.

Miss Posey and the other guests – all of whom resembled hungry trout in a glass tank as they swam in a slow circle around the dining room table scoping out and nibbling upon the spread of expensive goodies thereupon – rendered Larissa's hiding place the worst possible one she could have chosen on the downstairs level, except for maybe the hall half-bath that was also experiencing constant traffic flow.

Everyone had to ogle the bride, speak to the bride, admire the bride's ring. And who wouldn't admire a princess-cut diamond bigger than a mega-oily-ice-clear shooter marble with two sapphires set in platinum filigree worshiping it in reverence from both sides. Buddy broke into the line of fine jewelry aficionados to deliver cups of punch to the bride and groom. Said he about the ceremony, though not about the insane series of events leading up to it, "Went off without a hitch. Guess it was meant to be." He waited, gathering the courage to ask his grandfather a question he knew might be met with hostility. "Mind if I dance with your bride, Pop? It's expected, me being family and all, a close relative."

Bedon bounced his right thumb down, down, down. "Okay, okay," Bud said, his hopes dashed. "Just trying to be polite."

Caroline flounced up to rescue her de facto fiancé from being bored out of his mind by his boring old pop and "that girl" who did not know her place. Caroline had never spoken Larissa's name out loud and never intended to. She always played like she couldn't remember it. "Come on, Buddy," she said, taking his chin in her hand and wrenching it sideways to give him a close-up gander at her too-liberally-applied-mineral-madeup face. Breathing like a vampire, she added, "Dance with me, darling. It's a slow one, romantic. Remember how we used to do the 'Charleston Embrace' when were in middle school and took ballroom lessons at Society Hall?"

Larissa watched with searing heat as the desperate Caroline tugged the desperate Buddy into the parlor and arranged his arms and legs into some semblance of a dance partner. The almost-fiancé then half-closed her eyes in an effort to be sultry and executed a series of contorted tango-like moves all around Buddy's box-step (courtesy of his inadequate training in ballroom). Larissa didn't know whether to laugh or cry at the spectacle, or to go over and snatch Caroline's big greenish feather fascinator right off her big greenish-blond head. It was the hypnotizing effect of the riffling, molting fascinator feathers floating to the floor that kept Larissa from realizing right away that Bedon's whole body had begun to tremble with the violence of a grand mal seizure. Not until his punch cup hit the floor did she pull in the reins of her galloping jealousy and begin attending to what she was supposed to be attending to all along, instead of to things none of her business; i.e., Buddy and Caroline's laughable love life that Larissa knew for sure would register *pa-thetic* on any Richter Scale.

On hearing Bedon's punch cup shatter, his new bride looked down in shock at the lake of lemon-lime liquid spreading into a misshapen circle all around her second-hand shoes. On reflex, she knelt to begin the clean-up process with her linen napkin, but was interrupted by a different, more troubling sound emitting from Bedon's throat. Broken cup and spilled punch forgotten, she clamored onto her knees in front of her patient. As he fluttered his eyelids and rubbed his temples, she tried to comfort him with soft words.

"Listen to me, Bedon. I have to go tell Buddy to call an ambulance. But don't you worry. We're going to take care of you. We're going to take care of you together."

Still kneeling before her beloved Bedon, Larissa turned to scan the parlor through the archway, but the box-stepping good-ole-boy and his tangoing seductress no longer owned the room. When Larissa finally spotted Buddy, he was already running toward her in dreamlike slow motion. She lost her balance and almost fell over as Bedon slumped forward and let down his upper body weight onto her left shoulder. Buddy charged through the crush of guests faster when he saw his pop had lost consciousness, and Larissa's small body was the only barrier between him and the heart pine floor.

# 73.
# Tearful Good-byes

Bedon lay still and bluish in a hospital bed. Buddy and Caroline stood on one side, Larissa on the other. Tears ran down Buddy's cheeks as he mumbled under his breath, "This stupid wedding thing…it was too much for him. I should've put my foot down."

Larissa had the look of a fawn whose mother had just been shot. "I'm scared," she whispered.

Caroline had the look of a jealous mean-girl who'd just burped up burrito-binge stomach acid. "Some nurse you're gonna be," she said to Larissa, whose name she never wanted to know, but did know, and wished she could forget.

Larissa, too terrified to be insulted, began crying in the same old way she had of producing copious tears with no emotional facial expression. She said to Buddy as though Caroline were invisible and inaudible, "If he dies, it'll be my fault." Then to her unresponsive patient, "Bedon...open your eyes. Please, Bedon."

Buddy cried harder than when his parents had been killed. "I shouldn't have made things so hard for him," he said, his shoulders shaking. "All he wanted was to do something noble. Something for someone less fortunate. I'm a moron."

That did the trick for helping Larissa unleash emotion normal for a girl her age. She screwed up her face and began sobbing like a young child. "Someone less fortunate like me, you mean, to make sure I'd be all right in case something happened to him. He knew you'd run me off like a stray dog once he died. But he didn't have to worry about that. I wouldn't have tried to stay around anyway. He was my friend, not you, or those two leeches from Florida. All I wanted was to pay him back for the things he did for me, the risks he took for me. I wanted to take care of him."

Bud didn't try to comfort her. He was too busy wiping his own eyes with the palms of his hands. "If you think Pop was worried that he had to protect you from all of us, you can rest your mind, 'cause I know what his new will says."

Larissa cringed. "I don't want anything from a will or from you." She let her weight down upon her loving benefactor and hugged and kissed him, then took his hand in hers and kissed it twice, gently. "Bedon...Bedon...if you can hear me, I want to tell you something. When you helped me learn how to take care of myself and gave me enough money to go to school, that was all you needed to do for me to make sure I'd be okay. I'm going to finish my nursing program and get a job and live a decent life. I love you so much, Bedon. Good-bye now."

She kissed him once more on the cheek, a long kiss accompanied with pitiful snubbing, then tore herself away and hurried out of the room. Buddy followed her, but stopped at the door and watched as she ran down the corridor. Pauline and Lawrence rose from the waiting room sofa and gaped in silence as Bedon's young bride flew past them and out of sight.

# 74.
## Coping with New Normal

Bo stood on his grandfather's piazza that now belonged solely to him. He was thankful, but also uncomfortable with the responsibility. How would he ever earn enough money to pay the insurance and property tax bills every year? How would he earn enough to keep historically correct paint on the historically correct trim of the main house, carriage house, detached garage, and vacant doghouse?

Bo came into the front yard through the lyre gate and climbed the piazza steps carrying a covered casserole dish. He stopped short on the top step to blink at the beribboned funeral wreath on the front door. Aunt Pauline opened up without waiting for Bo to knock. Solemn faced, she accepted the casserole and thanked its deliverer for stopping by. "Bo, dear…you know how much you and your family are cherished by us, especially at a time like this." She held the warm CorningWare to her ample bosom and looked down at it lovingly. "I know your nana and mama made this potato au gratin pie with their own caring hands. Will you give them our undying gratitude?"

Before responding, "Bo, dear" glanced toward the stone-faced Buddy, who was maintaining a healthy distance from his great aunt. Buddy fixed his friend with a cold stare worthy of a corrections officer, which put "Bo, dear" in the awkward position of having to bring closure to Pauline's performance without looking directly at her. "Yes, m'am," he said in a quiet voice, his eyes still glued to Buddy's face. "I'll be sure to give everybody at our house your…"

Pauline had to help him finish the sentiment. "...undying gratitude," she purred.

"Yeah," Bo said, "undying gratitude...from everybody at y'all's house to everybody at our house." The staginess of his speech would have alerted anyone that he was afraid his friend, Buddy, might shove him off the piazza if he went along with too much more of Pauline's drama.

Pauline, unaware or without care she was grating on Buddy's nerves so much that a descent into hostile psychosis had become a distinct possibility for her great nephew, continued making hard times harder. "Bo, dear, if you'd like to express your condolences to our dear Lawrence concerning his loss, he's in the backyard puttering around with a rake and a wheelbarrow. I guess he's trying to get his mind off things. He and I were Bedon's closest relatives...and Buddy, of course. We all have to go to the funeral home later today to finalize the arrangements. Poor dear Lawrence." She jostled the casserole into the crook of one elbow, and using her free hand, dabbed at her eyes with a damp tissue that had shredded into white fuzzies all over her knobby knuckles. "I don't know exactly when we'll be reading the will. Do you, Bud?"

Now who among you honestly thinks Buddy Calhoun answered that fool question?

After Pauline spent another long minute expressing hope that the will would be read before a *certain person* would have the chance to complicate matters, she excused herself to go get presentable for her required visit to the funeral home. "Lawrence and I have to look nice to represent the family, since we're the closest...blah, blah, blah, blah, *blah*."

Bo's feelings of pity for his friend, Buddy, had multiplied exponentially with every syllable the new self-appointed – and let us not forget delusional and narcissistic – queen of the house uttered. After she retired to attend to her toilette, Bo gave his best friend a soulful stare akin to a look one might give a recently diagnosed terminally ill pony. "I gotta tell you, man," he said, "I'm so broke up about all this, and not only about your pop, about everything that's gone on your whole miserable life. Seems like you are jinxed, like it was just yesterday my family was doing this same casserole delivery thing when your mom and dad got hit by that eighteen-wheeler, and then your grandma dying so sudden like she did, and now your pop?" He paused and congratulated himself on his ability to empathize with a friend with such sensitivity. He wouldn't have bet he had it in him to empathize so well, or that it would feel so good to pour it on. Pleased with himself, he began to empathize some more. "Here you are alone with not one soul left around you who's got a grain of sense, and me with good family scattered all over Charleston. Doesn't seem fair."

Buddy walked over and sat down in his grandfather's favorite piazza rocking chair. He picked up Bedon's pipe from the side table and examined its bowl inside and out, giving it the sniff test its perfect seasoning deserved. "I'll be all right," he said to the pipe bowl, and then to Bo, "I've still got Aunt Pauline and Uncle Lawrence."

Bo dropped his chin so far it almost touched the second button on his forest green golf shirt, the one with the Wildlife Exposition emblem emblazoned on the front pocket. "Dude...don't make me feel worse about this than I already do."

Buddy put the pipe stem in his mouth in imitation of his grandfather. "And I've got Caroline. I guess I've got her."

Bo abandoned his sensitivity act and returned to his normal self. "Caroline ain't family, man. A woman ain't family 'til you marry her. Even your pop knew that."

In addition to pretending to smoke his pop's pipe, Buddy lifted his right foot and rested his ankle upon his left knee exactly as he'd seen his grandfather do a million times. He wasn't listening to Bo, only hearing him. "You know," he said to the fresh air blowing off the harbor, "all this time since Grandma Hildie died, I thought I was taking care of him, but now I know it was him taking care of me, ever since I was a kid, right up to the end."

Bo looked all around the piazza and up and down the sidewalk to see if anyone was in earshot before asking his next insensitive question. "Listen here, Buddy. I've been thinking about something. What're you gonna do about your pop's hot new widow?"

Bud put the pipe down. "It wasn't a real wedding. No paperwork. Pop just wanted to make some kind of grand gesture in his old age. Go out in a small blaze of glory, so to speak. In his mind, it was a statement of principle, of doing the right thing no matter what other people thought. I didn't quite get it, but he did, and that's all that matters."

"What's to get?" Bo said. "He wanted to marry the girl, because he loved the girl."

"I told you it wasn't a real wedding. He knew it wasn't, and so did she. I don't know why he put her through it. She was dragging her feet the whole way. Looked like she might pass out the day-of."

Bo shuffled over and sat down in the rocker next to Buddy's. His pal was beginning to look uncomfortable in his grandfather's old chair. "Man," Bo said, "for a guy smart enough to go to law school, you sure are dumb. Your pop was the last gentleman left South of Broad Street. The term Old Charlestonian don't mean nothin' no more. Most people who live down here these days are new money from up north somewhere."

"I suppose. But what does all that have to do with her? When she realized Pop wasn't going to make it out of the hospital, she bolted like a busted car thief."

"I so hate she left. Who's everybody gonna talk about now?"

"Don't worry. She's not out of the picture. Pop meant it when he said he wanted her to be taken care of after he was gone. I'll have to track her down pretty soon."

Bo made a surprised face as bogus as any Pauline had the talent to conjure up. "Oh..." he said, not astonished, "...*the will.*"

Buddy gave him a dirty look. "It's not like that. She's not like that."

"Man, she is the most *like that* of anybody I've ever run up on."

"You don't know her. You're jealous."

"Ah…ha, ha. Got her hooks into you, too. Somebody needs to tell Caroline to stop working on her guest list."

"No-o-o. My dealings with her won't be that big a deal. I'll cruise the project in a couple of weeks to find her or get hold of her schedule at Trident Tech some way."

Bo skipped down the piazza steps to take his leave. His blinded pal was talking like an idiot in broad daylight, and he, Bo, did not want to be a witness to such an embarrassing event. "Take my word for it," he said as he departed. "You won't have to go on a search. She'll show up back here soon enough." He stopped when he got to the front gate and turned back to give Buddy a forgotten message. "Oh yeah, man. I meant to tell you, all the gals in my family said for you to call if you need anything. Although, I'm afraid they'd be mighty shocked if you told'em what it sounds to me like you really need."

# 75.

## How Will Larissa Pay for School Now?

Alone in the carriage house in the middle of the night, Larissa rummaged through the drawers of the small chest, finding nothing but a wad of dollar store t-shirts, a raggedy ball of sad-sack undies, and two pairs of threadbare jeans. Buddy stepped into the room from the outside door without her hearing him. "Hello," he said. "What are you looking for?"

The startled girl slammed the third drawer shut, catching her pinkie finger in the process. "Owwwww... Ouch, ouch, ouch," she said as red dots of pain bounced around in her parietal lobe. "Why did you scare me like that? You did it on purpose. Owwww..." She put her little finger into her mouth and squinted.

Buddy appeared less than sympathetic about her calamity. "Could it be you were looking for this?" he said, holding up an envelope with her name on it.

Slipping the hand with the throbbing finger into her jeans pocket, she said to the smooth intruder, "Bedon knew it would soon be time for the semester to start. I thought maybe... I shouldn't have come back here, him just dying and all. I don't know why I came back. If only I could see him, talk to him." She winced from a much more jagged pain than the one in her pinched finger.

Buddy tossed the envelope onto the daybed. "I found it yesterday on his bedside table, stuck in his *Bible*. It's yours, got your name on it. Cold cash for whatever you want, a trip to the mall, a donation to United Fund."

"Keep it. I'll figure out school another way. Stay out a semester maybe, save up for the next one. I wish I hadn't come back."

Puzzled, Bud retrieved the envelope from the bed and walked close enough to give it to her hand to hand. "Don't be stupid. He wanted you to have it. It'd be an insult if you refused his help, just because you don't like me."

She took it. She didn't want to, but she couldn't help herself. Classes were expensive. But Bedon would never have humiliated her by giving her money in person like this. He always left it for her to find. "This'll be it," she said, folding the envelope and stuffing it into her pocket, gingerly protecting her injured finger. "No more. I promise."

"You didn't know Pop as well as you thought you did. He meant for you to finish your schooling and then some. He was a good Samaritan, and you were his project. I know. I was another one of his projects."

"No, you were his grandson, which is different. But I have to say, prep man, you didn't know him as well as you thought you did. I could tell you some stuff that would make your straight blond hair go frizzy." She waited a beat before adding, "Really, this will be more than enough. I'll apply for financial aid from now on. And...I'm sorry everything got so messed up." She placed her throbbing pinkie in the palm of her other hand and closed her warm fingers around it. "Well, see ya."

With that, she attempted to go far around Buddy as she started for the door. But he, for reasons beyond reason, stepped in front of her and blocked her way. Before she could stop him, he pulled her close by her shoulders and kissed her aggressively. She struggled out of his grasp and slapped him hard with her uninjured hand.

"You're *nothing* like Bedon," she said. "*Nothing.*" Then she ran out the door, leaving Bud alone to ponder the fact that his ability to mimic his pop's mannerisms with pipe and posture could never turn him into the actual man.

# 76.
## Law Student Goes Looking for Larissa

Buddy, looking sharp in a navy sport coat and a blue-and-gold-striped Ben Silver tie, sat in his car in the parking lot of Trident Tech's Nursing Division, watching and waiting. For two hours, he'd been witness to an unending parade of students of every creed and nationality coming and going at their leisure, but he'd not been witness to the presence of the specific student whom he was seeking.

He checked the interior pocket of his jacket for the hundredth time, feeling for the slick, sturdy paper stock of the traditional blue legal folder that he was going to so much trouble to deliver in person. On spying the student he'd been watching for, whom he almost missed when she walked by his car at a smart clip, he snatched the folder free and let himself out of the Dodge Charger without keeping a low profile. She couldn't help but notice his bravado and changed her direction from east to west in a motion so smooth she looked like a roller derby jammer who'd left her starred helmet at home.

It was the neatest, cleanest one-eighty Buddy had ever witnessed. But Larissa's nimbleness did not dissuade him from catching up with her, no matter what direction she tore off in. He jog-trotted behind her, his statusy necktie whipping back over his shoulder. Waving the blue folder in the air like it might be a subpoena, he gave no thought to the nut case he resembled. Larissa made the mistake of glancing back at him, the reason she tripped on her own shoe lace and landed face down in the scraggly grass beside the gravel path. Buddy came speeding up with the intent of helping her get to her feet. Never mind she was crawling away from him as fast as she could on her hands and knees to the delight of a gathering audience.

"Stop," Bud said. "Look at all these people laughing at us."

And though she did sneak a quick peek at all the people laughing, she continued crab-crawling away from him with her ba-donk-a-donk high in the air, presenting the perfect view of her perfect backside.

"Hey," Buddy said, struggling to haul her up from all fours. "I came over here to apologize to you about the stunt I pulled in the carriage house last night. I was out of line, and it won't happen again. I'm sorry. My own life being in a shambles doesn't give me license to..."

"To what?" she said. "Take advantage of me?"

Buddy turned to address the already bored audience, thanking its members collectively for stopping by to help, assuring them he hoped if any one of their assembly ever took a nose dive on a campus walkway, a few good souls as kind as they would happen along and give him or her a hand up. Larissa was unimpressed by the eloquence of Bud's speech, but thankful he was willing to confront the mob of five doing the staring, one of whom was a full professor in the English department who ought to have known better.

She herself decided on delivering an eloquent threat instead of an eloquent speech, toward Buddy, not the mob. "Get away from me," she said, "before I put in a call on one of those security phones they've got screwed to every other lamp post on this campus."

At that, the small crowd of five dispersed with neutrino speed. Nothing of its members remained, only a string of vaguely humanoid cut-out spaces in the atmosphere where living, breathing people had been standing not a second before.

Relieved the onlookers had vanished, Buddy pulled Larissa to a standing position against her will, and while she was brushing grass cuttings off her clothing, said to her in what was his idea of officious lawyer-speak, "I'll go, for now, but you're named in Pop's will, and I'm the executor, which means it's my job to make sure you know what's up."

She met his eyes straight on and spoke with the defiance of the project princess she essentially still was. "I don't want anything to do with that upper-class bunk. You've done your upper-class duty. Now leave me alone."

Again, Buddy tried to hand her the blue folder, and again she refused it. He shook the file in her face. "You have to take it," he said. "It's a legal thing for your own good."

With a satisfying swat, she slapped the folder away and said, "I'll tell you what's a legal thing for my own good. The red phone on that pole over there is a legal thing for my own good. Are you leaving now, or do I have to make another scene worse than the other scene? And don't forget, I'm a student here, and you're not."

"Okay, I'll leave, but not for good. I'm going to the student union to sit and wait 'til you show up. And if you call the campus cops on me there, well, I've gotten used to dealing with the blue wall over the last few weeks."

She smirked. "If you go to the student union in that coat and tie and hang around more than five minutes, I won't have to call security. Somebody else will."

Buddy stuffed the folder back into his jacket pocket. He held up both hands and sang a sing-song out of tune, "I'm cruising on over to the student hangout now to sit around looking like a loser parent trying to be cool with his two-dollar cuppa-ja-moke."

"Uh...prepster," she said and pointed in the opposite direction. "Student union's that way."

Bud saluted, course corrected, waved, then walked forward, backward, sideways, and every other way to keep an eye on her as long as he could while departing. "See me?" he said, still singsonging. "I'm walking...walking away."

Larissa couldn't keep her sweet lips from curving into a half-smile as she watched the young man, whose every physical feature and mannerism made her recall Bedon's every physical feature and mannerism. Except for the dorkiness. Buddy had a double helping of that, whereas Bedon had not a whiff. She contemplated if, in addition to everything else he'd done for her, Bedon would have been willing to at least act like a dork for her sake the way his grandson was doing right now, in public, on a community college campus where dorkism was an unforgiveable sin. He would, she thought. He threw a fake wedding for me, didn't he? I wish I could see him one more time. I never did tell him how much I loved him, not while he was alive anyway. Then, those odd tears that didn't alter her face except for the change in her complexion from tawny to crimson began to flow again. In an effort to quell them, she bit the blood out of her lower lip. But quell them she could not.

# 77.

# *Bud's Marathon Wait*

Self-conscious and uncomfortable, Buddy found himself sitting at an outdoor table of the student union drinking coffee from a "green" cup and waiting. His attire elicited two or three hate stares from boys in dreadlocks and Birkenstocks and two or three smiles from flirty girls in clingy dresses. After the first hour, he shed his coat, loosened his tie, and unbuttoned the top button of his shirt, making the Birkenstock boys more hostile and the flirty girls more come-hither. Bud scratched his head over this development, but never figured out what prompted it, not that he cared. By then his self-consciousness had taken a back seat to the pain in his rear caused by sitting too long in iron outdoor chairs.

By the time his third hour of waiting was inching closer to its painful end, Bud had become immune to all brands of looks-and-stares-and-glares from every type of student and other folk in the area. He sat in miserable repose with his feet propped high on a stone picnic table, uncaring that the bottoms of both his Weejuns had holes in them the size of fifty-cent pieces. Those embarrassing holes made his compatriots at the next stone table, the one with fewer pigeon droppings on it than his own, seem to like him more.

Bud ignored his friendly new neighbors and concentrated on the sports section of a two-day-old *Charleston Post and Courier*. Never mind he'd already read it three times, really four, counting the one on the morning it first came out. Of particular interest was an article on

297

page 4F justifying why it made sense for college football coaches in South Carolina to get paid three times more than doctors and lawyers and pastors. Bud wondered if his grandfather had known about this shocking state of affairs in his home state. Weary and bored, he refolded the paper and laid it among the many used green coffee cups that had stacked up on his table. There were so many of them – all discarded by one guy, Buddy himself – their green value was coming into question.

A quarter of the way into his fourth hour, Buddy figured out an ingenious way of taking a nap by balancing his backside in one iron chair, locking his arms over his chest, and propping his big feet in the seat of another iron chair. How he could achieve sleep after downing so much coffee was a curious thing, but achieve it he did.

This was when Larissa walked up. She stopped and studied his disordered state with frank horror – mussed hair, coffee stained tie and shirt, bad breath that could be detected from a surprising distance, and were those holes clear through to his socks in the bottoms of both preppy shoes?

She stepped closer and touched Bud's right shoulder. As he grumbled awake, his zoo-animal breath whooshed out, making Larissa step back. She chose not to hurt his feelings by commenting on his halitosis, since it appeared he had bigger problems.

She spoke to him in a condescending tone in exact imitation of the biology instructor whose class she'd just left. (What a pompous know-it-all *he* was.) "Please, tell me, Mr. Calhoun, you haven't been sitting here four hours straight."

Bud got up and stretched, which he was aware of doing, and stunk broadly, which he was unaware of doing. "No, I haven't been sitting here for four hours straight. I walked around some."

She sighed in dismay. "Come this way, Mr. Calhoun. I know where there're some park benches down by the duck pond. You're going to get arrested if you stay here one more minute."

# 78.

## A Sweeter Kiss

Larissa was right about the park benches and the pond with ducks, six Pekin whites, serene and aloof as they glided along the water's edge trolling for shoots of ribbon grass and black-back swimmers – those wiggly little critters more delectable if they remained alive and kicking on their slide down the gullet.

Buddy and Larissa sat beside each other on a stone bench no more forgiving than the iron chairs, watching the domestic bliss enjoyed by the ducks. Buddy, yielding to a masochistic tendency he'd been experiencing of late, took another shot at delivering the folder. Without removing his gaze from the Pekin whites, he thrust the shiny blue file before his lovely bench companion. Skating fast over his words to get them out before she could react, he spluttered, "I-have-to-give-you-this-by-law."

But he wasn't fast enough. She swatted the folder away again, this time with a more dramatic thwap. "Look, Calhoun, if you don't stop putting that thing up in my face, I'm going to scream bloody murder down here, and Duckville will never be the same."

Fearful of another scene and of attracting another audience, Bud made the dilapidated folder disappear again into the sweaty darkness of his jacket pocket. "You don't have to get so bent out," he said. "Sorry for bringing it up. Sorry for kissing you. Sorry for...breathing your air."

He studied the placid scene before him. Calm pond, if smelly. Calm ducks, if greedy. "I don't know exactly how Pop did it, but he made me feel like I'm supposed to pick up where he left off when it comes to looking out for you."

"I'm not sorry," she said.

He turned to enjoy her profile. "Not sorry for which thing?"

She faced him and enjoyed him enjoying her. "That you kissed me."

They shared a moment in dreamland, but she cut it short by returning to the muddy bank of the pond. Taking off the diamond ring her groom had given her, she held it out to Buddy. "I shouldn't be wearing this now. That playlike wedding was to satisfy Bedon. Not to say I didn't appreciate everything, but it's over."

Bud grinned and held up the stop-talking-nonsense flat of his left palm. "If you don't put that thing away, I'm going to scream bloody murder down here, and Duckville will never be the same."

She smiled, puzzled. "But wouldn't your girlfriend want it?"

"Caroline? Caroline wants a boulder, not a rock, although she did tell me carbon spots weren't a deal breaker, or pesky little flaws like occlusions. *E-normous* is what she's after."

Larissa had no idea what he meant by carbon spots or occlu-somethings. She closed one eye and took a deep look inside her own flawless diamond. Seeing nothing but the glittering universe flashing inside it, she shrugged one shoulder and started to put the ring back on her finger, then reconsidered and slipped it deep into her jeans pocket to keep company with a clump of lint. Then, drilling a hole clean through Buddy's heart with a single glance, she said in a catty tone, "Your girlfriend wouldn't like it if she knew you kissed me, the way you kissed me."

He reached over and kissed her again, this time sweetly, tenderly, minus the purple passion of the time before. "As long as I'm in trouble, I may as well get the goody out of it," he said when he came up for air. And since she didn't slap him again, he tried his luck once more. But she dodged and pulled away. "Hey...just because I grew up in the project doesn't mean I'm easy."

"I don't think you're easy. I think you're fine. Super fine."

Larissa looked down at her hands resting in her lap. In the afternoon light, Bud became aware of how heartbreakingly dark her lashes were against her cheeks. He saw, also, a thread-thin scar on her face that he hadn't noticed before. Larissa made eye contact with him another brief moment before rising and walking away. And though the Pekins quacked her a cheerful good-bye from their duck Heaven, and the late afternoon breeze whistled her a happy farewell from among the dwarf bamboo canes, she would not allow herself to dwell upon a paradise she felt sure would never be her own.

# 79.
# Good-bye to Bedon, Hello to Bud

Larissa, on foot, guided her Fendi Abici along the asphalt bike path that wound around the perimeter of Quiet Meadows Cemetery. It was high noon and hot, too hot for the regular parade of exercise addicts to be out and about, those conscientious folks who walked the bike path a couple of hours every day in hopes of staving off permanent residence in the cemetery proper. Their swelling ranks had driven to distraction the graveyard's diligent battalion of groundsmen.

Larissa forsook the path when she figured out it was lunch time for the grounds crew. She hunched over and skulked like a guilty thing across a hallowed grassy stretch that was off limits to walkers, but a shortcut to Bedon's grave site. Stopping every step or two to take a look at the engravings upon markers along the way, she read the names and thought about the birth and death dates. How far removed those dates seemed from her own life, with the exception of the set of dates on Bedon's stone, which didn't seem far removed at all, in fact, still had the power to twist her heart into a knot.

Out of her backpack she took a droopy bunch of day lilies she had scrounged from a clearance bucket at BI-LO and laid them between the two headstones on Hildie and Bedon's plot. It took only a moment to scan the engraved remembrances on both stones: Hilda Manchester Calhoun - loving wife, mother, and grandmother; Dr. Bedon Lautrec Calhoun, Sr. – loving husband, father, and grandfather.

Distracted by leaf debris inside the low shale wall around the plot, Larissa dropped to her knees and began clearing it away. Buddy walked up behind her, his footsteps quiet in the well-tended cushion of Zoysia grass, pride of the Quiet Meadows' groundsmen, who took seriously their responsibility of overseeing a service described to Buddy by the cemetery owners as Perpetual Care, all for a mere twenty-five dollars a month or an initial lump sum payment of twenty-five hundred. Buddy had chosen the pay-as-you-go plan until he could find time to sort out everything else that needed sorting, especially the disbursement to Lawrence and Pauline whatever they were going "to get" from Pop's will. Since Bedon's demise, Buddy had come to understand that Great Uncle Lawrence and Great Aunt Pauline were already in need of perpetual care, though they were both still very much alive.

Larissa knew Buddy had appeared behind her, but she kept working at her debris-clearing project without acknowledging him. Therefore, he acknowledged her. "Hello," he said. "Hope I didn't scare you like I did in the carriage house the other night. Is this the first time you've been out here?"

She spied a thriving mass of tall weeds and began pulling at them. He watched her work for a second before raising his eyes to look around at the peaceful landscape. "Beautiful place" he said. "So quiet. How did you know...?"

The kneeling girl decided to give up trying to ignore her stalker, since she knew he had no intention of going away. "The day of the funeral," she said, her voice melancholy, "I followed the line of cars to the church on my bike. Didn't go inside for the service, though. Waited around on the street 'til it was over, then followed everyone and watched what went on from behind those palmetto trees up there. Don't know why. I couldn't hear a thing y'all were saying."

Buddy nodded. "Some of the people who came asked where you were, the nicer ones anyway. Miss Posey Montegue told me it made her sad you stayed away. But she was sad about everything that day. Said she hated losing Pop and was beginning to feel like she was outliving everybody worth a dang in the whole town."

Bud squatted down beside Larissa and began helping her pull weeds as he talked. "Miss Posey surprised me with all the kind things she had to say about Pop that day, particularly how glad she was he finally broke out of the awful grieving period he went through after Grandma Hildie died and found someone like you to make him happy. Pop liked you so much, Larissa...loved you in some screwball way."

She rocked back on her haunches in the grass and studied the side of Buddy's face. "Screwball way?" she said, her eyes shining with tears. "You keep insulting me with things you say, and don't even seem to know you're doing it."

"I'm sorry. What I'm trying to do is ask you to eat lunch with me, so we can sit and talk like normal people."

"I don't want to."

"Eat lunch, or sit and talk like normal people?"

"Neither one." She sniffed and went back to her weeding, then said offhand, "Who's Miss Posey?"

"A friend of the family. A neighbor. She was the one at the wedding with the sunflower sticking straight up on her hat like a CAUTION sign."

"Ohhh...yeah. I remember her. Not long before Bedon died, she came over to the house for a visit and told him all about how she was relieved he'd come to his senses. I didn't know what she meant. And she's got that yappy little dog she walks every night. I used to see her sometimes when... Yeah, Miss Posey."

Taking advantage of Larissa's change in mood, Buddy pressed her again about lunch. "Come on. Aren't you hungry? It's almost one."

She stood up and brushed leaf bits from the knees of her jeans. "Okay, but only if you promise not to drag that blue folder out again."

"I won't, but I do want to take you somewhere nice downtown, somewhere you couldn't ordinarily afford."

"There you go again, saying things."

"There I go again, having to say I'm sorry." He flipped the kickstand up on the Fendi and pushed it along as they walked together down the grassy slope toward the bike path. To his pouty companion, he pointed out, "You've got to stop being so sensitive."

"Maybe I will," she replied, "when you stop being so *insensitive*."

# 80.
# Caroline Flies Mad

Buddy picked at the Cobb salad fresh off Magnolia Restaurant's midday menu, while Larissa demolished a burger made delicious beyond belief by extra bacon, blue cheese crumbles, and a massive side order of sweet potato fries. She had already made a respectable dent in the appetizer of homemade Irish potato chips with blue-crab dip still tantalizing her from the center of the table. Bud, astonished someone so slender could get her mouth around a burger that large, watched in amazement as she ate. Taking advantage of the fact she was distracted, he summoned the courage to speak to her frankly. "Listen here, Larissa. I've been thinking about something idiotic. Some people might say it was, anyway. But when you look at it from Pop's point of view, it makes sense. Don't freak out when I tell you, all right? Think about it a minute."

She nodded and blinked assent, but did not slow down on her frontal attack upon the burger bigger than she. Buddy knew this fast-talking specimen of a gal wouldn't remain silent for long, so he said quickly and with conviction, "You know, Larissa...Pop had something special going on in his life, something he lived out in his everyday dealings with people. He...uhh...always tried to do the right thing, no matter what. And I've decided to follow his lead. I'm asking you to marry me, straight up. That way I can finish what he started and take care of you in the right way from now on. What do you say?"

She took another huge bite of charbroiled beef, and, ignoring the au jus running down her chin, said as if pleased, "Great...if we can eat lunch here every day."

"Be serious. What do you really think?"

"I am being serious. This is the best cheeseburger I ever put in my mouth, better than Hardee's' and McDonald's put together. And I didn't know you could get potato chips anywhere except out of a bag. Those things are off the chain."

"You'd marry me for a lifetime supply of cheeseburgers and hand-cut, deep-fried potato chips?"

She chased the bite of juicy beef with a clover-shaped, greasy-greasy chip. "Come on, prep boy. You don't want to marry me. You've got it in your head I was Bedon's special project, and you want to be like him when you grow up, and so on and so on..."

"What's wrong with wanting to do the right thing?"

"I have issues in my life is what's wrong with it, issues like on TV. Stuff in my past you could never handle, not if you lived to be a hundred years old."

"What past could you possibly have? You aren't twenty-one yet."

I'm twenty-five, and I do so have a past, big junk that would make a guy like you go blind and deaf. But my past isn't the problem at the moment. Caroline is. She just walked in, and she doesn't look happy."

Bud jerked around in his chair and leveled his eyes on the entrance to the restaurant, where he was met with a stinging stare from the monstrously miffed Caroline. She was standing more rigid than postmortem in the entryway, exactly like the manikin in Bo's description, while a bevy of her clique girlfriends hip-wiggled around their clique queen like hula girls in silky dresses, the hues of which covered the spectrum of God's rainbow, with a few never-before-seen techno colors from outer space thrown in for general interest.

Unexpectedly, Caroline turned animate. Buddy stood up when he realized her intention was to hoof it in record breaking time straight to his and Larissa's table. His tablemate didn't care enough about Caroline's dangerous approach to stand and assume a defensive posture. She remained seated, took another bite of her burger, and licked the mingling, dripping, delicious ketchup-mayo-and-mustard mixture off each one of her fingers. She didn't even bother to look up when her female foe appeared tableside and struck a pose.

Caroline now ruled the room in all her Southern belle glory, skinny except in the chest area, her backbone straight as a mast, her knockers jacked up to a height so unattainable that it could never have been achieved without the support of a seriously engineered Spanks undergarment.

Buddy was terrified, mortified; Larissa was indifferent. Caroline tried to impale the hated Larissa with a look, but gave up when she found it was impossible to impale someone whose full attention was on her own lunch plate. So she turned and impaled Buddy, instead. At the squirming young man, she spat, "What do you think you're doing, Buddy Calhoun? Bringing her out in public like this. How dare you?"

Buddy Calhoun held out both hands and said, "It's lunch...don't get so mad."

"Oh, I'm not *getting* mad, you conceited worm. I'm *already* mad. I've had it with you humiliating me." She broke her Rockette pose, picked up Buddy's salad plate that was dripping with his favorite Gorganzola cheese dressing, and ground it with wicked pleasure into the front of his sky-blue shirt. But what she expected to happen next...didn't. What she expected was to have the satisfaction of flouncing back in the direction from which she had come and make a dramatic exit with her handmaidens clicking along behind her in their stilettos. But what actually happened was far more interesting, particularly to the other patrons of Magnolia's. It consisted of Larissa springing out of her chair and snatching Caroline backward by her greenish-blond hair. "You can't treat him like that," she said to the Southern belle in reference to the gorgonzola-dressed Buddy. "He's not your boyfriend anymore. He's mine."

The other diners enjoyed the show immensely: Larissa pulling Caroline's hair hard enough to make her fall backward to the floor; Buddy struggling in vain to help her up; the maitre d' zooming through the air with the speed and accuracy of a military drone programmed to shoot down any vile weed that dared raise its ugly head in the utopia of Magnolia's main dining room. "What is the problem here?" the maitre d' enunciated fast and clear like a radio pitch man. "You'll have to take whatever this is about outside. *Out... side*, I say."

Larissa agreed with the maitre d'. "Yeah...she doesn't know how to act in a nice place." This all while Caroline and Buddy continued engaging in a kind of wrestling match on the floor as Knight Gorganzola tried in vain to rescue Lady Caroline, whose bought-and-paid-for boobies were in danger of popping out of the top of her cling-thing dress due to the strain put upon them when their owner had landed with a thlunk on the floor after being attacked by a *gen-u-ine* project princess. The maitre d', seeing the possibility of indecent exposure of a sort that had never before occurred in the history of "refined" Magnolia's, joined Buddy in his effort to help Caroline regain her dignity. While the two men were thus engaged, Larissa smiled a reassuring smile at the audience/patrons in accidental attendance at this theater-in-the-round performance. Then she wrapped up the rest of her cheeseburger in a cloth napkin and stuffed it into her red-sequinned purse.

Meanwhile, as the other three performers continued scrambling on the floor (the first and second scramblers being Caroline and Bud, and the third scrambler being the outraged maitre d'), Buddy somehow managed to get a grip on one of the Southern belle's arms (though it was slippery with wayward gorgonzola), and the maitre d' a grip on her other arm (though it was slippery with bright red tomato pulp). Larissa stood up from the table then and gazed at the performers with surprising calmness right before leaning over sideways to get face-to-face with Buddy. "Don't worry about me," she assured him. "I'll be waiting for you in the car." After which she took her leave with the poise of Catherine Mountbatten-Windsor, the famed Duchess of Cambridge and Stepford wife of Harry's brother, William. The other patrons followed the blue-jeaned baby doll with their eyes as she crossed the expanse of the restaurant, half expecting her to honor them with a strictly-wrist-action, screwing-the-top-off-a-mayonnaise-jar, British royal wave.

# 81.

## Larissa Introduces Daniel's Law to the Law Student

Buddy, angry and apparently oblivious he might get arrested again, raced his Super Bee like a Nascar driver along the washout road on Folly Beach. Larissa tightened her seat belt and scrunched down low in the passenger seat. "Slow down," she yelled. "Cops are gonna stop us."

"I am so *over* being threatened by cops."

"Well, I'm not. Let me out."

Bud yanked the Super Bee's right wheels onto the sandy shoulder of the road and reached over his distressed passenger's lap. Opening the door and shoving it back hard against its hinges, he said to the frightened girl, "Un-ass the vehicle. I've had all I can stand of you for one day."

On her way out, Larissa fell to her knees in the white sand of the shoulder. Leaving the car door open, she crawled out of Buddy's reach, the second time within days that she'd found herself crab-crawling away from him, then got up and began a comic march along the roadside, sequinned purse held tight against her small, though real bosom. Buddy let the car creep along beside her with its passenger door hanging open. "Okay, okay," he said, "you've made your point. You're furious; I'm an idiot. Now get back in. It's dangerous out there with all those cars flying back and forth."

"Yours is the only car out here, prepster. And you can't make me get back in."

"Come on, Larissa. You're the one who didn't want the cops to pick us up. Get in before somebody in one of those houses across the road calls the island cop, the same guy who moonlights as bartender at the Sand Dollar Club on Center Street every other Saturday night."

Larissa marched on. Buddy apologized again. How many apologies did that make since he'd known her? Six? Seven? Eight? "All right," he said. "I had no business spouting off like that. I *do* care about getting locked up."

Larissa stopped walking and took an apprehensive look along the row of houses overlooking the street and ocean. Who knew what tattle-tale lurked behind the shutters of any one of them? Buddy allowed the Super Bee to ease to a stop, so she could climb back inside safely. He laughed when she locked her door and slumped against it like a sulking teenager.

"Well, doll face, are we getting married or not?" he said in a carefree voice that let her know he was no longer concerned about how she might react. "Caroline has given me the official boot."

Although her driver's improved attitude rubbed some ointment into Larissa's stinging feelings, she retained a tone. "I told you, I can't," she said. "There's stuff I've done..."

"What could you possibly have done at your age? You act like you killed somebody or something."

"I did."

"Did what?"

"Killed somebody. And worse than that, I had a baby boy and put him under Daniel's Law protection. Anything else you want to know?"

Buddy wheeled back onto the shoulder and cut the engine. He stared at his young passenger, whose face was now contorted in pain. Confused, he looked away from her and fixed his eyes on the parking fee-box near the boardwalk to the beach. He didn't know what to say. He didn't know what to ask. When neither the fee-box nor the steering wheel he was gripping too tightly volunteered any advice on how to go forward, he turned back to the tearful Larissa. "What...is Daniel's Law? I don't..."

She sniffed, the one and only sign tears had begun tracking down her cheeks. "I can't believe you don't know about something that important legally. You're supposed to be the law student, not me."

# 82.

# Seventeen?!

$\mathcal{B}$uddy and Larissa sat on the beach at the washout while she told him her whole story. He listened without interrupting, without asking a single question. When she'd finished explaining what had really happened the night of the shooting, she punctuated the ending with her famed, one-shouldered shrug. Bud pulled his knees up and wrapped his arms around his shins. He looked out to sea and thought about all she had said, then released his knees and wrapped both arms around Larissa's shoulders. As she rested her head against his chest, he intoned quietly, "I wish I could be half the man Pop was."

To which she responded deadpan, "I wish you could, too. But all that stuff I just told you was about me, not him. Yeah, he took care of me through everything, but I was the one going down the toilet without a life raft." She shivered as a hard chill took over her whole body. "I'm cold," she said. "Let's go."

Bud took a last look over the top of her head at the immutable Atlantic Ocean. "I'm glad to be named after him," he said. "Bedon Lautrec Calhoun, Jr. My mother told me they didn't know quite how to handle it, since he was my grandfather and not my father...the junior part, I mean."

Larissa wriggled out of his arms, irritated that he seemed to have no interest in the fact she was freezing. "And who do you think cares about that? I cannot believe how full of horse feathers all you uppity-ups are." (Clearly, Bedon's sophisticated use of language was still ringing in her ears.) "Didn't you hear me when I said I was turning into a popsickle out here? Give me the keys. I want to get back in the car."

Bud took his coat off and draped it over her shoulders. "You're right. It's time to go...back to your apartment to pick up a few things."

"No way. Mom and..."

"Your birth certificate and social security card."

Larissa questioned him with her eyes. He responded matter-of-fact. "When you look as young as you do, they make you prove your age to get a marriage license even in North Charleston. And we both have to show our social security cards."

Buddy sat waiting in his muscle car on the curb of Logan Street outside Larissa's apartment. As nervous as a race horse anxious to break out of the shoot, he tapped the steering wheel with both thumbs without realizing he was doing it. After forever, she emerged from the brick building with a large brown envelope tucked under her arm. Her mother followed her out onto their tiny stoop, looking wistful as her only daughter, her only child, ran to get into a parked car with a young man she said she was going to marry. Buddy allowed the anxious mother to meet his eyes with her own. He nodded to her, slightly. She nodded back, slightly.

Larissa, unaware of the drama playing out between Buddy and her mother – the mother whom she had defended to Bedon not so very long ago (*"She's good, perfect. No one could ask for a better mother. Not unfit like those DSS case workers say."*) – jumped into her new fiance's car and handed him the envelope containing the absolute truth about her age. He pulled out a jumble of papers, studied the top sheet, counted on his fingers, and looked, incredulously, at Larissa.

"Seventeen?" he said.

"Mom told me eighteen is the legal age to get married in South Carolina. She knows, 'cause she looked it up when she was almost gonna marry one of her teenage boyfriends. That was a long time ago when she was a cougar. Anyway, my birthday's next week, and I'll be eighteen. See right there?"

She pointed to a line on the paper. Buddy shut his eyes, thinking. "Let's see. I was still a junior in high school when I was eighteen. They held me back twice in kindergarten, the reason I was always two years behind."

Larissa laughed out loud and said, "I dropped out of high school a year early, 'cause I was so smart, and who knows how many years I skipped in elementary school? Got my GED the summer after I dropped out and went into the nursing program at Trident Tech. My guidance counselor arranged it all. You don't have to have a high school diploma to go to college, just the right credits. The counselor told me."

"I didn't know that."

"It's true," she said, grinning her cute grin. Buddy stuffed the sheaf of papers back into the envelope, handed it to Larissa, and cranked the car, the single skill he possessed that she didn't, or he hoped she didn't. It would be nice to have one ability left all to himself.

As he backed out of the parking place, and as they both waved their last farewells to her "good, perfect" mother before driving away for good, Buddy said to his bride-to-be, "I'm sure you'll be a college professor by the time you're twenty-one."

"Probably," she responded.

"I was kidding, brainiac."

"I know you were, prepster...but I wasn't."

# 83.

# Bo Gives Buddy Advice; Buddy Doesn't Take It

Bud paced back and forth beside the gazebo in White Point Garden, his smart phone at his ear. "Bo?" he yelled. "Is that you? What's all the racket?"

Bo stood in his kitchen talking to Bud on his landline, while wifey, Susannah May Eleanor, fed Baby Bo in his high chair. Dodging her child's jelly paws, wifey/mom spooned orange mishmash from a baby food jar into his baby-bird mouth. The other three children she had produced with Bo, all girls, ran around the kitchen in Super Woman headpieces yelling and beating drums. The tallest girl stuck out a foot and tripped her two younger sisters, both of whom crashed into their father's shins before plopping to the floor and setting up a howl for some adult to punish the great offender, who was now giggling at them from her stronghold under the table.

Bo never glanced down from the phone. "What're you talking about?" he hollered at Buddy. "It's quiet time over here. What's up where you are?"

Back to Buddy next to the gazebo: "I've decided to marry Larissa...for Pop's sake. I want to do something noble for a change, something out of the norm."

Bo's kitchen: "Out of the cosmic cube, you mean."

Gazebo: "Maybe. Anyhow, I called to ask your opinion on a fine point. Larissa's seventeen. I just found out. Would you marry somebody seventeen? Wasn't Susannah May Eleanor seventeen?"

Bo's kitchen: The great offender, Bo's eldest daughter, crept from under the table and pounced like a kittycat on top of her bawling siblings to remind them with a fierce tickle-fight of her birthright supremacy. The two little girls now squealed in joy instead of misery, thrilled to be attacked by a merciless monster in the form of their big sister. The brood of three tumbled about on the floor in a tight ball resembling poodle puppies at play. Bo came close to pitching forward when they rolled, en masse, into the calves of his legs. He caught himself by grabbing the refrigerator door, causing the giant white box to wobble. He steadied it with a forearm while dodging the ball of children barreling down on him again.

"Listen to me, man," he said to Buddy. "Don't marry anybody, and don't ever have kids. Shoot yourself instead. And seventeen isn't legal. Don't you remember Susanna May Eleanor and I had to wait 'til she turned eighteen, 'cause her mama and daddy wouldn't sign for her?"

Susannah May Eleanor beamed up at her romantic husband from her post at Baby Bo's high chair. He gave her the same I'd-do-it-all-over-again-honey smile that he seemed to be giving her more and more lately and meaning it less and less. She ate it up with more gusto than Baby Bo was eating up his orange goop. And the three-child fun ball on the sticky kitchen floor rolled merrily on.

Back to the gazebo: Buddy, cell phone still pressed to his ear, stopped pacing for a moment and scoped out a group of hottie little tourist girls jiggling by. They giggled in the same manner they jiggled, and Buddy nodded approval, winking at them like a pro, forgetting for a split-second that life as he knew it was hanging on a question Bo would not take seriously. "What's your take on it, man?" he shouted at Bo into the phone. "She'll be eighteen on her birthday next week, legal in this state."

Back to the Gaillard kitchen: "Oh-h-h..." Bo said. "That makes all the difference. Maturity wise, y'all might equal out."

Gazebo: "What do you think Pop would say about it?"

Gaillard kitchen: "Man...your Pop married her and was dead within twenty-four hours. He'd say think it over."

# 84.
# Marital Bliss

uddy in his rumpled navy-blue blazer and wrinkled tie, and Larissa in the same second-hand wedding attire she had worn for the first ceremony – except now she was holding a bouquet of pink plastic roses arranged artfully among white plastic baby's breath – stood side by side opposite a magistrate in a mobile home wedding chapel deep in North Charleston. *Family Feud* played on the mute setting on an ancient portable TV set complete with defunct rabbit ears covered in aluminum foil and sitting precisely in the middle of the magistrate's chrome-and-plastic dinette table, under which an aged bluetick hound napped on his flea-infested dog bed. When the magistrate pronounced the dazzled Buddy and Larissa man and wife, the hound dog jerked awaked and snapped at a fly buzzing by at the same touching moment that the groom kissed the bride.

As Bo would have said had he been present, which, mercifully, he was not, *"Congratulations, y'all!"*

# 85.

# Lucky Moonbow in the Mist

Larissa, now in a t-shirt and boxer shorts, stood in front of a mirrored dresser in Buddy's room in the Murray Boulevard house and brushed her hair like she'd seen girls do in the movies. Buddy, also in a t-shirt and boxers, lay on his bed playing idly with the Build-A-Bear that his wife seemed to like better than she liked him. He watched as Larissa brushed her hair. To complete the archetypal scene, the "watcher" and "watchee" could see each other's faces in the dresser mirror.

Larissa smiled sweetly at Buddy, then let her expression go thoughtful. Using her slender fingers as lifts to encourage her shiny curls, she said, "Do you think I'll ever fit in...this neighborhood, I mean?"

"South of Broad Street?" Bud said. "Oh, baby. Fitting in is a done concept down here. We've *di-verse* now."

His mocking manner told Larissa that Buddy's opinion was she'd never "fit it," though it mattered to her less than a Nine-Thousand-Series-Trap would matter to a mole.

She turned around to face her new hubby. "What did Bedon leave me?"

"Oh... now your real motive for marrying me comes slithering out."

"What?" she repeated.

"Not a boatload of cash, if that's what you were hoping...a little bit of green with stipulations about age and dispersal."

"Oh."

"Disappointed?" he said. "Whatever were you expecting, Anna Nicole?"

She shrugged, one-shouldered. "I don't know. I thought maybe he might leave me the carriage house."

"Nope, the carriage house goes with the main house, which he left to me, including Thomas Turner, although I did vow before that magistrate in North Charleston to share all my worldly goods with you from now on. Which means you can always sleep in the big house except on days when you're mad at me. Then you may retreat to the carriage house for no more than twenty-four hours at a time."

She thought this over, returning his warm gaze with a cool one of her own. Tilting her chin, she spoke in a tease. "I think you married me for my little bit of green, ever how much it is. And you can have that busted clock. It struck about a million times when you carried me over the threshold downstairs. What's wrong with that thing anyhow?"

"It struck twenty-four times, not a million. Pop told me to expect it to do that if I ever got married and brought my new bride back here to live. Same thing happened when he brought Grandma Hildie home." Bud threw a pillow at his bride. She ducked. "And, no, I didn't marry you for your money, sweet thang. I married you for your jogging shorts."

"Buddy, will you be serious for one minute? Is it all right with you if we keep using the carriage house as a safe house for girls having a hard time?"

"Sure, as long as it's legal. You need to make some phone calls, get connected to some organization or agency already in place."

"I will, and thanks. It was the reason I was hoping Bedon had left it to me. He and I helped another girl one time. We did it together. She was fourteen when her baby was born, and Bedon let her stay in the carriage house..."

"*Stop*," Buddy said and fell over on the bed. "I can't take hearing about any more wacky stuff Pop did behind my back." He raised his head and looked at her with weary eyes. "I'm 'tard' from getting married," he said. "Bo's right, it's like being hit by a Greyhound bus that knocks you into the path of a speeding freight train. Would you be hurt if I rested my eyes a few minutes? And do not tell me any other off-the-wall activities my late grandpaw used to be involved in. I can't handle it."

"Larissa put her forefinger to her lips and whispered, "*Shhhh.*" When certain her new husband wasn't going to open his eyes again, she slipped into the closet and switched on the light. Running her fingers over the row of Buddy's hanging clothes, she called out in a voice loud enough for him to hear her from the bed, "Are you asleep yet, Bud? I can't believe I have to put up with you the rest of my life, even if you abuse me by hugging and kissing me too much, and I have to call the police over here. I'm on first name basis with some of those guys, you know."

As a response, Buddy increased the volume of his snoring. Larissa stepped to the closet door and peeped out at him. "Bud...wake up a minute. I want to ask you something else. Can we name our first baby Bedon?"

"Huh...what?"

"I said can we name our first baby Bedon?"

"I already thought of that. Bedon, the third."

"I want to call him Bedon, not some dumb nickname like Bud or Buddy."

"Thanks for thinking so highly of the names I'm known by in this town. I think I'll call you something more formal. How about... Queen of the Nile?"

"How about Queen of the Universe?"

"You aren't even pregnant yet, and the first one could be a girl. Give it time. We'll have everything, oh my exalted Queen of the Universe, the monumental universe that is the tiny tip of the tiny peninsula known as South of Broad Street."

"And, Bud, will you get me a cell phone? I've never had one, not in my whole life."

"You can have my smart phone. I hate it."

"Does it text? I want one that texts."

"I don't know. Never tried it. I told you, I hate the thing."

"But I want to text you, Bud. And if you give your phone to me and don't buy another one for yourself, who am I gonna send messages to?"

"Okay, we'll get you a new one, and I'll keep the old one I hate. Are you happy now?"

"And can I have a pink Otter case for mine?"

"Okay, a pink Otter case. Otter cases are good, whatever Otter cases are. Are you happy *now*? I don't deserve to be badgered like this."

"Well...I would be happy...if I could get a tattoo."

"Now that right there I deserve. Have you been talking to Aunt Pauline? I suppose you want a red and white battle flag on your shoulder blade."

"No, I want a heart with a B in the middle."

"Aw, that's sweet. B for Buddy. You do love me, don't you."

"I do, but the B stands for Bedon, not Buddy, except for on Fridays. On Fridays, I'm going to let it stand for my baby boy, 'cause he was born on a Friday."

"What about me? I'm the one who'll be paying your phone bills."

"Okay, the B can stand for Buddy on Saturdays and Sundays when you're home from class all day."

"I am truly honored, Larissa. Truly honored. So where're you gonna let 'em ink your tattoo, on your hiney?"

"No, over my heart."

"That's too low. I want it to be higher up and right in front, in the middle of that sweet spot where your two little collar bones come together, so everybody in Charleston can see it when you're jogging South of Broad, especially Bo's sisters and his mama and nana."

"I love you so much, Buddy. I knew you'd let me get a heart, and you can get one, too, but yours can have an L in the middle for

Larissa, or an M, if you'd rather have it stand for Moonbow in the Mist. We can be twinsies."

"Larissa, I love you more than anything in the world, but I ain't getting a tattoo."

"Bedon would'a gotten one for me."

"I'm sure he would'a, considering what all else he did for you, but I am *not* going to do that."

"Please, please, please..."

"No."

"Plea-e-e-se, Bud...I already made our appointment in North Charleston for this afternoon."

"Well, shoot a mile and why not? What time do we have to be there?"

"Oh, Buddy, I can't wait to see you with a red heart tat with my initial in the middle right on your upper arm. Isn't Bo gonna be so jealous? And tomorrow we can talk about whether you want me to get a boob job. Who knows? You might like it..."

Buddy groaned into his pillow as Larissa disappeared into the bathroom and shut the door behind her. The new bridegroom fell asleep again quickly and began snoring extra loud, for he wasn't joking when he said he was "tard." Larissa, having given up on trying to have a reasonable conversation with him until he got some rest, walked over and opened a small box sitting on the oak linen chest. Taking a baby's receiving blanket out of the box, she unfolded it. It was the blanket the hospital nurse had given her when she'd brought her baby in on that heartbreaking night. Stroking her cheek with the soft flannel, Larissa stared at herself in the mirror above the chest. "*Bedon*..." she whispered. "It's a good name, a strong name. I wish I'd been able to give it to you." Then she tucked the blanket back inside its box and looked around for a safe place to hide it. Settling on the bottom shelf of the same linen chest, where it fit perfectly behind a stack of hand towels, she placed it there carefully and closed the cabinet door to protect her baby's memory.

Wandering back into the bedroom, she checked to see if Buddy was still sleeping and giggled when she saw how he'd propped his head up on two pillows and was puff-puffing away with Bo Bo Newsome clutched to his chest.

"Sleep, sweet prince," she said softly and smiled at her husband with the same love and warmth that always flooded her heart after daydreaming about her baby's innocent face. She crossed the room, covered Buddy with a blanket, and slipped Bo Bo Newsome out of his arms. "Sleep," she whispered again to Bud, "like my other sweet prince, my baby, and Bedon, too."

Taking Bo Bo with her, she glided to the window overlooking Murray Boulevard and stared in amazement at the expansive harbor view. For a moment she watched a three-masted schooner coursing through the harbor's calm waters. Then she held the teddy bear up to eye level and expressed her heart to him. "Do you know what, Bo Bo? I am one lucky girl. Even with Bedon gone, I still have two loves left, three if I count God, four if I count my mom, five if I count you. But those aren't the same as how I love Buddy and my baby boy."

Hugging the bear tightly, she looked out at the harbor again, at the schooner racing along as if nothing in the world mattered but sailing. "So many loves for Larissa," she said. "Lucky Moonbow in the Mist."

# 86.

# *Imagination*

All Buddy and Larissa's neighbors stared out their windows in horror at the gleaming new motor home parked on the curb of Murray Boulevard. Lawrence and Pauline's Ford Fusion rested on a car dolly that hugged up proudly to the RV's rear end, waiting in high anticipation for its thrilling tow to Central Florida. The Fusion contributed the most gaudy color combination to the tacky panorama with its blood-red flames licking along both kryptonite blue doors. In a side window of the forty-foot Winnebago Coach, Aunt Pauline had placed a professionally painted sign with a stunning background of metallic ore gold, upon which she had paid thirty dollars to have stenciled an elegant line of Charleston green script reading, *"Lazy Days Campground or Bust!"*

Larissa and Pauline stood by the lyre gate of the Calhoun house and admired both their husbands' acuity as they worked together removing four giant orange chocks from behind the mighty wheels of the moveable mansion. Buddy yanked out the last chock and stood proud and tall as he waved it in the air. "Done," he shouted to please the two gals watching from the gate, in addition to pleasing the cowardly neighbors watching in silent judgment from behind their lace window treatments, the kind you can see through from the inside, but not the outside, insuring complete privacy for any nosey homeowner who could afford them.

Bud placed the chocks in the cavernous storage compartment yawning from the motor home's belly. He checked and double-checked the lock on the bin's horizontal door to make sure Pauline wouldn't lose her card table and matching chairs that she'd need when it was her turn to play hostess for the regular ladies' Mahjong club party at Lazy Days, and Lawrence wouldn't lose his extensive collection of fishing gear Buddy had given him, reluctantly, out of Bedon's garage workshop as a remembrance of his only brother. When sure the bin lock would hold, Buddy shook his favorite great uncle's hand. "She's tight," he said, "and all yours, thanks to Pop."

Lawrence grinned so hard he added a set of new wrinkles to the geography of his dear old face. Still grinning, he said to his great nephew, "We'll be the envy of everyone at Lazy Days. I can't believe we're going to be full-timers now. Just what we always wanted."

Aunt Pauline, purse hanging on her forearm by its short strap handle in the style of great ladies all over the world, to include the Queen of England, bustled toward the passenger door of the handsome new RV that had never been slept in nor driven by another human being other than the lot salesman, and honorably obtained by Pauline and Lawrence beyond all possible accusations of deceit. Larissa, maidservant to Queen Pauline, followed her mistress foot to foot to help her up the steps of the royal vehicle and into its passenger throne. Lawrence hurried around to the driver's side and climbed into his own throne with no help, despite Buddy's sincere offer. Lawrence cranked the powerful diesel motor and listened joyfully to its rumble and roar. Pauline clapped and cheered from the passenger seat. Buddy and Larissa clapped and cheered from the sidewalk. As the great bus lumbered off with only minor lurches and grinding of gears perpetrated by Lawrence, its new owner, Aunt Pauline waved and blew kisses to Buddy and Larissa from her open window. "We'll call you when we get there," she shouted. "You know how much we love you. We're your closest relatives."

Bud and Larissa, arms around each other's waists, waved and grinned, grinned and waved, over and over. Said Buddy to his new wife as the RV wobbled around the curve that bounded the grounds of the Coast Guard Station, "It won't be long before they'll be back. You know that, right?"

"Oh, yeah. I give it a month, maybe two."

"Give it a week, maybe two. Can you handle it?"

"You're talking to a girl from the project. I can handle anything. The question is can you handle my mother moving in with us next week. I can't leave her in that apartment. She can sleep in one of those twenty-five guest rooms on the top floor. We can't put her in the carriage house. You promised we could keep that open for..."

"Bring her on," Buddy said. "I ain't afraid of no mama-in-law, but she can't move her boyfriends in. That's the only rule."

"Oh, she broke up with all her boyfriends. Told me on the phone last night a woman thirty-two years old shouldn't be carrying on like a kid anymore. She's going back to school to be a nurse like me."

Buddy released his hold on Larissa and gave her an I've-just-been-walloped-in-the-stomach look. "Are you telling me your mother's not but thirty-two years old?" He did a quick calculation in his head. "She was fourteen when you were born?"

"Uh-huh," Larissa said. "Fourteen going on fifteen."

"Do you realize I'm twenty-nine now, which makes my mother-in-law only three years older. Listen, Larissa, if you never do another thing for me in your entire life, you have to promise me you will never tell that to Bo Gaillard. I'm serious. You have to promise."

Larissa laughed like the school girl she still almost was. "Okay," she said, "but only if you promise to buy me all the Cocoa Crispies I want and not tease me about it when I eat'em with chocolate milk."

"Deal," Buddy said and made her shake on it. Then he redirected his attention to a noisy commotion developing on the sidewalk, where he saw and heard Miss Posey's spaniel, Hamp, yapping like a bad dog while pulling his mistress along by a brand new leash, his old one having been chewed into leathery strings. "Morning, Miss Posey. Morning, Hamp," Buddy said to the only neighbor lady and neighbor dog who'd had the courage to judge him and his new wife straight to their faces.

Miss Posey gave Hamp's halter a mighty wrench with his fancy new leash (monogrammed WH for Wade Hampton) to slow him down a notch. Without returning Buddy's pleasantry about the morning, the old woman began a discourse of her own that was so sensible, Buddy never forgot it. Neither did Larissa. "Take my advice, Bud Calhoun," she said, "you and that pretty bride of yours follow right along in your grandfather's footsteps. Bedon had what I call *imagination!* Got it a little late in life, but got it just the same."

Buddy hesitated, though relieved his grandfather's old friend and neighbor had developed such an encouraging attitude in her dotage. With sincere kindness of heart, he said, "Thanks, Miss Posey. That's exactly what we plan to do. Bye now."

As Posey and Hamp tottered away, Buddy and his "pretty bride" smiled at the retreating backside of the not-so-sour-anymore spinster and the twitching nubbin tail of Hamp. Buddy pulled his wife close again in a sideways hug and kissed the top of her head full of curls. Then he squeezed her until she squeaked as they walked together across Murray Boulevard toward the battery rail on their way to enjoy the divine view of Charleston Harbor that Bedon, Sr. had loved so much. Together, in utter gratitude for the utter happiness that had flooded their lives of late, the two young people gazed across the deep-blue water of the harbor and upward at the deep-blue sky.

The End

# Church Lady Rum Cake
## Courtesy of Margaret and Wendell Edwards Of Charleston

<u>Basic Cake Mix:</u>
2 cups cake flour
1½ cups granulated sugar
4 teaspoons baking powder
1 teaspoon salt
½ cup butter, cut into bits
3 tablespoons vegetable oil

<u>For the cake:</u>
½ cup finely chopped walnuts
1 (3.5 ounce) package instant vanilla pudding mix
½ cup milk
4 eggs
½ cup Whaler's Vanille Rum – Hawaiian-style
½ cup vegetable oil
1 teaspoon vanilla extract

<u>Rum Soaking Glaze:</u>
½ cup butter (NO SUBSTITUTE)
¼ cup water

1 cup granulated sugar
½ cup Whaler's Vanille Rum – Hawaiian-style

<u>For the cake:</u>
Heat oven to 325°F. Spray a large (12-cup size) Bundt pan with nonstick cooking spray. Sprinkle the chopped nuts into the bottom.

Place Basic Cake Mix, pudding mix, milk, eggs, rum, oil, and vanilla extract into a large bowl and combine on medium speed with an electric mixer for two to three minutes. Scrape down the bowl halfway through. Batter should be very smooth. Pour into prepared Bundt pan and level out top.

Bake until fully golden, tester comes out clean and cake springs back – about 55 minutes. Remove from oven and place on cooling rack while making soaking glaze.

<u>Rum Soaking Glaze:</u>
In a small saucepan combine butter, water, and sugar. Bring to boil carefully as mixture boils over easily. Reduce to a simmer and cook until sugar is dissolved and syrup is combined well and a little thicker. Remove from heat and add the rum. Mix to combine.

While cake is still cooling, pour hot syrup into and on top of cake. There is a lot of syrup and if cake doesn't soak it up right away, just wait a couple of minutes before adding the rest. It will take time to soak in.

Cool cake completely in Bundt pan before turning out onto serving platter.

This cake is delicate, so once it is turned out, it cannot be moved around easily. It can be eaten when fully cool, but is better the next day.

# Great Aunt Pauline's Shrimp and Grits Courtesy of Buster Blalock of Charleston

One pound bacon sliced
One green bell pepper diced
One sweet onion diced
Three pounds shrimp peeled
Flour and water
Old Bay seasoning
Grits

1. Fry bacon and hold on side.
2. In same pan, sauté diced onion and green bell pepper in bacon grease.
3. In same pan, sauté shrimp with diced onion and green bell pepper.
4. Add flour, water, Old Bay seasoning, salt, and black pepper to make gravy to taste.
5. Return bacon to pan and mix with other ingredients.
6. Follow instructions on package to cook grits.
7. Top servings of grits with shrimp and bacon gravy mixture.

# Burning Questions for Book Club Fun

1. How does the action in *Moonbow Over Charleston* address the human tendency to behave and speak in judgmental ways?
2. Recall incidents in which culture-clash causes sparks among the characters.
3. Remember scenes in the story informing the idea that the human spirit is ageless.
4. Share your favorite funny incidents and funny characters. Describe how the surprise of entertainment popping up at unexpected times relieves the tension created by serious subject matter.
5. What do you think the future holds for Larissa and Buddy?